SLEEPING WITH PATTY HEARST

SLEEPING WITH PATTY HEARST

MARY LAMBETH MOORE

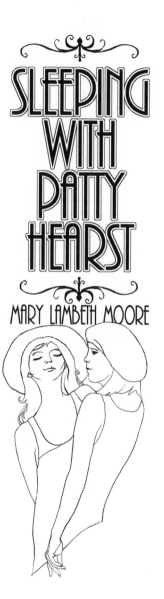

A Tigress Publishing Book

ISBN: 978-1-59404-035-1
1-594040-35-4
LCCN: 2010936064
Printed in the United States of America

Design and original cover illustration: Steve Montiglio
Editor: Carole L. Glickfeld

10 9 8 7 6 5 4 3 2 1

Grateful acknowledgement is made for permission to print a portion of "Thirteen Ways of Looking at a Blackbird," written by Wallace Stevens, copyright 1954 by Vintage Books—an imprint of Random House.

Tigress Publishing
4831 Fauntleroy Way SW #103
Seattle, Washington 98116
Copyright 2010 Mary Lambeth Moore

*With love and gratitude to
my parents, Jess and Barbara Moore,
and to Bill.*

"…from what we cannot hold the stars are made."
"Youth"
W.S. Merwin

PROLOGUE

You were twelve and I was eleven when we sewed our fingers together. I clutched my hands behind my back while you threaded the needle, the thinnest you could find. You said I was being a baby. "We'll be blood sisters," you said, and that had been enough to make me give up my finger to you. The secret is to sew only the very edge of the skin. It's tricky, but you managed a stitch. With ring fingers joined, my right and your left, we sat on your bed and listened to the Top Forty countdown until Lorraine called us downstairs. Then you found the scissors and snipped us apart, just like that.

It was the winter of 1970, February. Lorraine closed the shop early that day because nobody came to her sale. Not one person. Do you remember? She put the "Closed" sign out well before five and pulled a silver goblet off a display shelf. She poured a splash of Scotch, drank it, added more. "I will never waste money on another ad," she announced defiantly, as if we might argue. She was still wearing her wool suit trimmed with fur. "The damn newspaper has gone downhill. Nobody reads it anymore." She drained her drink again and went from table to table, snatching up all the tent cards she had labeled in her best cursive: "Just in from Austria." "50% off today only." "Bargains Galore!"

She had called us to do chores, that's what we thought, but she never gave us anything to do, so we settled at the bottom of the staircase to play gin rummy with our sore fingers. You were winning, of course. I don't remember that specifically, but you always won. Lorraine stalked over to a table next to us

1

and began straightening a row of crystal figurines, her hands moving in a distracted fury. We could hear her breathing. When she reached for the unicorns, she knocked a large toad onto the floor. It shattered, raining tiny shards of green glass over our jeans and shoes.

She pressed her fingers against her temples and swore under her breath. "Connie, go get the broom and sweep this up."

"I didn't do it," you said in a low voice. We had no use for the unicorns and ballerinas, but we had liked that toad.

"Excuse me?" Lorraine said.

"I didn't do it," you said, louder.

Lorraine grabbed your cards, tossed them aside and clamped her hand on your shoulder. "I am your mother and you'll do what I say." When you didn't answer, Lorraine's long fingernails dug deeper into your shirt before she released her grip. "Do it now, please." She stepped between us and went up the stairs. We heard her sniff before she closed the door, the first sound of a longer cry. You rubbed your shoulder and looked at me. The frames of your glasses were taped across your nose, and somehow your face looked crooked.

"I'll sweep," I whispered.

You shook the glass off your clothes and wandered off to the parlor. I got the broom and swept carefully, making sure I got every piece. After the job was done, I went to the kitchen. Lorraine had left a box of macaroni and a can of soup on the counter, but I ignored them and fixed a plate of crackers and sardines and carried it to the parlor, where I found you sitting on the floor with an open book on your lap. "Harper Valley PTA" was playing from one of the old radios lined up on a shelf, all with price tags dangling from their knobs. You patted the space beside you without looking up from your book and reached for a cracker. I sat close, so that our knees touched.

2

Customers often came in and saw us like that: two girls sitting cross-legged, listening to a radio that might be sold before the next song played. We had come to dread the parade of women who crept around the first floor of our house, searching for bargains, eyeing us with the same calculating assessment they gave to armchairs and candle holders. These were strangers with bad teeth who lived out in the country, not the well-off town ladies who had grown up with Lorraine, the ones who used to visit the house for birthday parties and barbecues. It's funny to remember how easily you talked to our customers if Lorraine wasn't there. You said you didn't mind people you didn't know.

Once, when you were about seven, you told a customer we were twins. The woman wore red lipstick and big rings, and she had found a crystal butter dish she wanted to buy. The lady looked at us in turn—me, small and dark, and you, so pale and tall for your age—and she seemed puzzled, but ready to believe. As you rang her up, Lorraine came in from the kitchen.

"Well, I never would have guessed they were twins!" the lady remarked.

Lorraine gave a little laugh. "Well, they are nearly Irish twins, only eighteen months apart." Even then we could see she was pleased to have this rare kind of customer, a prosperous-looking woman who was her equal, someone who could appreciate quality.

"They're smart girls," the lady said, watching as you expertly punched in the price and made the cash drawer spring open.

I was standing next to you; I was never more than an arm's length away. Lorraine came and rested her hand on my shoulder. "This one is my angel."

My neck and shoulders locked up. When she said things like that, I always felt ashamed.

"Did you find everything you need?" Lorraine asked as the woman turned to leave. "We have some lovely things on sale."

Lorraine often called us Irish twins, but never what we were: half sisters. You and I never said the half part, either.

❦

Anytime of the year, Lorraine's inventory included dozens of framed mirrors collected from estate sales, the kind people hung to reflect their prized possessions and make their rooms look larger. Lorraine liked them because they didn't take up much floor space and they moved well. "You can always sell a shot glass and a mirror," she liked to say. Some of the mirrors were set on the floor or propped against walls, but she hung the fanciest ones in the dining room, so that they surrounded the long mahogany table where we kept the cash register on one end and ate our meals on the other.

When I think of our time as little girls, so briefly captured in all that reflecting glass, I see us at odd angles and in blurry multiples. Each of us saw more than the other two knew, but everything was a secret. Why did ladies Lorraine had known for years barely speak to her in the grocery store? Why did you and I have different fathers and where were they? Lorraine was careful not to reveal too much, even when she was drinking. You and I lied to her routinely. "We don't have any homework." "These shoes fit fine." "No, we didn't hear the rain last night." Much of our lying wasn't significant or even necessary, but it seemed natural to us, almost a courtesy, to match her caution about giving anything away.

❦

Most people would say it was lucky we weren't killed, but now it doesn't seem that way to me. You were just born with certain skills, like knowing how to make a fire, how to read a map, and how to drive.

The first time we went out on the highway you were eleven. As soon as Lorraine went out that evening—her friend Jo Penny offered to drive that night—you grabbed her car keys and flew out to the driveway, heading for the ancient Plymouth that Lorraine despised. I followed behind you and got in on the passenger side.

"I'm cold," I said, trying not to sound scared. "We should have worn coats."

Outside the sky was dark and thick with clouds. Beyond the long slope of our yard, headlights glided across the bypass, the busy street that had been Lorraine's nightmare when we were toddlers. You fumbled in the pocket of your jeans, pulled out a book of matches, and struck one. We stared at the flame flickering above your steady hand. "For the god of driving," you said, then blew out the match. "Help me remember exactly where the car was parked, okay?"

"What if Lorraine comes home early?" I asked.

You scooted up to the edge of the seat, stretched your leg to reach the gas pedal, started the motor and put the car in gear. It jerked, then began rolling.

We crawled around the driveway until you got the hang of it again, then you sped up. On the first stop, you hit the brakes too hard and we pitched forward. "Damn," you said. We rode around the loop of the driveway again, circling the oak tree and the bare bones of the grapevine. "Turn on the radio," you said, and then you sped up a little and whisper-sang along with "Respect."

I kept glancing over my shoulder, even knowing Lorraine wasn't there. Our house loomed under the milky clouds in the sky, looking as menacing and out of place as ever with its rounded portico and four giant columns. The kids at school called it "the haunted house," emphasizing that our place was an oddity among the compact and practical ranch houses where everyone else lived. In the yard, Lorraine's discreet wooden sign, "Fine Crystal and Antiques," swayed in the breeze.

"We should go in now," I said, but you headed down the driveway toward the bypass. You were sitting up straight, your elbows pointed out like wings.

"We're going out," you said.

"I'm getting out." I reached for the door handle, but didn't pull it.

"Go ahead." You stopped at the end of the driveway and looked in both directions. A transfer truck sped by; it made a whistling sound like a bullet.

"We'll get arrested," I said.

The car rolled a couple of yards, then you pressed on the gas and we zoomed forward. I grabbed the side of my seat and closed my eyes.

"I'm only doing thirty-five," you said.

Headlights sprang up from a hill ahead, coming our way. "Oh, hell," I whispered. You gripped the wheel tighter and leaned forward. The other car went by like we were like any other vehicle on the road.

"Ha," you said, settling back in your seat.

We passed the Baptist Church, then the small boxy houses that lined the road beyond. We went by the mini-mart and the "Leaving Carlington" sign. Two, then three more cars passed from the other direction, only inches away, but no one gave us a second look. We sped by the crooked silhouettes of tobacco sheds and empty fields that lay by the road like wide, black pools. A deer's cotton butt flashed through a tangle of brush, followed by another, then they were gone. I felt a tingling in my legs, as if we were running, too.

I kept thinking something terrible would happen. When we got home, I half expected to see Lorraine standing on the porch waiting for us, ready to kill, but all was quiet, and no one was there. You parked the car exactly where it had been and plucked the keys from the ignition. When I started to get out, you reached over and gripped my arm. You pulled me close and kissed me, a hard, ecstatic stamp on my lips. "Do you know what this means?"

I inhaled your breath and looked past you toward the house. I tried, but I couldn't imagine being any other place. I closed my eyes and nodded. "We can get away."

On Thursday afternoons, my sister Connie worked the cash register and waited on customers in the next room while I had my piano lesson. The lessons took place in the west parlor, where we sold second-hand musical instruments, dishes, kitchen gadgets and colored bottles. A small white tag hung from the hinge that propped open the old Steinway: "NOT FOR SALE (will consider trade)." It wasn't unusual for prospective traders to examine the piano's trusses and the action of the hammers while I plodded through "Hong Kong Holiday" or "Sheep May Safely Graze."

All the Thursday lessons have melded in my memory, an indistinguishable blur, except the last one in August 1975. It was hot and humid that day, the final free week of summer before Connie and I both went back to high school.

"Let's try it again, Lily," my teacher, Mrs. Turner, said. "Pay a-tten-tion to the rhy-thm."

I slid over to the middle of the bench and looked down at the keyboard, imitating an expression of concentration. I was drowsy. The tip of my right ring finger throbbed. Connie and I had stayed up most of the night playing gin rummy, and I had been careless when she handed me a cigarette.

"Quarter, quarter, quarter, quarter, ha-a-lf note," Mrs. Turner chanted in her quavering voice. She was a thin, mournful woman who got emotional about scales and proper hand position. When she asked about the blister, I told her I had burned myself baking cookies.

Mrs. Turner was a widow of little means or she probably

wouldn't have put up with lessons to an indifferent student in a room open to shoppers. Over time, she stopped complaining about fumes from old perfume bottles, but she never got used to the interruptions as browsing customers moved in and out, occasionally trying out a battered violin or rattling saucepans and rotary beaters. It was like having a piano lesson in Woolworth's, except our merchandise was old and randomly displayed.

I had been taking lessons for over three years, since I was twelve. All the hours spent on finger positioning, laborious scales and halting songs never made a musician out of me. Connie played much better than I did, though I was the only one who knew it. She worked out tunes by ear, but only when our mother was out. Lorraine said Connie would need to improve her behavior if she wanted lessons. She had no idea that Connie could play the theme song from *M*A*S*H* and anything from *The Wizard of Oz*.

I, on the other hand, read music note by note and tried to play whatever Mrs. Turner put in front of me. I was slogging through "Let a Smile Be Your Umbrella" when Lorraine came to the doorway.

"Excuse me, Mrs. Turner," she said. "I want Lily to know I'll be leaving shortly. For a meeting."

I knew she and her boyfriend were going out for drinks and dinner. She was wearing her frosty lipstick, her hair was teased, and she would probably change out of the beige pants she was wearing and put on her black miniskirt.

She stood very straight and looked at me. "Lily, you and Connie will need to tidy up the shop after your lesson. Don't close until six. And you two are not to go anywhere." She glanced sideways at Mrs. Turner. "Connie is grounded. Indefinitely." Connie had been caught with a joint in the parking lot at school, and I could see Lorraine was worried that the news had spread. If everyone knew, she would make sure they also knew she was addressing the problem. She flashed her teeth at Mrs. Turner and gave a little wave before closing the door.

"Quarter, quarter, quarter…" Mrs. Turner began again, sounding like a woman throwing herself against a wall. She stamped the time with her narrow black pumps while I went on butchering "Umbrella." I heard my mother's boyfriend, Denis, clatter into the house, shouting for Lorraine. Mrs. Turner paused for a second and winced before going on.

Denis's car had just roared out of the driveway when the telephone rang out in the hallway. I didn't pay any attention— Connie would have to get it, or more likely, she would let it ring—but then the door opened and she was standing there. "Excuse me," she said, pushing her glasses higher on her nose.

Mrs. Turner looked at her with a twitchy squint. During the years of my lessons, Lorraine always banished Connie from the parlor, commanding her not to "distract your sister." I wondered if Mrs. Turner even recognized the seventeen-year-old standing there. Connie was wearing what she called her summer uniform: cut-off jeans, strings hanging down from the hem, and a green baseball cap. Her eyes were hidden in the glare behind her big black glasses.

"Yes, what is it?" Mrs. Turner asked.

"Lily's doctor is on the phone. He needs to talk to Lily right away."

"Oh," said Mrs. Turner, giving me a quizzical look. "I hope everything is all right." She looked at her watch and reached under the piano for her battered satchel. "We might as well adjourn early. You are excused, Lily."

I couldn't imagine why Dr. Ellington was calling, and

why he would ask for me instead of Lorraine. I tried to catch Connie's eye, but she was holding the door open for Mrs. Turner and didn't look at me.

"Lily, I want to hear some improvement next week," Mrs. Turner said on her way out. "You want to be ready for the competition, don't you?"

"Indeed she does," Connie called after her.

I picked up the receiver, but there was only a dial tone. "Who was it?"

"It wasn't anyone," Connie said.

"But it rang. "

"I made it ring, there's a number you can call," she said over her shoulder, already moving to the cash register to pluck out a couple of bills. She disappeared into the kitchen and came back twirling Lorraine's car keys on her finger. "Closing time!" she shouted, loud enough for any straggling customer to hear.

Ten minutes later, we were cruising down the highway in Lorraine's Thunderbird, The Who blaring from the eight-track player, a pack of Lucky Strikes on the seat between us. The car was brand new, a trophy to Lorraine's business skills and her persistence in courting the Country Club set, ladies who were always on the prowl for furniture and good crystal. After being shunned for years, she was finally getting a steady stream of their business and even an occasional invitation to their parties. When Connie was caught with the joint, Lorraine paced around the parlor crying into her hands. "You're trying to ruin everything for me, aren't you?" she said.

"No," Connie had answered. "I was trying to get high."

"Help me look out for cops," Connie said now. Her cap was pulled down to the rim of her glasses; she steered with the tips of her fingers. She sped up to sixty-five, then seventy, relaxing back in her seat. She loved to drive, especially when she was supposed to be grounded. I sang "See Me, Feel Me" loudly and out of tune.

Not 'excitement at your *feel*,'" Connie said. "It's *feet*."

"Oh." I thought about Joseph's feet, which looked so big and solid in his football shoes. "Let's go to the lake." I said it because I thought that's where she would want to go.

She shook her head. "Earl's."

"Why? You're not working tonight." I tried to sound matter-of-fact. It had been a blow to me early in the summer when she suddenly announced her new job as a waitress. It meant nights alone without her, but it was even worse that she had applied for the job without even telling me. When I got upset, she accused me of being just like Lorraine.

"Why not? You could practice driving in Earl's parking lot."

I was silent. I had no desire to drive and she knew it, though she didn't seem to understand why someone wouldn't want to be in control of a complicated machine that killed thousands of people every year. The very thought of being behind a wheel made me want to throw up. "I don't feel like going to Earl's," I said.

"Do you expect me to drive you around forever?"

"Why should I drive when you're so good at it?"

"When we go to California, I can't drive all three thousand miles."

As soon as we saved enough money, we were running away. That had been our plan since we were little girls in ankle socks, for so many years it no longer seemed like a real plan. At first the thought terrified me. I had stayed awake nights thinking about the two of us alone in strange and dangerous cities, about leaving Lorraine, who told me she didn't know what she'd do without me but never said anything like that to Connie. Connie needed to get away from her; I knew that. I wanted to get away, too. Part of me did. But we had been talking about it for so long I could no longer imagine it, any more than I could imagine levitating or becoming a Hare Krishna—things we also talked about.

"We'll go to the lake," she said, as if I had never mentioned it. "After we get beer."

"Do you have any more pot?" I asked a bit stiffly. The pot had been another thing she hadn't told me about until after she tried it.

She shook her head. "I didn't really like it. I don't care if I ever smoke any again, but I'll probably be grounded forever. Lorraine's stupid boyfriend guzzles beer like it's water, and she doesn't say a word."

She never said Denis's name. We ignored him as much as possible. I would answer if he asked me a question, but Connie could look right through him as if he weren't there.

She pulled into a gas station and fished out her fake ID from her pocket. While I pumped the gas, she bought a six-pack, and then we headed out of town, down a narrow two-lane road lined with picked-over corn fields and junked cars until it turned into a big divided highway, running by dilapidated motels and small farm houses with handwritten signs in the yards advertising things like cantaloupes and fresh eggs. We passed the fancy horse estate where Lorraine had known the owners before they sold it to somebody else, and then Connie slowed down and started looking for the turnoff to the lake, an unmarked gravel road. We turned in, and after riding nearly another mile we came to a scattering of VWs and battered vans parked off to the side. Connie pulled in behind an old Ford painted in psychedelic swirls.

We got out of the car and stood in the heat. The air was muggy, but it carried the gold sheen of the last hour before sunset. In the distance, we could hear voices and splashing. A dirt path ran through a pasture and down to the lake, but we walked past it and trudged up a hill. At the top, Connie squatted down and scrambled to the edge of a large, flat rock. I followed with the beer. The lake was below us, maybe a hundred yards away.

We settled on the rock, taking care to position ourselves so we were partially shielded from view if anyone looked up. The lake was really a pond, a large brownish-green pool with a wide strip of gray sand on the near side. About a dozen people were there, either in the water or lying on faded towels on the beach. They were older than us, guys and girls in their twenties and thirties, and they all had long hair. Some wore a bathing suit or shorts, but several had abandoned all clothes.

We loved watching them; we wanted to *be* them: these older, naked hippies, the same ones who went to rock festivals, marched in protests and held love-ins and be-ins. We had discovered this pond-beach about the same time that Patty Hearst, the daughter of a rich family in California, was kidnapped by a band of radicals who demanded that Patty's parents distribute food to the poor. Only a few weeks after the kidnapping, Patty denounced her parents and joined her captors. The instant we saw these hippies at the pond, we knew they were Patty's people, people who recognized the greed and hypocrisy of America.

As Connie and I drove around the outskirts of town, we played a game we called "I Spy Patty." The newspapers were full of stories of people who thought they had spotted her. We half-jokingly fantasized about finding Patty and offering her refuge, since Carlington, North Carolina would be the perfect place to escape notice. We would hide her in our basement with blankets and canteens. After Lorraine went to bed, Connie and I would sneak down with food and spend our nights with her, making plans for revolution and sleeping side-by-side until dawn. We didn't think about who Patty and her comrades had killed or might kill; that part was blurry. All we knew was that, like Patty, we wanted wars stopped and hungry people fed, and, like her, we wanted to become someone else.

I opened our beers and gave one to Connie. She lit two cigarettes and handed one to me. We gazed down at a couple walking out of the water after a swim, a skinny guy with a mustache and a plump girl. The guy's dick was long and droopy, like his mustache, and his thin hips gleamed white next to the tan on the rest of his body. The girl took his hand and swung it in the air; her round breasts bounced like they were packed with springs. Connie and I lifted our cigarettes at the same time and took a long drag.

"A boy at school tried to kiss me," I said.

She blew her smoke out in a thick stream. "Who?"

"Joseph."

"Satterfield? The preacher's kid who wears creased jeans?"

I nodded.

She took a swig of her beer. "This is bad. This is very bad."

"I didn't let him do it."

And that was the truth, even though I had regretted it until this moment, when I looked at Connie's face and saw that she was really disturbed. I had been right not to talk about him before. She had secrets from me, I suspected; things more important than the job or smoking pot. I would have this one secret from her.

"He asked me if I was saved," I said, hoping it would make her feel better if I offered an easy target for blasting Joseph some more.

"Like 'come-to-Jesus' saved?" she said.

"I guess so."

I had seen Joseph for so many years in school, since we were in grade school, that his newly expanded senior-year body still seemed startling—his height and the width of his shoulders, the faint shadow above his lip where he had started to shave. His eyes were the same—dark brown, almost black. They would look intense and maybe even a bit wicked except they had lashes thicker than mine. I took the stick of gum he gave me, but I didn't unwrap it; I didn't want to chew in front of him. When he asked if I was saved, I wasn't sure what he meant, but at that moment I thought I might be.

"Don't get near him again," Connie said.

"I won't."

We finished our cigarettes and sipped on our beers. Twilight was beginning to set in. One by one the swimmers waded out of the lake, which had turned pink and gold from the sunset. A group on the beach had gathered on a blanket; I thought I caught a whiff of marijuana in the breeze. Connie was quiet. She was often quiet, but it felt like we weren't speaking. We watched as two girls wearing T-shirts stood and shook sand out of their towels. I pointed at the slight one with brown hair. "She looks like Patty."

"It's not," Connie said.

"I know. She just looks a little like her."

"No, she doesn't."

"*Okay.*"

She turned and walked back to the car, and I followed. She started the car and we headed back toward town.

"I don't think you'll really do it," she said.

"Do what?"

"Go to California. When it comes down to it, I just don't think you'll go."

I was shocked. "I'm going wherever you go. Why do you think I wouldn't?"

She didn't answer right away. We drove past the city limits sign and stopped at a light. "Once we leave, we're never coming back," she said. "We'll never see Lorraine or anybody."

"I don't care."

"What about Joseph?"

"What about him?"

"You can't lie to me, Lily. I know you like him."

"Would it be such a big deal if I did?" But as soon as I said it, I knew it would be.

She reached for the cigarettes. "It's just that you're lying to me, that's all."

I thought if we could get home and put on our pajamas and deal a hand of cards, then everything would be okay. We would play gin or spades, and Connie would beat me until one of us fell asleep. I would wake up in the morning in her bed, and we would tell each other our weird dreams and read for a while, then we'd go downstairs and make ourselves French toast, which is what we did every Sunday morning while Lorraine slept late.

The car suddenly slowed down, throwing me forward. We were almost home, maybe a quarter of a mile away. Connie was squinting at the silhouette of our house on the hill.

"What is it?"

"Lights."

Bright rectangles of light glowed from two windows downstairs and in the hallway on the second floor.

"Maybe we forgot to turn them off." But I knew better.

"Shit," Connie whispered. "Shit, shit, shit."

For years customers had come into our house, our shop, and commented that Connie and I didn't look anything alike. These were always people from out in the county or newcomers to town. Anyone who was a true Carlington native knew our mother's story. When she was sober and talking to strangers, Lorraine would call us "modern-day Irish twins." When she was drinking and the three of us were alone, she sometimes called us her "youthful indiscretions." If we asked questions, she would only say, "I'm sorry, your father passed away years ago, and I don't want to talk about him," even after we knew we had different fathers and they probably were living somewhere.

"If they were really dead, there would be pictures, and Lorraine would visit the graves," Connie said. We rode our bikes to the Baptist church cemetery and examined all the headstones, including the two for our grandparents, and that's when it dawned on us that Lorraine was still Lorraine Stokes, the same last name she had always had. We didn't know anyone else who had a mother who had never been married, much less a mother who was dating.

I was born on November 30, 1959, a year and a half after Connie. When I was three, I would only eat from her plate, even when Lorraine tried to tempt me with shrimp and candy bars. On Connie's first day of school, I grabbed the hem of her dress as she tried to leave the house, and it took all of Lorraine's strength to pry my fingers away. Later that same year, when Connie wanted to practice flying, I arranged a pile of straw beside the old tool shed and boosted her up. She called me a baby because I was too timid to try it myself, and she landed on me to help break her fall, making me feel useful and redeemed.

We have the same first memory of Lorraine: bedtime in a dim room, the two of us placed on a mattress on the floor. The mattress felt like our raft, a temporary refuge that might float away in the night. We lay quietly but alert, shoulder to shoulder, our nearest legs entwined. Lorraine was sitting near a curtained window, smoking and swinging one crossed leg. Her cigarette glowed and faded, glowed again. Each time the ember burned bright, we got a glimpse of her sharp, pointed nose and the gold lights in her dark blonde hair, and then she was gone again.

For a long time it puzzled me that Lorraine never liked Connie, even from the beginning. Later I realized Connie's birth had been the first event in Lorraine's unexpected transition from a pampered daughter to a single mother, weighed down with responsibility and sometimes short on cash. It didn't help matters that I came along so soon after Connie, but Lorraine had a gift for overlooking inconvenient facts. Through years of saying the right things to the right people and earning the money necessary to keep up appearances, she was well on her way to making a comeback in Carlington society. But Connie lacked the looks and charm to assist. Without realizing it, Lorraine viewed her as constant and irritating proof of a mistake she wanted erased.

On the other hand, I roused something softer in her. She seemed physically drawn to me: She loved to pick out my clothes, brush my hair, paint my fingernails. I accepted these attentions, and even enjoyed them when Connie wasn't watching.

"You're lucky to be so pretty," Lorraine told me time and again. "You have your grandfather's eyes."

I was much older and on my own before I realized that Lorraine's father had hazel eyes; they weren't like mine at all. Even later I found a picture hidden in Lorraine's jewelry box, a man with thick hair and eyes that were distinctly blue. When I picked it up, it was like looking in a mirror. My father's name was Jack. I never knew him, but I came to understand that, in a way, he lived with us for many years.

"Keep driving," I said. The lighted windows seemed to get brighter as we stared at them.

Connie pulled the car over to the side of the road, but left the engine running. We sat very still, watching the house as if it were in flames.

"Let's keep going," I said.

She leaned back and rubbed her eyes. "We only have a couple of dollars, so we can't go far. If you don't come home, Lorraine will have every pig in the state looking for us."

We sat in silence until she pulled the car out on the road again. I swallowed, tasting stale beer and a threat of vomit. We turned into our driveway slowly. Denis's car was gone, but our headlights flashed across Lorraine, who was standing near the porch, one hand on her hip. Even in that glimpse, I could see she was ready to spring.

Connie parked the car under the oak tree and cut off the motor. Through our open windows, we heard Lorraine's heels snapping down the driveway. She was wearing a short, tight skirt; the outline of a cigarette pack showed through the sheer fabric of her red blouse. She strode to Connie's side of the car and spoke through the open window. "Get out." Her voice was dangerously low, and her breath was heavy with whatever she had been drinking. "Both of you get out of the car right goddam now."

We got out and stood shivering in the driveway in shorts and bare feet. I felt cold inside and out, and I needed to pee. I stayed on my side of the car, protected by the width of the hood. Lorraine's face was pale and livid, with narrowed eyes and gleaming lipstick. A strange man brandishing a knife wouldn't have scared me more.

"Where have you been?"

"We didn't go far," I said hoarsely, but she was looking at Connie.

"It doesn't matter what I tell you, does it?" She lunged at Connie and grabbed her by the shoulders.

Connie wrenched herself away and batted Lorraine's face with her forearm. I ran around the front of the car, but it was too late. Lorraine was swinging at Connie, and Connie's hand was wrapped around a clump of Lorraine's hair.

Lorraine and Connie had fought for years, but nothing physical. This seemed unimaginable even as it was happening, too awful to take in, yet later I knew we had been waiting for it.

I forced myself between Lorraine and Connie, trying to pry them apart. "Get out of the way!" Lorraine screamed, and she mashed her hand against my face. I groped for Connie and tackled her. We both fell to the ground, my stomach draped across Connie's. I got up on my knees and held out my arms, prepared to take punches. But Lorraine stood where she was, shaking and panting. The pocket on her blouse was torn and drooping on her chest. Broken cigarettes lay scattered on the concrete and in the grass.

"Get out," Lorraine said. "You can leave on your own two feet, and I don't care where you go."

"Fine," Connie said. She stood and began limping toward the house.

"Where are you going?" Lorraine shrieked.

Connie whipped around. A thin streak of blood ran across her cheek. "Do you mind if I take a change of clothes and a fucking toothbrush?"

"You have five minutes."

"That's all I need."

I got up to follow her, but Lorraine stopped me. "No, Lily. You stay here."

Connie went into the house, slamming the door behind her.

"Don't make her go," I said.

"I can't worry about her anymore, Lily. I've done all I can do." Lorraine searched the ground until she found an unbroken cigarette. I did the same and lit one, silently daring her to say a word. I sat on the ground with my back against the car and smoked. The fender was still warm; a soft ticking sound came from beneath the hood.

Lorraine paced around the driveway. "I'll give her one more minute," she kept saying.

When Connie finally came out, she had changed into her bell bottom jeans and her Army surplus jacket. She was carrying a knapsack I had never seen. I got to my feet. She walked past Lorraine without looking at her.

"You'd better not have anything of mine in that bag," Lorraine said.

Connie stopped in front of me. "Come on. Let's go."

I stepped toward her, but Lorraine reached out and gripped my arm. "Lily is staying here," she said.

Connie kept her eyes on me. "I packed enough for both of us."

I tried to wrench away; Lorraine's fingernails dug into

23

my arm. She shoved me behind her, blocking my view, but Connie's voice was clear. "She can't stop you, Lily."

"Let me go, I'll come right back, I swear it," I said to Lorraine, not sure whether I was lying.

"Go on," Lorraine shouted at Connie. "You're not Lily's real sister. Just go."

Connie took a few steps down the driveway, then whirled around. "Come with me now, Lily, or I'll never see you again. Push her and run."

Lorraine was stronger than I was; I couldn't move. It was as if my body had died and all its contents had been sucked out—bones, heart and brain—everything gone except a paralyzing fear. Lorraine put her arm around me to lead me toward the house. My legs were rigid, they wouldn't bend. Lorraine pulled harder, and my knees slammed down on the driveway. I didn't feel anything.

"Here, let me help you," she said.

She hauled me up and clamped her arm around me again. When we got to the porch, I twisted around to look. I hoped to see Connie coming back, or at least waiting in the driveway, ready to give me a signal. But I only caught a glimpse of her in the distance, walking fast, the hem of her jeans dragging in the dirt by the road.

Our grandparents built our house in 1915, a three-story mansion with a round portico in the center, topped by a balcony and supported by four columns. The ground floor, later dedicated to the shop, had two parlors, a large dining room and kitchen, and a sun porch on the back, as well as smaller utilitarian rooms. A long staircase led to a large, windowed landing and curled into two exits, both leading to a spacious hall and five bedrooms (two became store rooms, packed wall-to-wall with Lorraine's excess inventory). The third floor, where Lorraine seldom went, was an enormous ballroom festooned with cobwebs and tattered wallpaper, a room she intended to renovate one day. Connie and I were embarrassed to live somewhere so old and showy when all the kids at school had regular ranch houses.

Lorraine's relationship to our house was both intense and legal. Her mother, Cecelia, bequeathed the property to her, while directing all cash assets to Lorraine's sister in Atlanta. The will stipulated that the house be kept in the family until twenty-one years after Lorraine's death. Lorraine called this clause Cecelia's Curse. Even when we were small children, Lorraine asked Connie and me how we intended to pay the taxes when the property became ours. Her own solution was to turn the house into a shop where she sold virtually anything, with a specialty in glass and crystal. Current inventory was displayed downstairs—stacked, arranged and crammed in the two parlors, the dining room and foyer—and we slept upstairs.

Lorraine worked hard to make the shop attractive for Carlington's elite, the people she had grown up with. Her father, Rob, had owned the town's only newspaper, the *Carlington Eagle*. It was a decent paper, but it never generated as much money as Rob could spend. He was a generous man who needed to be surrounded by people, and he liked to open the house for big, lavish parties. Lorraine smiled when she thought of those days. "Back then, people knew how to entertain properly," she often said. "We were invited to everything, and when we had a party, *everybody* came."

Lorraine made only the barest distinction between the house and herself. She fussed over it, planned for future improvements, and alternately raged and reveled in it. Any deterioration or breakdown was received as a personal affront. Connie knew this very well.

After Connie left, Lorraine escorted me to my room. When I sat on the bed, she leaned down to kiss me on the forehead, but I jerked away. "You'll feel better after sleeping," she said calmly. She left, closing my door behind her.

I stayed where she left me, still numb except for a throbbing pain I was just noticing. I looked down and saw brownish-red spots on the knees of my jeans where blood had seeped through. I was thinking about going to the bathroom to clean up when I heard Lorraine scream. It was a long, high wail that got louder as it went along. It was the most alarming sound I had ever heard, the kind of sound Connie would love to cause. *She came back*, I thought. I imagined Lorraine's battered body and a pool of blood. I jumped up, wincing at the pain in my knees, and ran to Lorraine's room.

She was standing on the other side of her bed by the

windows, clutching a glass of Scotch. I glanced around; she was alone. She looked all right, only a small purple bruise on her neck from the fight in the driveway. She pointed at the floor beyond the foot of her bed. "Look."

The carpet—new yellow shag, recently acquired after Lorraine spent weeks looking at samples—was covered with a jumble of open jars, cans, bottles and broken tubes of lipstick. Everything that had been on the vanity table, Lorraine's cold creams and powders and blushes, her Noxzema and Chanel No. 5, was dumped and mixed into a heap of wreckage on the floor. On the vanity mirror, Connie had scrawled a message in bright red lipstick: "Death to FASCISTS."

Lorraine stared at the message uncomprehendingly, then sank down on the edge of the bed. "It will cost a fortune to replace all this stuff. The carpet is ruined."

Something in her tone surprised me. I studied her face and was puzzled by her expression of relief.

"We did the right thing, Lily," she said. "We could not allow her to live in this house any longer, she is incorrigible. I'm sorry as I can be, I know you two were close, but you see that we can't put up with this, don't you?"

Then I understood: she had harbored some doubts, but now was vindicated. Connie had justified her own removal. If anyone questioned Lorraine, if anyone should be bold enough to imply that perhaps she had been too hasty, she could simply point to the stains on her new carpet.

I went back to my room and lay down. When I closed my eyes, I saw Connie's accusing stare, I heard her say, "I packed enough for both of us," I saw the lights in the windows, I heard Lorraine scream. Finally I opened my eyes in the dark and concentrated on my last glimpse of Connie, the knapsack dangling crookedly on her back, the bulk of her army jacket beneath it. Her gait was fast and certain, the walk of someone with a specific destination.

All these years later, I'm still not exactly sure where Connie went that first night. There's much I'll never know. Still, I try to imagine every detail. Beginning with the bare facts, an outline, I trace Connie's steps then embellish and edit until it all seems plausible. It's the same thing I have always done with Lorraine, piecing together parts of her life she never directly revealed. I know both of them better than they want to be known; it feels like my job. I'm like someone with amnesia, inventing when I can't bear the panic of a blank, the loss of a connection. In my mind, I have followed them everywhere.

Connie strides along the bypass, avoiding streetlights, deliberately staying in the dark. Even when a truck stops and a vampirish-looking man asks if she wants a ride, she isn't afraid. She shakes her head and keeps walking.

She goes to the park with the broken swing sets and a creek we used to play in. A thin old man with a grizzled face is propped against a tree, sound asleep with an empty paper bag in his lap. She kneels beside the creek and splashes her face with cold water. Her cheek stings where Lorraine scratched her. She dips the end of her shirttail in the water and holds it against the scratch. The old man stirs, snorts, and finally lifts his head to look.

"Hey," Connie says.

"Hey, yourself," the man mutters, and he's asleep again.

She goes to a bench in the shadows and furtively counts the money in her pocket. There isn't much, but she has taken all of the bills from Lorraine's cash register, leaving the change. She counts forty-seven dollars. Enough for now, she thinks.

She feels something warm rising inside her, not exactly joy, but a light breaking through. It's as if she has lived her life walking along an endless wall and now, suddenly, has found a low place to jump over. She can think of nothing to miss from the other side. Fuck Lorraine, she thinks. Fuck Lily, too. Her only regret is not leaving sooner. It galls her that Lorraine gets the satisfaction of kicking her out. She never should have wasted so much time waiting to turn eighteen, waiting for Lily. It's clear now: Lily will stay at home and do exactly what Lorraine wants her to do, and she will end up with some boy, and even then she'll sink deeper and deeper into what Lorraine wants her to be.

A police car cruises down the street, and she hides in the bushes until it passes. She and Lily could have hidden together, she thinks. They could have avoided the cops, no sweat. She wonders how many times in the past year Patty Hearst has gone out in disguise, maybe even to movies and concerts, maybe even walking right past cops. It's not hard to not be noticed.

It begins to rain, softly at first and then harder. She walks out of the park and heads downtown, looking for a place to sleep. The rain splatters down on her until she reaches the awnings hanging in front of the stores. She walks beneath the shelter, peering into the stores as she goes along. It occurs to her that it would be easy to throw a brick through one of the big glass windows, to help herself to anything she wants. She looks critically at the displays: preppy sweaters, floral Granny gowns, impossibly high platform shoes, and a hot pink wraparound skirt that Lorraine would love. There's nothing worth stealing.

No cars are out this time of night, but a few are parked here and there on the curb. Hardly any of them are locked; she can take her pick. Leaving the shelter of the awnings, she goes down a side street until she finds an old van, pale lavender and rusting. She climbs in the back and locks the doors. She sleeps on the wide back seat with her Army jacket draped over her and the knapsack under her head.

In the morning, she goes to the Carlington bus station. The waiting room is empty except for the same old man she saw sleeping in the park. He's slumped in a metal chair watching a small television that sits in the window. A spider web circles overhead, stretched between the blades of an ancient ceiling fan.

Her hair is tucked up in her baseball cap; she hopes she looks like a boy. She walks across the gritty floor and studies the bus schedule. She stands there several minutes, calculating her resources and considering where to go and how long she can live. She doesn't have enough money to travel far and buy food, too. When she has made up her mind, she goes to the old man and asks him to buy a ticket for her. The man watches with a toothless smile as she counts out some bills. "There's an extra dollar for you," she says.

She steps outside and watches through a window while the man limps up to the ticket counter. Asking him to buy the ticket is probably an unnecessary precaution. She doesn't think anyone will look for her here, but Lorraine might try to trace her just for show.

Please take out the garbage in the kitchen—it smells!—
and sand the legs of this Parsons chair. I have a headache,
but will get up later to fix dinner for us. Mother

The note, written in Lorraine's neat cursive, lay on the kitchen table. For *us;* I resented the false cheer and coziness. She had placed the chair—an old tweed-covered thing—near the kitchen table, where I wouldn't miss it. She must have gotten up briefly before going back to bed, something she often did on Sundays. I stood in my bare feet on the gray linoleum floor and looked around. Everything was the same—the ruffled curtains at the kitchen window, the bowl of plastic fruit on the scarred wooden table—but it all looked odd to me, as if I had suddenly been beamed into someone else's house. I felt dangerously alone, but the thought of seeing Lorraine felt even riskier. Without the distraction and protection of Connie between us, I had no idea what we might do to each other.

I had stayed awake all night with the lights on in my room and the window open, straining to hear footsteps in the driveway or a rock thrown against my screen. It seemed possible—I convinced myself it was even likely—that Connie would circle back to get me. As the night dragged by, I decided she was waiting until daylight. Toward dawn I got out of bed, shivering in the cool morning air, glad not to be warm if Connie wasn't. I got dressed and packed a small bag. I kneeled beside my window and looked out at the road. For the next five hours I scanned all the horizon I could see, wanting to spot her the first instant she was visible. I alternated between praying and trying to use ESP to call her back, knowing Connie would roll her eyes if she knew.

Connie was suspicious of any kind of religion, especially after she read Marx. "God is a figment of our overactive capitalist imaginations," she said. "You don't believe any of that crap about having your sins washed away, do you?"

I wasn't sure what I believed. Being saved sounded too much like Disneyland or Las Vegas, faraway places we weren't likely to visit. But sin was familiar. I knew it was a sin to steal jewelry from the shop and sell it at school, as Connie sometimes did when she needed money. On the other hand, when I told a lie to keep Connie out of trouble when she was always in trouble anyway, it didn't seem so bad to me. All of my real faith was in Connie, but I had a secret wish to believe in God, too, especially if God could overlook necessary sins and bring Connie home.

I looked at Lorraine's note again, and it told me everything: She was going to act as if nothing had happened. I snatched up a pen and scribbled under the message: "Sand the damned chair yourself." I stared at this message until the words blurred, then I balled up the paper and threw it in the trash. *It's a sin to hate,* I thought. And, *Connie's not coming back.*

I had just spread newspapers under the chair when the bell tinkled at the side door, and I heard Denis come in, whistling. I didn't want to see him, I didn't want to see anybody except Connie, but there was no escape. If I left the kitchen, I would run right into him. I stayed quiet, hoping he would go up to see Lorraine, but he breezed into the room, wearing cut-off jeans and his old sea monkey T-shirt.

"Hi there," he said in his booming voice. "Your mom still upstairs?"

That's what he said, but it sounded more like, "Hi theah, your mom still upstiz?" No matter how many times I heard him speak, his Boston accent came as a small jolt to me, as if he were from another country. His hair was still damp from the shower, combed into a subdued nap that would spring up in dark red ringlets as it dried. He kept his hair longer than Lorraine liked; it was one of the things they fought about. Some days he shaved, some days he didn't; that day his face had a shadow of reddish-brown stubble.

"Yes, Lorraine's still in bed," I said shortly.

He looked around. "Where's Connie?"

Whiz Connie, I echoed in my head. Denis had been Lorraine's boyfriend for four years, and he had seldom seen one of us without the other. "I don't know," I said.

He walked over to the fruit bowl and picked out three oranges. Tossing each one in the air, he began to juggle. "Man, what happened last night? When Lorraine saw you had 'borrowed' the T-bird, she went apeshit."

"She made Connie leave. She kicked her out." I picked up a scrap of sandpaper and began rubbing it across a chair leg. Denis could get very talky, and I didn't want to encourage him.

He gave a low whistle, caught all three oranges neatly and set them down. "Where did she go?"

"I told you. I don't know." My mouth trembled, and I felt my throat tighten. I sanded harder.

"Come on, I'll take you for a drive. We'll get ice cream." His voice was several decibels louder than usual, loud enough for Lorraine to hear if she was awake and listening.

"I don't want any, thanks."

"Lily." His voice went quiet. "Let's go look for her."

33

Denis's blazing red Mustang had been almost new when he met Lorraine, but now it was dented on one side and dusty enough to write on. I started to get in, but the passenger seat was covered with a jumble of envelopes, books, candy wrappers, and a magazine with a nearly naked woman on the cover. "Just throw that stuff in the back," he said, but he reached in himself and tossed it behind the seats. He settled himself behind the wheel, filling up the car and seeming alarmingly close. He wasn't a tall man, but he was thick and muscular. Wherever he was, he seemed to take up more space than you would expect. He reached across me and fished out his sunglasses from the glove compartment, clamped them over his ears, then twisted around to pull a beer out of the cooler in the back seat. "Where shall we start?"

"Downtown." If she was still in Carlington, I couldn't think of where else she would go.

He started the car and began to back out. "Wait," I said. "We didn't leave a note for Lorraine."

"It's okay. We won't be gone long."

That gave me a sudden flare of hope. "Do you think we could find her right away?"

"Maybe," he said. "Carlington's not a big town."

As we headed toward town, he surprised me by not trying to make conversation. It was strange to be alone with him, and following Connie's lead, I had always kept my distance. He and Lorraine were in love sometimes, but they broke up every few months. During their good spells, she wanted to marry him; occasionally he wanted to marry her, too, but they never seemed to have the desire at the same time. Lorraine often said Connie was "a major obstacle in the relationship." It's true that Connie was rude to Denis, but he didn't seem to mind. "I'm a Yankee," he would say to Lorraine. "I'm used to rudeness."

He twisted a knob, and classical music filled the car. "Saint-Saens," he said with satisfaction. "Do you know this one?"

I shook my head. As far as I knew, no one in Carlington listened to classical music. Denis didn't grow up with it, either, but he called it one of his acquired passions, along with good wine and antiques. He liked to talk about his blue-collar upbringing near Boston, where his father had worked for a construction company and his mother was "a professional alcoholic." Denis had done well enough in school to win a scholarship to Boston College—a fact he broadcast to Lorraine early on, failing to mention, until much later, that he never actually graduated. He ended up working as a freelance journalist in Richmond and Washington, D.C., then inheriting land from an uncle who lived outside of Carlington. When he came south to claim his property, he had stopped by our shop to browse.

He and Lorraine still bicker about whether he first fell in love with the house or with her. But he definitely pursued Lorraine, plying her with fancy dinners, roses and jewelry. She had loved everything about him, including the novelty of his Boston voice and the fact that he was a writer. She had especially loved his status as a writer-landowner. He sold some of his land immediately—"This will give me a chance to work on a book," he said—and made plans to develop the rest. When Denis sold his land, he had plenty of cash while Lorraine had been struggling financially. Since then, the situation had gradually reversed. Lorraine's business expanded while Denis's resources dwindled. Denis didn't seem overly concerned, but it caused Lorraine much distress. After she and Denis went out to dinner, Lorraine's friend, Jo Penny, always asked who paid. Once I heard Lorraine tell her to shut up, something I had never heard her say before, even to Connie.

Denis turned the car onto Main Street, with its staid houses and wide, groomed yards. These places were occupied by old well-to-do people—retired doctors, lawyers and bankers— many of whom had been friends of our grandparents. Just in the past couple of years, they had begun inviting Lorraine to their open houses at Christmas. Every embossed card that appeared among our mail was a triumph; she never missed a single event.

A commercial came on the radio, and Denis reached over and switched to a Top Forty station. The car filled with "Love Will Keep Us Together," a song Connie hated.

"Would you mind turning that off?"

"Sure," he looked amused. "Don't you like love songs?"

"Not that one," I said.

He cut off the radio, and I regretted the silence.

"So I hear you have a boyfriend," he said.

I jerked my head toward him, outraged. "Did Lorraine say that?"

"Just kidding, nobody told me that. But I thought you might."

"Well, I don't." I had already made up my mind. If I talked to Joseph, Connie would know somehow, just as she had always known everything about me. If I refused to have anything to do with him, Connie would let me find her. It didn't matter that this connection wasn't provable or even rational; I felt sure of it. "Turn here," I said, pointing to the right.

Carlington's downtown consisted of three streets lined with old stores where nobody shopped much, and a train depot surrounded by boxcars that never seemed to go anywhere. Across the tracks the colored people had their own stores and a pool hall. To the west was the tobacco factory, where troops of workers made cigarettes all day and through the night.

36

Customers who came to the shop from out of town sometimes asked about the sweet, heavy odor that hung in Carlington's air, but Connie and I couldn't smell what we had breathed all our lives.

"Go across the tracks," I said. "Please."

Denis glanced at me and raised an eyebrow, but he made no comment as we bumped across the track. "Now what?"

"Take a right there." I pointed toward the corner ahead. "Go straight for a couple of blocks, then take a left."

We turned at the corner with the pool hall, then headed down a street lined with tiny houses topped with low-slung roofs. Black people still dressed in their Sunday clothes were visiting with each other on the front porches. They looked up as we rode past, lifting a hand or nodding, but not smiling. I remembered Connie telling me that no one ever came here, no one white, unless it was the Ku Klux Klan, who all through the '60s made surprise visits, riding around firing their shot guns and starting fires.

"What are we doing here?" Denis asked.

"We ride our bikes here sometimes."

"Why?"

"I don't know. Connie likes it here."

Lorraine had strictly forbidden us to go beyond Main Street, but we went everywhere—Connie on a rusty bike someone had left at the shop, I on my Schwinn from Santa Claus, with the white wicker basket hanging from the handlebars. The first time we hadn't meant to end up in colored town, but suddenly we were there, staring straight into the eyes of three girls squatting in the dirt of a vacant lot. They were playing jacks with the normal red ball, but instead of the little star-shaped metal pieces, they had a scattering of rocks. Connie surprised me by parking her bike, and we stood and watched the game until they asked us to play. The girls were sisters: Denitra, Sandra and Jackie. After that, we often came back when we could get away from the shop. We traded trinkets, played hide-and-seek, or walked over to the store that was really an old house and bought a single Coke and a package of crackers that we passed among us, everyone getting exactly the same. For a while, those girls were the closest things to friends that we had.

Denis drove slowly, passing the vacant lot. I stared out the window, scanning for Connie, but there were only broken bottles, paper litter, and clumps of weeds poking through the dirt.

"Does Lorraine know you come here?" Denis asked.

"There's Jackie. Stop."

Jackie was the youngest, a thin girl with small, sleepy looking eyes. She was sitting in her front yard, listlessly holding a doll. I rolled down my window. "Hey. Have you seen Connie?"

She eyed Denis suspiciously. "Naw. I ain't seen her in a long time."

I gave a little wave as we moved on; she didn't wave back.

There had been a time when she and her sisters had eagerly run up to our bikes anytime we appeared. As we had gotten older, something shifted. Maybe their parents had cautioned them against us, or maybe the separateness we felt in our uneasily integrated schools had seeped into everything. For whatever reason, they seemed more distant and wary. As I watched Jackie get up and walk away, I knew Connie wouldn't have come here.

"Where now?" Denis asked. "What about Earl's? Would she go there?"

I shook my head. "It's closed on Sundays." It felt odd to be asked, to be in charge.

38

I thought he would take us home, but instead we drove in the opposite direction, past the tobacco factory. Even though it was Sunday, thick gray smoke poured silently from the main stack. He headed straight until we were outside the city limits, moving north toward Virginia. I didn't ask where we were going. It didn't matter to me; nothing mattered. Denis picked up speed. I watched the speedometer tremble to the right.

He saw me watching. "I like to go fast. Does it bother you?"

"No, it's okay." I looked out the window at the farm houses, the junked cars by the road, tattered cornstalks and empty fields. The furrowed rows of dirt made a zigzag pattern as we flew by. I stared at them dully, slumped in my seat. My bra strap drooped over my left shoulder. Without thinking, I stuck my hand inside my collar—an old flannel shirt of Connie's—to pull it up.

"You know, Lily, I don't think you need to wear a bra."

Denis sounded so matter-of-fact I wasn't embarrassed. "Lorraine says I do."

"Your mother's a fine lady, but sometimes I think she's been in Carlington too long. These days a lot of girls are going without bras."

"And burning them," I added.

"Hell, there's no need to burn them. Just throw 'em away," he laughed.

We turned onto a gravel road, and I recognized the place as his property. He and Lorraine had dragged Connie and me here a number of times before we were old enough to stay at home alone. Then there had been kudzu and groves of pines and oaks; now nearly all of the trees had been cleared away, leaving lots that were divided into precise squares of red mud. Denis drove slowly up and down the road, squinting at the sites.

"This is a great place for a development, don't you think?"

I nodded, but I couldn't imagine anyone who would want to live here.

"After we get through construction and sell, I'll get twenty-five thousand dollars of clear profit," he said. "Thirty, if I can squeeze in another lot." He drove around twice more, sipping on his beer and nodding to himself. "All right," he said, stopping the car. "Do you have any other ideas about where to look for your sister?"

I felt grateful that he said "sister," without the half part. I shook my head.

He gave me a sharp look. "Are you sure?"

"Yeah," I said, barely audible.

"Come on. Where did she go?"

I took a breath. "To California."

He nodded slightly and sat there thinking, tapping the steering wheel. "You know what I think?"

"What?"

"I think you had better start learning how to drive."

I looked away. "I'm not old enough."

"Well, yeah, you're not quite sixteen yet. But soon."

I shook my head. "To me, driving...it would be like jumping from a plane. With no parachute." I tried to laugh to make it lighter, as if the very thought of being behind the wheel didn't make me sweat. I would never drive, I was sure of that.

"Driving is just a simple matter of physics," Denis said. He sometimes talked like a professor; it made Lorraine nuts. "Newton's third law, and all that. 'Every action has an equal and opposite reaction.'" He grinned. "Especially when you're dealing with Lorraine."

"We need to get home," I said. "She's bound to be up by now, and she doesn't know where I am."

40

"Come on, take a turn at the wheel," he said. "A few more minutes won't make any difference."

"No," I said. "No, thank you."

"Okay," he said. "Your call."

When we pulled into the driveway, it was late afternoon. I looked up at the house, and through the gray air, I saw a figure hunched on the glider on the front porch. For a brief, breathless moment, I thought it was Connie, but then I saw that someone had left a bundle there, probably merchandise for Lorraine.

We walked in quietly through the side door, and immediately I could feel that Lorraine had been pacing and fuming; her anger was in the air even stronger than the smoke from her cigarettes. The instant we entered the foyer, she appeared at the top of the stairs, fumbling with the sash of her old bathrobe. Her hair was in tangles, and she was pale and witchy looking. She glared down at us. "Lily, I thought I told you never to leave this house without letting me know."

Denis stepped forward. "It's okay, Lo. She was with me."

"Don't either of you know how to write a note? Where have you been all this time?"

"We went to look at my properties. There was a surveyor working on the lines, he was having some problems, and I had to stick around and help him out."

I marveled at how easily this lie came. He said it so calmly and reasonably, I found myself trying to remember the surveyor.

"There was a man working there on Sunday?" Lorraine asked suspiciously.

"Yeah, well, it surprised me, too," Denis said.

She turned to me. "Lily, as I recall, you had chores to

do today. I needed you to vacuum, and you didn't even start sanding that chair."

"I'll do it now," I said.

"I brought you something, Sugar." Denis took the steps two at a time until he reached the top. He handed Lorraine a coffee mug decorated with yellow smiley faces; I had seen it rolling around behind the seat of his car. Lorraine looked at it as if it were an object she didn't recognize.

"You can sell it if you don't want to use it," Denis said.

"I won't sell a goddamned thing if I don't get some help. There was plenty to do around here today, and you two just vanished."

She flounced to her room, and Denis followed, saying, "I'm sorry, Baby" and muffled words I couldn't hear.

I went to the hall closet and dragged out the vacuum cleaner. As I pushed the machine back and forth across the floor, Denis came trotting down the stairs, and I knew Lorraine had ordered him to go, as she often did. He gave me a cheerful wave as he left the house.

By the time I finished sanding the chair later that evening, Lorraine had already gone back to bed. I found her cigarettes and took one out to the front porch. It had turned cool outside, but I had been sweating over the chair, and the air felt good. I sat in an old rocker and smoked. Up in the sky I could see the moon hanging over the hills beyond town. It was full and large, floating in wisps of clouds. I wondered if Connie was hitchhiking, something we had talked about doing together. I wondered what it would be like to ride alone with strangers, speeding through the dark without looking back.

School started on Monday, and I did what I was told to do. When the bell rang between classes, I was the first to jump out of my seat. I rushed to the bathroom and sat in a stall, avoiding Joseph and everyone else I knew. During history, a classmate named Sally, a buck-toothed girl who liked to follow me around, kept pecking at my shoulder with her forefinger. "What's wrong?" she whispered.

"Nothing," I finally hissed, turning away and hunching over my textbook. At lunch, I took a pack of Nabs behind the library and smoked cigarettes until a teacher made me go to the next class.

As soon as I got home, I went to Connie's room and sat on her bed. Her bureau drawers were gaping open; T-shirts and sweaters lay scattered on the floor. Without looking, I knew which jeans and shirts she had taken, the few favorites she wore all the time. Her baseball cap was gone and also her rabbit's foot. Otherwise there wasn't much obviously missing. Her tape player and speakers were on the shelves. Her Eldridge Cleaver poster still raged on the wall. The radio was in its usual place on the floor beside the bed. She must have decided it was too heavy to carry.

I heaped her remaining clothes in my arms and took them to my closet, where I hung them up, even the T-shirts. Her things were too big for me, but I would wear them anyway. I was surprised to find her Frank Zappa sweatshirt, the one with the perfect ripped sleeves. I slipped it on over the shirt I was wearing.

Lorraine knocked on my door several times, but I said I was trying to sleep. When she went downstairs, I saw my chance, and I tiptoed to her bedroom to call Mrs. Turner. The call took only a minute. I spent the rest of the afternoon standing at the window, peering out until it was too dark to see.

Lorraine knocked again and said, "Dinner's ready, Lily. JP is here. I insist that you come down to eat with us."

Every time Lorraine broke up with Denis, she called Jo Penny Medcastle immediately, even though she and JP often had their own bouts of bickering. They envied each other intensely. Lorraine resented Jo Penny for being thin without trying and for having only one daughter who never gave her any trouble. Jo Penny suspected she wasn't as smart as Lorraine, which made Lorraine's frequent corrections and contradictions even more maddening. Lorraine conceded that Jo Penny had the best wardrobe, but Jo Penny had an unfair advantage since she worked part-time in a Reedsboro clothing store. Lorraine had bigger boobs, Jo Penny looked better from behind. The comparisons were ongoing, endless.

Maybe in a bigger town they would have had other friends, but in Carlington there weren't any other unmarried women over thirty who were "their kind"—that is, who had come from old, well-to-do families. Jo Penny was divorced, which was semi-scandalous, but most people were relieved when she ended a match with a ne'er-do-well who had been considered unsuitable from the beginning. "We both have a gift for finding jerks," Jo Penny had once commented to Lorraine, which had triggered another battle, since on that particular day Lorraine happened to be madly in love with Denis. JP often blurted out anecdotes and opinions without thinking. Over the years, Connie and I had gleaned a lot of useful information from her.

Tonight I suspected Lorraine had invited JP over as a

buffer, to avoid our first meal together without Connie. When I finally forced myself to go down to the dining room, the two of them were already seated at the long mahogany table. They looked up expectantly as I came in. Large mirrors lined both sides of the wall, with tiny white tags tied discreetly to their ornate frames. The mirrors meant I didn't need to look at Lorraine and Jo Penny directly to see that they were eating on my grandmother's pink-and-white china, that they were smoking, even though they both agreed that smoking at the table was a horrible habit, and they both wore charm bracelets, which tinkled as they flicked their ashes.

"Come on in, girl, and get something to eat!" Jo Penny shouted. She always spoke in a party voice, as if she were talking over a crowd.

Lorraine sat at the head of the table, as she always did, and Jo Penny sat in my usual seat on the right. Lorraine smiled nervously and tugged at the chair on her other side; she didn't seem to even think about the fact that it was Connie's place. Ignoring the chair she offered, I went to the other side of the table and slouched down next to Jo Penny. I avoided looking at Lorraine directly, but the rows of glass showed broken glimpses of her: the gleam of red on her mouth, the ribbon perched on her ponytail. The sight of these festive touches sent a cold fury through me. My own reflection stared back from the wall: red and swollen nose, greasy hair, sullen expression. There was nothing pretty about me, and I was glad.

"Oh, you're sitting next to Jo Penny," Lorraine said, trying to sound cheerful even as she eyed my torn sweatshirt. "Here, let me move your plate."

She passed a plate heaped with meatloaf, mashed potatoes and a Jell-O salad crowned with a dollop of mayonnaise. Even though I hadn't eaten all day, I didn't want any of it.

45

"What would you like to drink?" Lorraine asked. "Jo Penny and I are having Tab, but there's tea."

"Water," I said, starting to push away from the table.

"No, no, stay there," Lorraine said, uncharacteristically. "I'll get it. Do you need anything, Jo Penny?"

"I'm fine, honey," she yelled.

As soon as the swinging door to the kitchen closed behind Lorraine, Jo Penny turned to me and spoke in a normal voice, which she must have considered a whisper. "Ooh, honey child, sounds like it was rough around here over the weekend."

I looked down at my Jell-O and shrugged.

"Didn't surprise me," Jo Penny said, stubbing out her cigarette. "I knew the instant your sister turned seventeen she wouldn't stick around. Chuck and Frances Wheeler's kid ran away when he was seventeen, and there's really nothing they could do. It's legal then, you know, though God knows they tried to get the police to do something. They don't like to get…"

"She didn't run away," I said.

Lorraine bustled in as I spoke, pretending not to hear. She set a water glass in front of me. "You must be starving," she said. "I was worried when you didn't come down for a snack this afternoon, but I'm glad you got some rest. I'm sure you needed it."

I stared at her: Since when did she notice whether I ate a snack? Jo Penny handed me a basket of rolls, and I automatically took one. There was a brief silence.

"We met a couple of dream boats at lunch today," Jo Penny said brightly.

I looked at Lorraine questioningly. She said, "I closed the shop this afternoon. You know how slow Mondays are. I just thought…"

"Looks like your mom and I will be stepping out soon," Jo

46

Penny cut in, wiggling her shoulders.

"We were introduced," Lorraine said quickly. "We went out for lunch and bumped into some friends of Don and Trish Snyder."

I knew them well enough to know the real story. They had gone to a bar in Reedsboro and flirted with some strange men who happened to know somebody from Carlington. I automatically looked across the table, but there was no one to exchange glances with except my own alien reflection.

"I think the lawyer really liked you," Jo Penny said. "Denis would be so jealous!"

Lorraine smiled and took a quick sip from her Tab. "We came home and watched a movie on TV. It was a really cute Shirley Temple show, just what I needed. Watching her made me feel so excited about your piano competition, Lily." She beamed at me.

"I'm not doing the competition."

"What?" She put down her fork. Jo Penny's eyebrows raised and disappeared under her teased bangs.

"I called Mrs. Turner today. I told her my piano lessons are over."

"Are you out of your mind?" said Jo Penny. "There's a waiting list. Everybody's trying to get on with her."

Lorraine pressed her napkin to her mouth then lay it carefully back on her lap. "Lily, I know you've been upset, but I want you to give this more thought. I certainly wish someone had offered me a chance like this when I was your age. I am afraid you will have serious regrets if you fail to develop your talent."

"Have you heard me play lately?" I picked up my roll then put it back on the plate. The smell of meatloaf made me feel sick.

"It's such a great opportunity," Jo Penny exclaimed. "My Marlene loves dancing, of course. Do you remember when she took tap? I still have all of her costumes."

Lorraine sighed and shot her an exasperated look. "Lily, honey, I'm sure it's not too late to call Mrs. Turner back. You're probably just nervous. That's natural, but you'll be fine."

She kept talking, with frequent interruptions from Jo Penny. All around me, the mirrors created rows of Lorraines and Jo Pennys, reflected from the front and the back and in various poses: Jo Penny's sharp nose, Lorraine's bouncy ribbon, the flash of their bracelets and the rapid movement of their lips.

"Lily, are you listening?" Lorraine asked. "I'm sure I can call Mrs. Turner and straighten all of this out. It will be hard to manage without you in the shop on Saturdays—you will need to do extra rehearsals before the competition—but I don't want you to worry about that. I'll just try to find more help if I need it."

"You just fired your best help," I muttered.

"What was that?" Jo Penny asked.

"Excuse me," I said, pushing away from the table. "I'm not hungry tonight."

"She wasn't helping, Lily," Lorraine said evenly. "She hurt me every chance she got."

"Excuse me," I said again, running out of the room.

"Lily, you're not leaving this house," Lorraine yelled after me.

I went to Connie's room and threw myself across her bed. When I couldn't cry anymore, I sat up. The sight of Connie's radio was comforting. It was an old Sylvania from the 1950s, a rectangular aqua-colored box with a dingy clock built in on one side. Years before it had sat in the shop for weeks without being sold. One day Connie had simply taken it up to her room and plugged it in. Afterwards we spent most Sunday afternoons lying together on her bed and listening to the Top 40 countdown, trying to guess the next song.

I reached down and turned it on. "One of These Nights."
I stretched out on the bed and listened, not thinking about
anything. I was still listening hours later when the station
signed off. I should go to my own room, I thought, but I stayed
on Connie's bed until I fell asleep.

Connie savors the bus ride, moving down the highway with
no effort, taking pleasure in being among strangers. There are
maybe a dozen passengers, all sitting as far apart from each
other as possible. She looks out the window, she doodles on a
scrap of paper. When she gets hungry, she eats a pack of Nabs
she bought from a vending machine at the station.

The bus moves along at an unhurried pace, much more
slowly than if she were driving, but she arrives in Reedsboro
sooner than she expects. The driver turns off the highway and
rumbles down a street lined with small, squalid houses and
dingy stores. Eventually the bus makes one last roar into the
station and stops.

She hangs around the parking lot for a while to give herself
time to think. She notices a diner across the street called Blue
Jay's; there's a help-wanted sign in the window. She goes inside
and buys a cup of coffee, checks out the place. When she leaves,
she has a job. They ask for a year-long commitment. She agrees,
but she knows she'll be gone as soon as she has enough money.

One of the other waitresses there tells her about a place for
rent, a one-room garage apartment three blocks behind the
diner. The place is cheap, the girl says, but the landlord lives
in the house right there, and she's crazy. Old Lady Brooks, a
religious nut who sometimes preaches on street corners.

Connie walks until she finds the address. She stands in front
of a small brick house with a gable over the door shaped like a

witch's hat. The garage is a separate building just a few yards away. She runs a comb through her hair and tucks her shirt into her jeans, then walks up to the front door and rings the bell. The door swings open and Mrs. Brooks appears wearing a long black dress with a gold cross pinned to her collar. She has long gray hair, but there are no lines on her face. Her eyes are clear and blue as a baby's.

"Is your apartment still for rent?" Connie asks.

Mrs. Brooks takes her time looking Connie over, her blue jeans and hiking boots, her neatly combed hair. When her gaze moves up to her eyes, Connie does not look away.

"Do you believe in the Lord?" Mrs. Brooks asks.

"Yes, I do," Connie says solemnly.

Mrs. Brooks nods. "Let me show you the place."

At dinner, with the two of us alone, I told Lorraine that I wouldn't take another piano lesson. Ever again. I got her attention and said it very quietly, and then I looked down at my chicken bones and untouched lima beans, waiting for her tirade. To my surprise, she said nothing, then she handed me her glass. "Would you freshen my drink, please?"

I went to the kitchen and poured three fingers of Scotch and a splash of water. I gave it to her and sat without eating. The beans had come from a can and had been served in a silver dish, which, as always, was set on a white tablecloth. We were on our end of the table, nearest to the kitchen. Eight feet away, the cash register sat on the other end alongside a display of teacups and saucers. I couldn't get used to the fact that Connie wasn't sitting across from me. The larger view of the mirror played tricks; the slightest movement by Lorraine or me made it seem as if we weren't alone, as if there were another woman smoking, another girl with hunched shoulders, glancing around and twitching to leave. I mumbled to be excused and started to get up to clear the table, but Lorraine said, "Lily, let the dishes wait. Sit down for a minute."

She pinched a cigarette from her pack and licked her lips. The relief I had started to feel was gone instantly. Something I didn't want to hear was coming, something she was bursting to say. We never wanted to be around when Lorraine decided to speak her truths. Connie and I had seen this too many times, the slow warm-up of self-pity that escalated into accusations and ended with a slap across Connie's face or a glass thrown across the room. I thought of the fight-or-flight response we had learned about in science class. I'd never win a fight, and there was nowhere to go. I sat.

"Lily, this might be hard for you to understand, but when Connie left, it was the best thing that ever happened to you."

I looked at her without blinking. In my lap, my fingers curled into fists.

"Connie has problems, and she has always held you back." She took a deep swallow from her drink and set it down. "You have been like..." she paused. "Like a plant. A geranium that never got enough sun. She blocked you from the light." She nodded, looking pleased with herself.

"I won't do the piano competition."

She lifted her palm. "Fine. The competition is not that important. The important thing is now you can make new friends. Lily, Connie left you. You need to stop moping about it and take advantage of all the opportunities you have."

Connie left you. The thought was too horrible to focus on right then. I only heard that Lorraine was finally saying her name, and it gave me an opening. "Do you know where she is? Have you heard anything?"

She shook her head without looking at me. "But I'm sure she's fine. Connie can take care of herself."

"She has *always* taken care of herself," I said.

She did look at me then, and I saw she had gotten my meaning. She narrowed her eyes and scanned my face. "You're smaller than I am, Lily, but you have nice features. You have lovely lips and good cheekbones. I bet the girls at school envy you, just like they used to envy me. All the girls thought I was trying to steal their boyfriends, but I didn't have to *try.*"

I had heard this before, but maybe this time she was deliberately trying to distract me. When she said she didn't know anything, I didn't quite believe her. Maybe someone had seen Connie and told Lorraine. Or maybe Connie had called or written. If Lorraine had a letter, she wouldn't give it to me, I was sure of that. The thought made me livid and, at the same time, gave me hope.

"May I be excused?" I asked, as required.

"One more thing. I need to tell you one more thing."

Most of her dinner was still on her plate, but her glass was nearly empty. She lit another cigarette, taking her time. She liked to keep me when she knew I wanted to go. I wanted to knock the cigarette out of her hand. I wanted it for myself.

She inhaled deeply, then blew the smoke to the side. "It has become clear we need some new rules around here. I have allowed you and Connie…" She stopped. She hadn't intended to say her name again, but she went on. "I have permitted you a certain amount of freedom, but you're only fifteen. A lot of bad things can happen…" She looked at me directly, waiting until I looked back. I could see the glaze in her eyes. "I need to know where you are at all times," she concluded.

"I always tell you where I am," I said, ignoring the outing with Denis.

"You cannot ride your bike around town or wander around in the woods. It is simply too dangerous. You may go out with my approval, but I need to know exactly where you'll be. Do you understand?"

I did. She was keeping a close eye on me so I wouldn't have any chances to find Connie or to run away. "Yes, ma'am," I said tightly.

Washing the dishes wasn't my usual job. Connie had always been the one to wash while I dried. We had a system: silverware first, then glasses, plates last. She was fast and efficient, and I was careful. Now it felt wrong that I was the one filling the

53

sink with water and wondering how much soap should go in. There weren't many things to wash, but my hands felt clumsy and the job seemed endless. As I finished soaping the last glass, it slipped from my hand and shattered on the floor. I took a step to fetch the broom, but felt a stab. I lifted my foot and saw the tiny gleam of a shard stuck in my heel. It stung more than I would have thought. Good, I thought. Great.

          ❧

As I was trudging down the hall between classes, a teacher named Mrs. Gorser motioned me to stop. She was tall with a long nose; Connie always called her Mrs. Horser. She put her hand on my shoulder and guided me to the wall, away from the stream of kids changing classes. She leaned down and spoke loudly over the noise. She wanted to know if Connie was sick. Her breath carried a grassy odor. I nodded.

"I hope it's nothing serious," she said.

I looked past her and waved as if someone walking in the hall had spoken to me.

Mrs. Gorser cleared her throat. "I'm afraid Connie is getting behind in geometry. Would you mind taking some assignments to her? Perhaps she'll feel well enough to do some work at home."

I followed her high, broad backside to her classroom and dutifully copied page numbers on a piece of notebook paper. "She has her book at home, doesn't she?" Mrs. Gorser asked.

"Yes, ma'am." I turned to leave, but she stopped me.

"Lily." She didn't continue until I looked at her face. "Remind your sister that she must bring a note *from your mother* when she returns to school."

"Yes, ma'am."

As I walked into history class, I balled up the assignment

54

notes and threw them into the trashcan next to the door.

❧

For the first time in my life, the telephone mattered to me. I knew from conversations at school that most girls were crazy about talking on the phone; some of them were even getting their own lines. Connie and I had never had any need to talk with a wire between us. I tried to remember a time I had heard her voice on the telephone other than when she was making prank calls and I was sitting right next to her, laughing into my hand. It was hard to imagine her calling the house now; I think I knew she wouldn't. But still, instead of avoiding the phone as usual and hoping that Lorraine would pick up the daily stream of calls from Jo Penny, Denis, customers and salesmen, I was leaping at the phone when it rang.

Lorraine was anxious about the phone, too, because she was waiting to hear from the lawyer she had met with Jo Penny. If I answered a call, she lurked nearby to hear who it was, and I did the same when she answered. Twice I heard her hang up on Denis after yelling at him for not calling her sooner. "I will not be ignored," she said. I wondered if she was really that mad at him or if she were gambling that she would hear from the other guy.

On Thursday after school, the phone rang almost as soon as I got home. *It's her*, I thought. Lorraine was with a customer in the parlor, so I ran to the phone in the kitchen. "Hello," I said, sounding too hopeful. Lorraine required us to answer by saying, "Fine-Crystal-and-Antiques-this-is-Lily/Connie-speaking-how-may-I-help-you," but Connie and I never did it unless Lorraine was close enough to hear.

"This is Darlene Gorser. May I speak to your mother?"

Well, they can't do anything to her now, I thought. I called

Lorraine to the phone, and after she picked it up, I got a glass of water and lingered.

"Why hello, Mrs. Gorser," Lorraine said, putting on her best responsible-mother voice. After listening for a moment, she tersely said that Connie no longer lived with us. "As far as I'm concerned, the school can put her on the dropout list," she said. "You can send any necessary paperwork in the mail."

When she hung up, I put down my glass and stared at her. She looked at her wristwatch to avoid my look. "Lily, when you've finished dusting, be sure to get your homework done," she said as she went back to her customer.

Just like that, she had made Connie a high school dropout. "Dropout" was a word that had always been so despicable to her she could hardly speak it, even though we knew from Jo Penny that Lorraine herself had dropped out of school for a while. I thought of all the things Jo Penny had told us that we would never hear from Lorraine herself. I wondered again if Lorraine knew something about Connie that I didn't know, and whether maybe a letter had come. The mail was delivered in the mornings; except on Saturdays, I could never be the first to see it.

I went out in the hallway and listened. Lorraine and a customer were deep into a conversation about upholstery. Stepping quietly, I went upstairs to Lorraine's bedroom, closed the door quietly behind me, and began searching. I opened every drawer and riffled through her scarves, photos and old papers. There were envelopes that had been mailed way back, before I was born, but nothing with Connie's handwriting. I closed the drawers and went to her closet and searched through the shoes on the floor and the sweaters and belts on the shelves. I looked under the skirt of her vanity and the edges of the stained carpet and even under her mattress. There was

56

nothing except dust and a dog-eared copy of *The Valley of the Dolls.*

Later that evening I was in Connie's room doing homework when the phone rang again. Through the wall, I listened to Lorraine answer in her bedroom. The words weren't clear, but I could tell from her tone it was a call she welcomed. I assumed it was Jo Penny, but then I heard her step out in the hall. She tapped on Connie's closed door. "Telephone, Lily," she trilled. "It's Joseph Satterfield."

Shit. I imagined him breathing into the receiver, waiting for me. He wouldn't be sitting; Joseph wasn't the type to slouch in a chair. He would be standing by the phone, all six feet of him, pressing the receiver against his smooth, pimple-free cheek, ready to say whatever he had rehearsed. He was going to ask me out, I was sure.

"Tell him I'm not here," I called back to Lorraine.

Lorraine opened the door and poked her head in. "That's not very nice."

I met her stare. It wasn't easy, but Connie had taught me the power of a pointed silence. Lorraine sighed and turned away. Through the open door, I heard her say I couldn't come to the phone right then.

I hoped that would be the end of it, but she came back and stood in the doorway again.

"Yes?" I said, looking up from my homework.

"Why don't you go to your own room, Lily?" she said.

"Okay." But I rolled over so my back faced her, and I didn't move.

The next afternoon when I came home from school, Lorraine was dressed in old, dusty clothes, and she looked tired. "I did an unbelievable amount of cleaning today," she said. "Would you mind fixing dinner?"

I mixed canned tuna with mayonnaise and scooped it out on lettuce leaves. I arranged some crackers and apples slices on a plate and called Lorraine to the table. We were eating in silence when the phone rang. We both jumped, and then looked at each other, thinking the same thought: It was Joseph calling back.

"Lily, will you please get it?"

I gave her an evil look, but it wouldn't pay to directly disobey her. I got up and slowly made my way toward the phone in the kitchen, letting it ring twice more. "Lily, pick that up!" Lorraine yelled. I held my nose, a poor attempt to disguise my voice, and answered cautiously.

"Hey, is Connie there?" The voice was low and gravelly, but it was a girl.

I released my nose. "No."

"This is Earl. I was wondering if she's still working here since she didn't show up last night."

I hadn't seen Earl since we were both in grade school, even though she wasn't much older than Connie and me. Everyone in town seemed to know her and thought she was likable but strange, since only men or older couples owned restaurants. People said Earl was as tough and decisive as any man. Her parents, who originally started the restaurant as "Dixie's," had named their only child Earline, but nobody called her that. Like us, Earl started working while she was just a kid, running around filling waters and delivering plates, and then serving in the kitchen and behind the register as she got older. When both of her parents passed away within a short time of each other, she left college and took over the business, completely remodeling the restaurant and adding things like bean bag chairs and black lights. No one over thirty ever went there now, and that's apparently the way Earl wanted it.

I already knew Connie hadn't shown up for work; I had called the restaurant twice during her shift. "She's not here," I said.

"When do you expect her back?" Earl asked.

"I'm not sure," I said, just wanting the call to end.

"Lily, did she have a fight with her mother?"

I was startled that she used my name and by the question itself. I wondered if Connie had talked about Lorraine and me at work, but that didn't seem likely. Other than me, Connie didn't talk to anybody, not really. "Did someone tell you that?" I asked.

"I saw it coming," Earl said. "Look, can you tell me where she is now?"

My throat tightened. I was afraid I might cry, and I was also pissed. This girl had no right to be asking questions. "I don't think she would want me giving out any information," I said stiffly.

"I need to know whether she's coming back to work."

"I just don't know," I said.

There was a pause, and I could hear her shuffling through papers. "She's scheduled to work next this Saturday afternoon," Earl said. "If you hear from her before then, would you please tell her to call me?"

"Yes," I said. "Okay." Even though Earl's prying irritated me, it was good to hear someone mention hearing from Connie as if it were a real possibility.

After we hung up, Lorraine asked who it was and made no comment when I told her. She had a low opinion of Earl's as a place to eat and work.

"I'm dead tired," she said. "Would you mind taking those

clothes out of the dryer and folding them?"

I did as she asked and stayed up watching TV. It was late when I went upstairs, and Lorraine's door was closed, the crack beneath it dark. The door to Connie's room was closed, too, which was unusual—I had been leaving it open. As soon as I touched the knob, even before I entered the room, I could feel something wasn't right.

I turned on the light and felt I had stumbled into the wrong place. The room had been stripped. Connie's bed and bureau were gone, the floor was bare of any clothes or books, and the walls were blank. In place of Connie's things, Lorraine had stacked empty boxes, out-of-season inventory, and cans of paint and turpentine.

I sank to the bare wood floor, shaking, looking for even one thing that had been Connie's. There was nothing, only the clothes I had already taken to my room. I picked up a paint brush and hurled it across the room. It landed on the wall with a satisfying smack, sprinkling a white shower of dried paint flecks. I looked at the wall that separated the room from Lorraine's and whispered, *I hate you.*

I got up and moved into the hall like an animal hunting. Moonlight poured in from the window at the end of the hall; the wood floor was cold under my feet. I opened Lorraine's door with a loud rattle of the knob, as if it were broad daylight and she wasn't there. I turned on the light. She was sprawled under the covers on her stomach, her face scrunched against the pillow and facing the door. Her head was crowned with three giant rollers on top and small pink foam cylinders on the sides. The noise and light made her stir, but she was sleeping hard and didn't wake. I shook her shoulder roughly. Her eyes flew open.

"What?" she said. "What is it?"

I grabbed her arm. "Where are Connie's things?"

"I've put them away," she said groggily. "Just for now."

"She's been trying to contact me, I know she has," I yelled. "You've intercepted messages, haven't you?"

Lorraine pulled away from me and sat up on one elbow. I watched her face closely, searching for any calculation. She only looked bewildered. I clutched her arm again. "Don't lie to me," I hissed.

She started shaking her head. I wanted to see that she *was* lying, and I could always tell. If she acted dumb or outraged, then I would pounce. If necessary, I would beat the truth out of her. But she looked at me almost sadly.

I squeezed her arm harder. "Where will she stay when she comes back?"

She pulled away as if I had done something distasteful, like I had sneezed on her. "You're over-tired, Lily. Go back to sleep."

She rolled over and faced the other way, pulling the covers closer around her. My breathing was fast; I wanted to scream, I wanted to hurt her, but how could I when she had, for once, told me the plain truth: Connie hadn't tried to send a message. I turned off the light and stumbled back to my room. The next day, neither of us mentioned it.

The lawyer from Reedsboro, a man named Ben, triggered a major event by asking Lorraine to go out to dinner. She wasn't speaking to Denis; I heard her hang up on him twice. I don't know whether they were officially broken up, but when the lawyer telephoned, I heard her say, "Yes, that sounds nice." She chatted with him calmly as they settled on the details, then she hung up and let out an ecstatic shriek. Not counting Denis, this was her first date in years.

Connie and I had never liked watching Lorraine go through the dramas of courtship, especially since everyone else we knew in Carlington had a mother who was married to their dad. Lorraine and Denis had two basic ways of being together: passionately lovey-dovey or bitterly hostile. Connie and I could never decide which was worse.

I found out there was something worse by far: Lorraine's total perkiness as she anticipated her date. On that Saturday, the first full Saturday without Connie, she came to my room before nine, calling in a sing-song voice for me to "rise and shine." When I came downstairs, she was bobbing around the house with her hair in rollers. "I'll run upstairs if somebody comes," she assured me, as if I cared. I did my chores with quiet fury, depressed at the thought of an entire weekend alone and furious at Lorraine for everything. I gave a cobweb a vicious whack with the broom and knocked over a chair. Lorraine didn't seem to notice. She was busying herself changing prices, something she loved to do. It was time-consuming; she wrote the new prices on white tags, cut them out and hung them with tiny strings on each item. One day she would hike up the numbers, the next she might mark everything down. "It keeps people coming back," she said, as if she hadn't made this comment a thousand times. "Don't you think?"

The truth is she could never make up her mind about how much something was worth. I kept sweeping without answering, without even looking up. We moved around the shop silently then, only the small, discrete noises of my broom and her small scratches and snips. The quiet in the house seemed to swell around us until it felt hard to breathe. The phone rang, and I jumped.

It was Denis, and the conversation was short. Lorraine told him it was over, completely over, and she didn't want to see him ever again.

When she hung up, she continued working on her price changes, and the silence between us took on a different tone. We were used to Denis's constant appearances, always in and out of the house like a repairman or a large, friendly dog. Lorraine didn't tell him about her date, but I was sure that, in her mind, Ben was already her new boyfriend. As she placed new tags on crystal vases, she had the starry-eyed look she had always reserved for the man who was my father. I knew instinctively that she saw this new man as a path to everything she wanted, someone who could decisively wipe out whatever had happened before. He was Security, Respectability and Revenge all wrapped up in one. She had plans; she didn't want to deal with Denis, and she didn't want to deal with me, either—not today.

Around two o'clock, the bell rang on the door and Jo Penny burst into the house. "JP to the rescue," she shouted. "Beauty patrol!" I was sitting at the dining room table, sorting and rolling coins from Lorraine's change jar. Jo Penny flounced into the room, carrying a cosmetic bag and wearing her shiny turquoise raincoat designed to look wet even when it wasn't. She paused to take a critical look at Lorraine, who came out of the kitchen wearing an old, shapeless dress and no lipstick. "We'll need to re-do your hair and spray the hell out of it," Jo Penny said, "but we'll start with our nails."

She sat down and emptied out her bag on the table, an assortment of files, scissors, and little bottles filled with liquids that ranged from clear to fire-engine red. Lorraine spread towels on the table, and they went to work on each other's hands while I kept stacking coins in their stiff paper wrappers. My plan was to finish as quickly as possible and escape to my room.

"Guess what I just heard on the radio," Jo Penny said, dabbing cuticle oil on Lorraine's nails. "They found Patty Hearst. Finally. She was with some Oriental girl in San Francisco."

My fingers froze on a paper roll of nickels.

"Thank God," Lorraine said. "They should fry her little butt in the electric chair."

I put the roll down carefully as if it might break. Without saying anything, I got up and went to the parlor and sat down on the floor in front of our old TV. A soap opera was on, but I didn't have to wait long before it was interrupted with a "special news bulletin." It was odd to see Walter Cronkite on the screen during the middle of the day; he looked out of place. He said "kidnapped heiress Patricia Hearst has been captured in a San Francisco apartment" with another young woman. They didn't show any pictures from the arrest, just the outside of a three-story apartment house strewn with yellow police tape.

In the days that followed, I would hear more details: Patty had been so scared when the police came that she peed in her pants, yet when they made her fill out paperwork, she had listed her occupation as "urban guerrilla." Later I would spend a lot of time wondering how Patty had managed to hide in San Francisco and what it would be like in jail, but right then, sitting on the floor with the TV close enough to touch, I could only think of Connie. It seemed unfair that Patty had showed up when she was still missing. I wondered, again, if she was in California, if maybe she had been nearby when Patty was caught. Maybe she had even managed to make contact. Seeing the particular house where Patty had lived made California seem both more real and farther away. The story shifted to a San Francisco park, where a group of protestors was already gathering, rallying to Patty's defense. I leaned forward and scanned their faces as the camera panned across the crowd, all too quickly. Connie was among them; I just felt it. Right then I made up my mind that nothing would stop me from going there, too.

"Lily, you need to finish rolling the money," Lorraine called.

When I went back to the dining room, she and Jo Penny were sitting at the table, smoking and holding their fingers stretched apart as their nails dried.

"I don't think I've ever known a Ben," Lorraine was saying dreamily.

"Wasn't that the name of the rat in that movie? The sequel to 'Wilson'?" Jo Penny asked.

I knew Jo Penny was in the mood to be bitchy; the lawyer's friend hadn't called her. I felt no pity. "It was *Willard*," I said. "Not Wilson." A plan was beginning to form in my mind. This could be the last time I had to sit and listen to their bullshit.

Jo Penny ignored me. "Do you think this guy really is an attorney?" she asked Lorraine. "What if he's lying?"

"I looked him up in the phone book," Lorraine said, flapping her left hand through the smoky air and squinting critically at her nails, now painted in a flaming pink. "He's a partner. Do you have any idea how much money they make?"

"I've heard that lawyers are tightwads," Jo Penny said.

Lorraine turned to me. "What do you want for dinner tonight?"

"I don't know." I finished a stack of nickels and folded the ends of the roll.

"JP, maybe you, Marlene and Lily could go out together and get a pizza."

"I'd love to, but I have plans," Jo Penny said sweetly. She obviously had been waiting to drop this information.

"Plans?" Lorraine raised her eyebrows.

"Yes, Wanda called me. We're going to Reedsboro to try that new Mexican place. Marlene has plans, too. One of the other cheerleaders invited her over to spend the night." She glanced at me, checking to see if I would show any reaction to Marlene's popularity. I didn't.

"I thought you couldn't stand Wanda," Lorraine said, "and I hate for Lily to be alone."

"I'll be fine," I said quickly.

"For God's sake, Lorraine, she's fifteen years old."

Lorraine gave Jo Penny a withering look, but didn't reply. Later, she took me aside in the kitchen. "You're not going anywhere tonight, are you?" she said. It wasn't really a question, and my answer wasn't really the truth.

It was nearly closing time when the bell chimed on the door. I thought it was Lorraine and Jo Penny returning—they had gone out to search for a new necklace for Lorraine, Jo Penny had decided it was essential—but when I stuck a finger in my book and looked up, it was Joseph. He stood in the doorway, clutching a dripping umbrella in one hand. "Hey," he said.

"Hi." In spite of the umbrella, there were damp streaks in his hair. His dark bangs hung in a razor-straight line above his eyebrows, and the rest was cut neatly above his earlobes as required by the football coach. He looked even taller than I remembered, and bigger across the shoulders. Only the week before I would have panicked at the sight of him in the shop. The jumble of junk would have embarrassed me, and I would have been bothered by my ragged Zappa shirt and unbrushed hair. Now the worse I looked, the worse everything looked, the better.

"Um, what should I do with this?" He indicated the small puddle of water forming under his umbrella. "I'm afraid I'm making a mess."

"It doesn't matter," I said.

He cleared his throat. "I hope it's okay that I came."

"We're open," I said, too politely.

He looked hurt, then stoic. "I guess I'll just look around then."

"Go ahead." I retreated to the west parlor and tried to look busy straightening things. After a while he came in, meandering around displays, touching items here and there.

"Hey, this is neat," he said, picking up a set of bongo drums. He looked genuinely excited. "I didn't know you had instruments here."

"Sometimes we do." Denis had bought the bongos at a yard sale. "Got 'em for a buck," he had chortled to Lorraine. "I bet you can sell them for three."

"I've always wanted a set," Joseph said, lightly tapping the surface of the drums. "How much are they?"

"Fifty dollars."

He put the bongos down. "Lily, why won't you talk to me? What did I do?"

Hearing him say my name made me feel weak. My hands had been shaking then and they were shaking now. I put them behind my back. "You didn't do anything."

His face turned bright red. "Are you mad because I…" he swallowed hard. "Because I tried to kiss you?"

I nodded, relieved to be handed an excuse.

"I'm really sorry," he said. "I shouldn't have…"

"I think you better go," I said quietly. "My mother doesn't allow me to be alone in the house with boys."

"Oh, golly, you should have told me…" He jammed his hands in his pockets. "Well, I won't bother you anymore." He started to leave, but then stopped. "Marlene Medcastle called last night and asked if I would go to a concert with her this weekend. I told her no, but I guess there's no reason why I shouldn't call her back."

"I guess not."

After he left, I stared out the front window at the cars passing down the road, their headlights burning through the fog. I was still at the front window when Lorraine came bustling into the house carrying a box. She set it down on the floor with a crash and called, "Lily, where are you? Why on earth haven't you turned on any lights?"

When Lorraine's date came to the door, I was in my room, listening to the radio news and nervously chain-smoking out the open window. I was surprised that Lorraine didn't call me downstairs to meet him, but then I realized she didn't want to highlight her status as a single mother. If she had insisted on an introduction, I would have given Ben a genuine smile; that's the least I could do, since he was getting Lorraine out of my way. I watched at the window as they drove away in his car, my heart thudding.

The thought of searching in a big city didn't bother me, because once I was close enough, I had no doubt I could find her. When we were kids playing hide-and-seek, I was able to zero in on Connie's hiding place, no matter how weird or remote. Since generally I didn't have any practical skills, she had been surprised. Once, when I went straight to the window seat in the ballroom and opened it to find her lying inside, she was irritated, since she had thought it might take me hours. "How did you know?" she kept asking.

"I just did," I said, not having any words to explain it. Now the hard part was getting to California.

As soon as Lorraine and Ben left, I began throwing things in a duffel bag: underwear, shirts and jeans, cigarettes filched from Lorraine's room. I took a twenty from the cash register and several rolls of coins. After one last look around—good riddance to the rows of vases and figurines, the rockers and armchairs and dusty lamps, the glass beads, the fucking mirrors on the wall—I went out the side door and shut it behind me.

The cool air outside raised the hairs on my arms, and I wished I had thought to bring a sweater. It was a dark night; the moon didn't seem to be anywhere in particular, just scattered and smeared behind the clouds. I walked through the damp grass toward the road. Down the hill at the edge of the yard, a streetlight glowed where our driveway met the bypass. I stood under the light and held out my thumb.

Several cars whizzed by. I began to remember every grisly story I had ever heard that involved hitchhiking. I thought of Patty Hearst, pulled out of her apartment and stuffed into a car. From heiress to "urban guerrilla"—Connie would love that. Already people were speculating about Patty's defense; someone said her lawyers would claim brainwashing. I knew

70

Connie would be disappointed if Patty said it was all a mistake. Imagining the sour expression that would pass across Connie's face, I longed for her. I held my thumb higher.

Cars continued to ignore me. I paced back and forth between the streetlight and shadows, resting my arm during pauses in the traffic. Every minute dragged; I was cold and tired. Several times I nearly lost my nerve and considered going back into the house, but I would imagine Connie's look of contempt.

A car in the distance began to slow down, and I forced myself to keep my thumb up. I thought it would pass, like all the others, but it was definitely pulling over. The headlights shone in my eyes, blinding me. This is it, I thought. I'll either get to California or die trying. I pulled my bag tighter over my shoulder and began loping toward the car, and then I saw it was Denis's Mustang.

He reached across the passenger side and rolled down the window. "What in the devil are you doing?"

Through the dim light, I could see that he hadn't shaved for several days. If he was actually growing a beard, Lorraine would hate it. "Nothing," I said.

"Nothing, hell. Where are you trying to go?"

"California," I mumbled.

"From Carlington?" he said in disbelief. "Get in here."

Silently I got in the car and closed the door. It smelled like beer and peanut butter.

"Girl, do you know what could happen to you? I used to hitch all the time, but you're a lot better looking than I am. This is extremely hazardous to your health."

"I don't care," I said.

"Have you thought this through? How much money do you have?"

"I got some out of the register."

He shook his head and gave a disbelieving laugh. "There's barely enough in there to get you to Tennessee."

I felt stupid, and the determined hope that had been driving me was suddenly gone. My mouth trembled and tears leaked out.

"Hey," he said softly. He reached into his glove compartment and pulled out a crumpled napkin. I reached to take it, but he leaned forward and dabbed at my face and smoothed my hair back from my eyes.

"Thanks," I said, pulling away.

He glanced up toward the driveway and spotted Lorraine's car. "I don't suppose you informed your mother that you're out here by the side of the road. Where does she think you are?"

I didn't want to tell him anything. "In the house."

He looked at me sharply. "Then where is she?"

"Uh, she and Jo Penny…"

"Lily, don't lie to me."

"She's on a date. Some guy from Reedsboro."

His face darkened in a way that scared me, but then he tried to smile. "Where did they go?"

I knew then it was no accident he had driven by. "I don't know. Honestly."

He looked at my face closely and seemed satisfied. "Listen, I'll help you find Connie."

"How?"

"I don't know. Let me think about it; I'll come up with something. But right now, you go back into the house and stay there, okay?"

"Okay," I said, sounding reluctant but feeling relieved. "Please don't tell Lorraine I was out here."

"If you don't tell her you saw me, then I never saw you."

He waited until I got up to the front porch. I lifted a planter near the door and pulled out the key we always hid there. I waved at Denis, and he waved back before doing a U-turn on the road and speeding away. I watched until he was out of sight, not wanting to go into the empty house. I tried to think of what Connie would do. When it wasn't possible to get Lorraine's car, we often hung out in an old abandoned cabin in the woods behind our house. I had never been there alone, but after gathering the courage to hitchhike, the prospect didn't seem too daunting. I went to Lorraine's car and got the flashlight she kept in her glove compartment. Clicking it on, I could see the battery was weak, but it provided a dim light. I followed its pale glow to the back yard and then to the path in the woods.

The cabin—a one-room shack, really—had been built decades earlier to house the series of gardeners who worked for my grandparents. The one small window was now a gaping square with no glass. Inside there were remnants of simple furnishings and a rusty basin. The front door, the only entrance, had fallen off long ago and had been carried off by vagrants for firewood.

The first time Connie and I found the place, we were amazed, even enchanted, as if we had stumbled upon a cottage in a fairy tale. We ran home and breathlessly told Lorraine about it, our discovery, and instantly we saw it wasn't our discovery at all. She knew the cabin, and she didn't like it. She told us that it was the old gardeners' house, and we shouldn't play there. "It's dirty and…dangerous," she had said, closing the drawer of the cash register harder than necessary.

I was crushed, but as soon as Lorraine left the room, Connie told me not to worry. We went back to the cabin that same day and set about sweeping, cleaning and decorating.

Afterwards, whenever we disappeared and Lorraine asked where we had been, we said we were playing in the woods. We never mentioned the cabin to her again, even though she must have known we went there.

Now I hesitated in the open doorway, taking in the familiar smell of pine and rotting wood. Connie's voice came back to me as clearly as if she had spoken. Here in the cabin our talk had sounded different: closer, more solid and distinct, not like in the main house, where words could drift up and get lost under the high ceilings. We had liked the compactness of a space where even whispers carried weight. I waved the flashlight from one wall to the other. Dry leaves had collected in the corners of the room, and there were animal droppings, but also all the familiar evidence of our hours there: a checkerboard, a deck of cards, candles, tattered posters, discarded tins of sardines, and burned-out matches.

Sitting in there now, alone, would be more than I could stand. I turned away and went to sit on a stump in the clearing. I clicked off the flashlight and let the darkness settle around me. There was nothing that could be seen that I wanted to see. My loneliness felt unbearable, a tearing that seemed to go on and on, and it felt like it would kill me. There was nowhere to get away from it, so I sat, listening to the night sounds around me and my own breathing. After a while I could stand it. The thought came to me that Connie and I were alike, at least for this moment. No one knew my whereabouts, either. I kept thinking I should go back home, but I didn't move.

In the distance, I heard the honk of a car horn and the faint sound of a voice calling out. I thought of another time when we were playing out here, and we wouldn't go home. It was in the summer, and Connie was eight, I was seven. We had brought a picnic to the cabin—marshmallows, sardines and crackers—and we were in the clearing, arranging leftovers in the dirt for the birds to eat. From a distance, we heard the screech of the back screen door opening, and Lorraine called us to come inside. I started to open my mouth to answer, but Connie threw her hand up and shook her head. Lorraine called louder. We sat there for a while, it seemed like the longest time to me, listening to the sound of our names in the air: *Li-ly. Con-nie.*

When we finally came out of the woods, Lorraine made Connie cut a switch from the willow tree. "You're the oldest," Lorraine said, whipping the back of her bare legs while I watched. Later, when we were alone again, Connie smacked my face, and we both felt better.

At school, when kids talked about eating frozen dinners in front of the TV, Connie and I had envied them. Lorraine believed in having a formal meal in the dining room, complete with Cecelia's china and silver. Whenever Lorraine was too tired to cook, Connie and I fixed spaghetti or macaroni and cheese, which we were required to serve on ornate silver dishes. We gulped down our food and waited to be excused. Lorraine nibbled from her plate and smoked. "We don't have much," she often said, which puzzled us, since we seemed to have more stuff than anyone we knew, "but, by God, we will eat like decent people."

A week after her date with Ben, Lorraine closed the shop early because no one came by all afternoon. At dinner, we were both in a miserable mood. She sat at the head of the table with her legs crossed, the top foot kicking the air as she alternately smoked, picked at her food, and sipped on a glass of Scotch and water. She had slept with Ben (I heard their muffled laughter in her room and then later his car engine as he drove away before daylight), but since then he hadn't called. I was entering a new stage of grief over Connie. It was clear she didn't intend to contact me, and I lacked both the courage and the money I needed to find her. So Lorraine and I sat in gloomy silence over our china plates filled with fried apples, carrot sticks and bologna sandwiches.

Lorraine sighed and suddenly looked at me. "Chew with your mouth closed."

"I am," I said.

"Don't you talk back to me."

I finished chewing and swallowed.

"Did you hear me?" she asked.

I nodded.

"Answer me," she said sharply.

"Yes, ma'am."

During the silence that followed, the telephone rang. Lorraine sat up straight and jerked her head toward the sound. She listened for the second ring, then dashed toward the hall.

"It's not him," I called after her, just low enough so she could pretend not to hear. "He's not going to call you."

I heard her say hello in her lowest, most refined voice. There was a pause, then she spoke again, harder and more matter-of-fact. When she began describing a crystal clock, I got up to clear the table.

Later, I was surprised when Lorraine, carrying a fresh Scotch, came in the parlor to join me in front of the TV. She nudged aside a lampshade and settled on the sofa, curling her feet beneath her in the way she did when she wanted to be youthful and charming. "What's on?" she asked brightly.

"Nothing. *Hawaii Five-O.*"

"You should be more active, Lily. At your age, I was always practicing cheers. It paid off, too. When I was a junior, they made me chief, even though there were several girls who were seniors."

And the next year you were kicked off the squad, I added silently. Girls who got pregnant couldn't cheer. Jo Penny had told us; Lorraine didn't know we knew.

"Boys were always crazy about me. It'll be the same for you, Lily, just you wait and see." She scowled at the television, which showed a beautiful girl in a bikini, a girl with a body like Lorraine's, only smaller in the waist and firmer in the thighs. "Cut off that trash, would you?"

78

I turned off the TV. It was quiet then except for a row of clocks ticking on a shelf. A grandfather clock near the staircase suddenly began striking, making me jump. It gonged three times and stopped, though it was after nine. In California, it would only be six-something. Connie would have the whole evening ahead of her to do whatever she wanted.

Lorraine rattled her ice cubes to better mix her drink. "You'll be taller than I am, Lily, and you're a beauty, too. I bet the girls at school envy you. Believe me, I remember what that's like."

I stood and stretched. "I guess I should do my homework."

Lorraine reached for her cigarettes. "Sit down, Lily. You don't need to go right this minute."

I sat again, feeling trapped and insignificant in an essential way. She described the dances and parties she attended, the outfits she wore. She told the story about her thirteenth birthday, when her father flew her all the way to New York to go shopping. He took her to Sardi's for lunch and bought her three new dresses and her first pair of high heels. "Mother had a fit, but Daddy told her it was all right. He said a young lady must have a proper wardrobe."

It would have been harder if Connie had been around; she had no patience for Lorraine's reminiscing. We had heard a lot about Lorraine's past, but the best stories weren't the ones she told. The most interesting bits came from Jo Penny or from our summer visits to Aunt Becky, Lorraine's sister in Atlanta, where some information slipped and some was deliberately fed to us. Lorraine's history became like random fragments of a movie seen at different times. Nobody had all the details, but over time I heard enough to piece a story together.

In 1958, Carlington had a short list of unforgivable sins for girls from decent families, especially a pretty, high-spirited girl like Lorraine. The town could overlook almost anything except crossing the hard line between white girls and colored boys. Or murder. Or getting pregnant twice without the benefit of marriage.

Lorraine was found guilty on nearly all counts. People said Connie's father was white trash, "almost as bad as a nigger." The same people whispered that Lorraine's promiscuous behavior killed her mother. Years later, when Connie and I looked at pictures of Cecelia, we found it hard to imagine. She was a big, stern woman with broad shoulders and a bulky chest. She looked stronger and more serious than Lorraine, not someone to be trifled with.

But Lorraine said her mother was the nervous type, always worrying and praying. Cecelia's family had been moderately rich and very religious, and after her inheritance was spent building our house, Cecelia concentrated on her faith. She went to the Victory Baptist Church nearly every day of her life, attending services or leading committee meetings or serving iced tea at potlucks. She went without our grandfather, who was busy running the newspaper and having fun, spending his weekends on the golf course or in the air, flying the bright yellow Piper that had thrown them deeper into debt.

Lorraine and her sister were as different as night and day, with Lorraine more nearly like night. Becky was always appropriate. She made good grades in school and earned the most badges in her Girl Scout troop. When she finished high school, she went to a girl's college in Winston-Salem. There she met a young medical student at Wake Forest who eventually became her husband.

Becky belonged to Cecelia, but Lorraine was her daddy's

girl. Rob took his youngest daughter everywhere, even golfing. He liked to show off Little Lo, as he called her, who looked so fetching in her frilly dresses and white ankle socks. She perched between bags of clubs on the back of Rob's golf cart, sipping from her daddy's beer cans. "No matter what I did," Lorraine often said, "I was never as good as Miss Perfect Becky. But I learned pretty fast that you don't have to be a goody two-shoes to get ahead in this world, not if you have looks."

Rob liked to take risks, both financial and physical. Flying was his greatest pleasure. Cecelia hated the idea of Rob in the air; she and Becky refused to go up with him. Cecelia often predicted he would turn her into a widow before the children were grown. But Lorraine begged to go flying, and against Cecelia's wishes, Rob took her. Lorraine fell in love with speed and altitude. Rob said she had stronger nerves than a Marine, but to her it was no effort to seem fearless. She always felt safe with her father, even when he did stunts in the air. The two of them sat close together in the cockpit, laughing at Cecelia and Becky. They saw themselves as stronger, braver people, people who knew how to *live*.

Lorraine was fourteen when Rob died of a heart attack. It was a hot, sunny afternoon in June, the sort of day Lorraine spent lounging and flirting at the Country Club swimming pool. When Cecelia fetched her and took her home to tell the news, Lorraine refused to believe it. Her father wouldn't have died so suddenly, not without giving her some kind of warning or sign. When the truth sank in, she secretly blamed Cecelia, with all her talk of early widowhood. Her mother's predictions were disguised wishes, and wishes could make things happen.

Rob's funeral was enormous, drawing everybody in town who counted and people from out of town, too. Lorraine wore a black knit dress with a respectable hem that fell at her knees, but it had a tight fit that showed off her small waist and size C breasts. She looked older than fourteen, and she knew it. As she and Becky and Cecelia walked down the center aisle, all of the people in the crowded church rose to their feet. Lorraine had never felt so much concentrated attention. Everyone was looking sideways at the three of them. The men, her father's friends and business associates, were looking at her especially. She paused inside the reserved pew and smoothed her dress behind her as she sat down.

At the cemetery the crowd formed a thick semi-circle around the makeshift tent, the men sweating in their coats and the women shifting uncomfortably in their heels. Becky stood between Cecelia and Lorraine and held her mother's arm. The silver casket gleamed in the sun as the pallbearers rolled it toward the open grave. It was wrong to bury him, Lorraine thought, to cover him with dirt when he had loved being above the ground. It was wrong that the day was so bright, that all these people were there, secretly impatient to take off their stockings and neckties. Becky put her arm around Cecelia. Lorraine covered her face with her hands and cried, understanding for the first time that she was alone.

After that, the world lost its shine. Becky went off to college, and Cecelia became even more nervous and irritable. By the time she turned sixteen, Lorraine hated Carlington and everyone in it. She continued going through the motions—she spent Friday nights prancing and twirling through football cheers—but everything seemed pointless and dull.

This is how things stood on a Sunday in January, when Becky was still at home on her holiday break from college. Lorraine had been skipping church on a regular basis, but because Becky was there, Cecelia insisted that the three of them attend. To make matters worse, she also insisted that Lorraine wear "the world's ugliest dress," as Lorraine called it. It was full and blousy, a pink and lavender print, with lace at the cuffs and a large white collar with sharp points. The dress made Lorraine feel frumpy and child-like.

On the way home after the service, Cecelia and Becky decided it would be a good idea if Becky gave Lorraine knitting lessons. "You could make your own sweaters, like Becky does," said Cecelia. "Wouldn't that be grand?"

Lorraine didn't think it would be grand; she preferred to buy her sweaters at department stores in Reedsboro, but Cecelia wouldn't accept any excuses. So after lunch, she reluctantly went to the east parlor and watched while Becky eagerly took out brightly colored skeins of yarn. She picked up a scrap she had been working on, and began to demonstrate a simple stitch. "You can't pull the yarn too tight, or you end up with a mess," Becky said, "and we don't want that, do we? Here, you try it now."

Lorraine took the knitting needles. "Becky," she said, keeping her voice as low and controlled as possible, "if I don't get out of here right now, I'll jam these needles straight into your eyeballs, and we don't want that, do we?"

Lorraine threw down the needles and ran outside, still wearing the horrible dress and stiff patent leather shoes. If she had thought to snatch the car keys, she would have taken the car, but it was too late to go back. She headed to the back yard and then to the path in the woods, a place where Cecelia and Becky never ventured.

It was an unseasonably warm day, mostly cloudy with weak spots of sun. In the woods, everything was still except for the occasional squawk of a blue jay and the sound of her feet brushing through dry leaves. When her feet began to hurt, she took off her shoes and continued picking her way down the path in her stockings. When the stockings tore, she yanked them from the clasps on her garter belt, and threw them in the woods. She loved the feel of air under her dress and pine needles under her bare feet, but her soles were tender, and she had to watch the ground to avoid rocks and sharp fragments of cones. The path widened, and she was startled to look up and see that she had come to the clearing where Cecelia's gardener lived.

The man was sitting on the ground, leaning against a stump in front of his small brown cabin. Everything about him was thin—his body, his face, his wispy yellowish hair. Cecelia had mentioned that he was in his thirties, but his face looked older. His long legs, covered in stained dark trousers, stretched out before him as he smoked a cigarette.

"Hi," Lorraine said, thinking she would startle him. But he barely looked up with a brief nod, and she realized he had seen her coming. She wondered if he had watched her remove her stockings, and then she remembered a day from the previous summer, when she had been wearing her bathing suit in the yard and she caught him looking at her. As soon as she had noticed his stare, he turned away and returned to his business. His name was Chet. Cecelia called him the gardener, but really he was an all-purpose handyman who took care of everything from plumbing repairs to garbage disposal, tasks Rob previously had done or managed. He was rather old, Lorraine thought, but not as old as her father. He kept to himself and seemed very serious, the kind who would never flirt. She took this as a challenge.

"May I have a cigarette?" she asked, tossing down her shoes and seating herself on the ground across from him. She tried to arrange the dress around her in a flattering way, but there wasn't much she could do with all that pink and purple and lace.

He took a package of Lucky Strikes from his shirt pocket and handed it to her. His hands were rough and his fingernails dirty. She pinched a cigarette out and waited for a light, but he seemed to be looking at something in the woods. She spotted a book of matches on the ground, so she took them and lit it herself.

"I guess you have the day off on Sundays," she said.

He nodded. "Yes, ma'am."

"You don't have to call me *ma'am*."

He nodded and looked away again.

"Do you mind that I'm here?" she asked.

"Would it matter if I did?"

"No. I guess not. But I don't want to bother you."

He looked at her squarely for the first time. "You're not bothering me, Miss Lorraine."

His eyes were grayish-green and keenly aware. His gaze and the sound of her name startled her. She felt recognized in a way she hadn't since her father's death.

"I hate this dress," she said.

He said nothing.

"It's too hot." She stubbed out her cigarette and reached behind her shoulders to work on her zipper. "I need some air."

There was a long pause, then he frowned. "Don't."

"It's all right." She began shimmying out of the dress. "I'm wearing a slip."

He got up and walked to the cabin. "Take another cigarette and go home," he called over his shoulder. He went through the ramshackle front door and closed it behind him.

She stepped out of the dress and kicked it away, watching with satisfaction as it landed in the dirt. She went up to the door, feeling daring and mischievous. She knocked lightly and took a step inside. In the dim light, she saw him standing by a small table, his long, thin back facing her.

85

"What a chicken," she giggled, standing there in her slip.

He turned around, and she watched his face as he took her in. He sighed, but he didn't look away. She realized he *couldn't* look away, and she felt satisfied; that was all she needed. She started to step back, but he crossed the room in two strides, and then his hands were on her. His grip was strong, and it scared her. "No," she said, but it was too late, and when he began kissing her, she stopped resisting.

Half an hour later she left the cabin alone, moving slowly, blinking in the light. She shook out her dress and put it on, and made her way back through the woods.

She sneaked back into the house and took a bath. Afterwards, she helped Cecelia by snapping beans and arranging flowers for the table. That evening, she sat quietly while Becky measured her for a sweater and led her through another knitting lesson.

The next day the gardener resigned his post and left with all of his belongings. A rumor went around that he had hitchhiked his way across the country. Cecelia was indignant. "He didn't even ask for his last check, and it's a good thing, because I wouldn't have given him a penny."

When Lorraine confessed her pregnancy, Cecelia realized this hasty departure was a blessing, because she would have had him killed. She made Lorraine promise never to reveal his identity.

For years, Lorraine kept her word and probably would have died with the secret except for a hot summer night with Jo Penny that featured too many gins on ice. She made Jo Penny swear not to tell. She dug through stacks of books until she found a Bible, and she insisted that Jo Penny literally lay her hand on it while repeating a solemn, if somewhat slurred, pledge to God. But Lorraine's judgment was impaired; she forgot that Jo Penny wasn't much of a believer.

As much as I dreaded going to school, Saturdays were even worse. Connie and I had always worked in the shop together, managing to hang out in rooms away from Lorraine, sneaking in card games and forbidden snacks. Now Lorraine wanted me to work by her side, usually in the mirrored dining room. For years Connie and I had sprayed and cleaned the rows of glass, working on opposite walls. I had felt protected by multiples of her—the back of her head, her profile, the sweep of her arm as she polished. Now everywhere I looked it was Lorraine and Lorraine and Lorraine; there was no escape.

She tried. She asked me how my week had been at school.

I said, "Okay."

"Just okay?" she probed.

"It was fine," I said, spraying more Windex on a mirror I had just finished.

She started to tell me about an heirloom armoire she had acquired, then trailed off when she saw I wasn't listening. "When you're done with the mirrors, would you mind dusting in the parlor?" she asked, trying to be nice but grating on my nerves.

The usual oppressive silence set in between us. I began wiping things on one side of the parlor while she did paperwork at her desk on the other side. For long minutes, there was no sound other than the scratching of her pen and the occasional hiss of my spray. Just as I was wishing that a customer would come in, the bell tinkled at the front door. I expected to hear a yoo-hoo, but nobody spoke.

"Hello," Lorraine called without looking up from her work.

We heard quiet footsteps—deliberately quiet, almost stealthy—then Denis was standing in the doorway.

It had been a month since they had broken up or even spoken. His sideburns were longer, and there was the mustache I had already seen. Lorraine's hands flew to her hair. She half rose, then sat again. "Can I help you?" she asked coolly.

He was wearing a pink shirt with oversized silver cufflinks shaped like stars. The skin around his facial hair looked freshly shaven. He glanced at me, twitched his eye like a wink, and smiled ever so slightly at Lorraine. "I'm looking for a grand piano."

"Sorry," Lorraine said. "We don't have any."

"Then how about a pretty lady to take to dinner?"

"We're fresh out of those, too."

"*Au contraire.* I see one you must have missed."

He was still smiling, but his eyes seemed to turn a darker shade of blue. Lorraine lifted her chin and, for a long moment, they stared at each other. He looked confident; I guessed that he had spoken to Jo Penny and knew that Lorraine wasn't seeing the lawyer. Lorraine's face shifted like a prism, registering anger, caution and a glint of delight, a glint I was sure she didn't want to show. She was the first to look away. "When were you thinking of going?" she asked.

"Now."

"But it's way too early for dinner, and I have the shop…"

"We can get a drink first. Lily can take care of the shop."

"I'm not ready. I need to change clothes."

"Well, go get ready." He grinned, knowing he had won again.

Lorraine stood with as much dignity as she could muster, and he watched her walk away before turning to me. "Hi there,

Gorgeous. Thumbed anywhere lately?"

I shook my head.

He walked around the room, touching the clocks on the mantle, examining Lorraine's roll-top desk, perusing her papers. He picked up an envelope, read the address, put it down. "So she only had the one date with the lawyer asshole?" he said.

"How do you know he's an asshole?"

He just shook his head, as if it were too obvious to explain. As he had often told us, he "narrowly escaped" becoming a lawyer himself. When he began college in Boston, he had planned to go on to law school.

He picked up an old parasol decorated with red and yellow flowers, and twirled it. "This looks Asian. Makes me think of Saigon."

"But you weren't in Vietnam..."

"Nah, the government didn't take old farts like me, thank God." He had recently turned forty, a fact Jo Penny often mentioned to Lorraine along with her opinion that one would think a man that age would want to settle down.

"You know I might have liked being in the Navy," Denis mused. "There's something about being on the water. I've told you I worked on a cruise ship...that's part of what I'm writing about. You know I'm working on a novel, right?"

I nodded. He had been talking about his novel since he and Lorraine got together, and occasionally he disappeared for a few days or a week to "bang out some work on the book," but as far as I knew, he hadn't shown any pages to anyone. Based on various descriptions I had heard from him, the story involved an amazingly intricate plot set in half a dozen locations around the world, all of it focused on a dashing hero who kept encountering beautiful women in bikinis as he completed important political missions. "Kind of like James Bond meets the Jackal," Denis often said, "but it'll be better."

Before he could say more, the door bell tinkled, and a customer, a regular named Mrs. Pegram, came in. Connie always called her Mrs. Pigworm, even to her face; Mrs. Pegram thought she had a speech impediment. Lorraine couldn't stand her either. Mrs. Pegram was a constant complainer who liked to spend hours in the shop whining and not buying. She was a small, nervous woman with a perpetual crabby expression on her over-rouged face. Before I could say anything, Denis stepped forward. "Good afternoon, Madam. May I help you?"

She peered at him suspiciously. "You're Lorraine's boyfriend, aren't you?"

"Fiancé," he said, ignoring my look. Although he had never officially proposed to Lorraine, he liked to tell people they were engaged.

"Where's Lorraine?" Mrs. Pegram asked, looking around.

"She's with another client right now," Denis said. "May I be of service?"

"I'm looking for a chest of drawers," Mrs. Pegram said reluctantly, as if she were hesitant to reveal this information to just anyone.

"Excellent," Denis said.

"It's for my grown daughter," Mrs. Pegram confided. "I've been trying to tell her she needs something bigger. Her things are a mess, and she won't stop buying more junk."

"Ah, I see." Denis pressed his palms together and looked around the room. He spotted a battered-looking bureau. "Right here." He put his arm around Mrs. Pegram and led her to it. "You know antiques, don't you?"

She touched a chipped edge of the wood and nodded vaguely.

"It only needs refinishing," Denis said. He asked Mrs. Pegram

90

where her daughter lived, and he listened sympathetically as she described the perils of driving in Charlotte. Before I knew it, they were talking about her garden, and she was giving him the recipe for her special spaghetti sauce, which she said she had never shared with anyone. Denis was a very good cook himself, but he asked dumb questions and began recording all the details on a piece of scrap paper. By then he was calling her by her first name, and she was smiling and looking at the bureau with more interest. But when Denis mentioned two hundred dollars, her eyes flew open wide.

"I can't spend two hundred dollars."

"Of course not, Judy," Denis said. "Given that it needs some work, I could let it go for less. How about one twenty-five?"

She shook her head, but Denis kept talking, and in the end she wrote a check for ninety dollars. He agreed to hold the bureau for her until she arranged for pick-up. He told her she had a real bargain. Beaming, Mrs. Pegram left the shop. Denis smiled and waved. When the door closed behind her, he shook his head. "That lady doesn't know shit about a good tomato sauce."

"Lorraine would have let that thing go for ten bucks," I said.

"And ten bucks is all she would have gotten." He reached over and gave the back of my neck a little squeeze. "The more you ask for, the more you get, Lily."

The quick tap of high heels sounded from the hall, and Lorraine came in wearing boots, wool gauchos and a tight black sweater.

Denis looked her up and down and gave a low whistle.

"I assume we're going somewhere nice," Lorraine said. Her face was still set against him.

I told her Denis had made a sale.

"Really? I'm not surprised." She gave me a list of chores and warned me not to leave the house. From the porch, she called back, "We won't be late." As Denis closed the door behind them, he caught my eye and mouthed, "We'll be late."

I put the closed sign on the door and called a taxi to pick me up, praying that no customers would come. I had never ridden in a cab before; no one in Carlington ever used cabs except poor people who didn't have a car to get to work and people with emergencies. I'm sure the bearded man who picked me up was surprised to get called to our house, but he didn't say a word when I got in except to ask where I was going. When the car delivered me to Earl's parking lot, I paid him quickly and jumped out.

It was still early; the parking lot was nearly empty. I paused in front of the door to tuck in my shirt and run my fingers through my hair. I was wearing Earl's standard uniform, including a denim skirt that was supposed to be short, but because it was Connie's, it hit the top of my knees. The red T-shirt with "Earl's" scrawled across the pocket looked all right.

The sign on the door said "Closed," but when I pushed, it opened. I took a deep breath and went inside.

The main room was unlit; a few cracks of light slanted in from the edges of the windows. The smell of French fries, smoke and stale beer hung in the air. I looked around, letting my eyes adjust to the dimness. It had been years since I had seen the inside of Earl's. When Connie and I were little girls—when Earl's parents still ran the place as a regular diner—Lorraine had brought us here occasionally to eat things like dumplings and fried apples. The booths against the wall looked the same, with their plastic red seats and gray speckled Formica tops, but the seating had been supplemented with tables made out of giant wooden spools, several bean bags scattered nearby, and a church pew. The pew held a few paperback books, a backgammon board and a box of crayons. All around on the walls were large and small paintings on unframed canvases— bright geometric shapes and Picasso-like figures, all signed "E.M."—Earl Matthews, I assumed. There was also a macramé hanging and a large "Keep on Truckin'" poster that showed a cartoon man striding with oversized feet. Looking around at everything, I understood why Connie had loved it here.

An arched doorway was covered with long strands of pink and purple beads. From within, a radio played a faint jumble of music and static. I cleared my throat and coughed. When no one came, I pushed through the beads and stepped to the other side.

I expected to be in the kitchen, but it was a large pantry lined with shelves and cabinets. Beneath a rusty freezer, a puddle of water gleamed on the floor. A skillet the size of a manhole cover hung on the wall, and an enormous can of lard sat half-opened on a stool. Through another wide doorway I could see an old black stove with a dirty grill on the side. A girl was sitting at a table, chopping a pale head of iceberg lettuce. She looked older, maybe nineteen or twenty. With her prominent nose and heavy black eye makeup, she made me think of a raccoon. The name "Sherry" was scrawled in black marker on her work shirt. She gave me a belligerent look. "We're not open."

I took a step toward her. "I'm here to apply for a job."

This is one of many ideas that had occurred to me during the middle of the night. These evenings I went to bed exhausted and fell asleep quickly, but then I would open my eyes three or four hours later, completely awake. I lay in the dark and tried to come up with a plan. The need to do something was becoming unbearable. Somewhere in the dark hours of morning it occurred to me that I could apply for Connie's job. At the time, the idea seemed brilliant. I convinced myself that money was the biggest obstacle between us. Taking her job would help me feel closer to her now while helping me earn enough money for a cross-country bus.

Sherry kept chopping. "We're not hiring now."

"I want to take Connie Stokes' place. I'm her sister."

She narrowed her eyes and gave me a long up-and-down stare. "You don't look like her."

"Do you do the hiring?" I asked pointedly.

She gave a little grunt. "You'll have to talk to Earl. She's due here anytime."

I sat down at the table across from her. She chopped the lettuce slowly, like the work was tiring.

"I'll help, if you like," I said.

She shrugged. "There's plenty to go around." She gestured toward the end of the table, where there was a cardboard box filled with lettuce. I reached inside and took a head; it felt slick in my hands. "Doesn't this need to be washed first?"

She shook her head disdainfully. "Just pick off the bad parts. If you wash it today, it'll look like hell when we use it the rest of the week."

I started tearing the lettuce with my hands, the way Denis had taught me. She shook her head. "Use this. Here." She reached in a drawer and handed me a long, dull-looking knife. "I was really pissed off when your sister stopped showing up. I had to work by myself. It's lucky we haven't been too busy."

"Have you heard from her?" I tried to sound casual. I had called the restaurant several times, but it occurred to me that Sherry might know something.

"Hell, no. What did she do, run away?"

"My mother kicked her out of the house."

She shook her head. "I'm not surprised. That girl's not easy to get along with."

There was a clank, then a scuffling noise from somewhere in the back. A door slammed, and a skinny white guy with a reddish Afro came into the kitchen. He was carrying a tray filled with stacks of frozen hamburger patties.

"This is Connie's sister," Sherry said. "Unlike Connie, she claims she wants to work."

"Connie did her share of the work." He spoke in a slow, dreamy voice. "And more," he added.

"Are you saying I don't do my part, Fry-Boy?" Sherry asked.

"I ain't said nothing about you."

We heard footsteps in the dining room, then a hand parted the beads in the doorway and Earl breezed into the room. I had always pictured her as someone who would be short and stocky, but she was tall and slender in an athletic way, with a plain face and short, curly hair. Her white overalls, strapped over a tie-dyed T-shirt, were splattered on one knee with blue and yellow paint.

She plunked a sack of groceries on the counter and turned to Sherry. "Why is that mess on the floor out there?"

Her voice was low and rough, but somehow appealing— Mae West without any come-on. I remembered seeing her wait tables when she was just a skinny kid, only a few years older than Connie and me. Even then she had been impeccably competent, as if she had been born knowing how to keep orders straight and carry three trays at once.

Sherry looked sullen. "What mess?"

"There's a pile of cigarette butts on the floor. Looks like somebody spilled an ashtray."

"Oh. That. I'll get to it when I'm finished with all this lettuce."

Earl had already turned away and was looking at me. "That's Connie's sister," Sherry announced.

"Did you come for her last check?"

"Um, yes," I said, stopping myself just in time before saying "ma'am." "I want to apply for her job, too."

Earl gave a small laugh and said, "You and a dozen others who've been pestering me."

"Did you know Connie's got kicked out of her own house?" Sherry asked.

Earl kept talking as if Sherry hadn't spoken. "Do you know where she is?"

I shook my head. "Have you heard from her?" I had to ask.

"No. And I've checked around." She noticed my look of surprise and added, "I don't like it when my employees disappear."

She sat on a stool and eyed me as if she were sizing me up. "We've managed all right without her. I wasn't planning to hire anyone else for a while."

"I started using a cash register when I was six," I said. "I'm used to working."

Earl opened a drawer and rummaged through some receipts. I thought she might be done with us, but then she closed the drawer and squinted at me with an appraising look. "You're only fifteen, right?"

I wondered how she knew; most people guessed older. "Almost sixteen."

Earl nodded. "I could use some help around the holidays, beginning right after Thanksgiving. Can you work on week nights?"

"Yes," I said quickly, though I had no idea how I would

convince Lorraine to let me work here anytime.

"Okay, there are a few things you need to know, Lily. First, if guys come in here wearing a tie, stop serving beer. You're underage, and I don't need any trouble from the ABC Board."

"Got it," I said.

"Second, you need to hem your skirt. You look like somebody's grandma."

I nodded.

"That's it," she said. "I'll call when I've put you on the schedule." She turned to the cook. "Go ahead and fry up a bunch of cheeseburgers. There's a football game tonight."

"Okay," he said. "Let me have a smoke, and I'll be right back."

He went out the back door, and I started to go, too, feeling elated. I realized I had plenty of time to walk home and that's what I wanted to do. Just as I got to the door, Earl stopped me.

"Wait, take this." She handed me a check: fifty-eight dollars and twenty-three cents, made out to Connie. "Maybe she'll turn up and you can give it to her."

"You're still paying her?" I asked.

"She earned it," she said, already turning away.

When I went out, the cook—I never heard anyone call him anything other than Fry-Boy—was leaning against a dumpster, smoking a joint. I nodded at him, and from the other side of a cloud of smoke, he gave me a small smile. "I liked your sister," he murmured. "She was all right."

10

Sometime after midnight, I heard Lorraine and Denis making their way up the stairs, giggling and shushing each other. Around five in the morning, I woke up again when Denis started his car in the driveway and roared away. Lorraine rarely let him stay until daylight; she didn't want to risk her newly restored reputation on a chance sighting of his car.

Later, after I got up and started to go downstairs, she called me to her room. It was a longstanding rule that we didn't enter Lorraine's bedroom unless invited. It was her sanctuary, carefully decorated, with a blue-and-yellow bedspread to match the heavy, fringed curtains that framed her window. All signs of Connie's vandalism had been cleaned from the carpet, and the vanity table was restored to its usual clutter of makeup and potions. In addition to the large vanity mirror, there was a smaller one surrounded by little round light bulbs. When we were small, Connie and I had sometimes sneaked in to preen in front of that mirror, pretending we were movie stars.

Lorraine was lying on her bed, wearing only a slip. The pantyhose she had worn the night before were slung over a chair. The smell of warm nylon mixed with a trace of her perfume.

"Come talk to me, Lily," she said cheerfully, patting her bedspread where she wanted me to sit. I approached cautiously and sat on the very edge of the bed.

"I have some exciting news," she began, her eyes sparkling. "Construction is starting on Denis's property in two weeks. He's beginning with four houses, and he thinks he can sell them right away, even before they're done."

This didn't seem like news to me—Denis had been making similar announcements for at least two years—but I forced a smile.

"And guess what else," she said, her eyes bright. "We're getting married."

I cocked my head and widened my eyes, feigning surprise. She seemed to forget they had said this before, too.

"When?"

"Soon. He hasn't made a formal proposal yet, but he will." Lorraine looked at me appraisingly. "He likes you. That's lucky." She leaned back on the pillows piled behind her. "The timing is right now that..." She stopped. "Well, now that he's getting more financial security." She gave me a swift look; I tried not to show anything on my face. "Most men are scared away by children," she said, "but he doesn't mind. He was raised Catholic, and Catholics believe children are sacred."

I thought about the used condoms that Connie and I had often seen in the bathroom trashcan. Lorraine looked dreamy. "Last night we talked about our favorite names for kids. He wouldn't come right out and admit it, but I think he really wants a child."

This *was* new; I was stunned. "Would you have another baby?" She was almost thirty-five, so I supposed it was possible.

"Well, it wasn't really what I had planned. But if Denis wants to start a family, maybe I'll do it. Just one. He will be a wonderful father, don't you think?"

I nodded numbly. "I guess I'll go eat breakfast," I said.

"Great!" she said, as if I had mentioned something remarkable. "Would you mind putting on the coffee?"

Walking through the dining room on the way to the kitchen, I tried not to look in the mirrors as I passed, but there they were, and there was my face: small, pale, unfamiliar. It was a face that was easily forgettable, I thought, like an extra who crosses a street in a movie.

❧

When Lorraine was six months pregnant with Connie, she and Cecelia nearly had a wreck. They were on their way to the next county for a doctor's checkup. Lorraine had wanted an abortion, and she knew her mother could make the necessary connections, but Cecelia was horrified at the very idea. Neither of them ever considered going to old Dr. Sprayer, the family doctor in Carlington. The thought was too embarrassing to contemplate.

It was raining hard that day. Lorraine asked to drive—she secretly thought herself to be a better driver than her mother—but Cecelia said absolutely not, not in those conditions.

Neither of them spoke during the forty-five minute trip; the only sound was the squeaky work of the windshield wipers. Lorraine had already left school, and the long days at home were excruciating. Except for the grudging performance of chores ordered by Cecelia, she spent most of the time in her room brooding. Once she went to the library, hoping to find a book with a simple solution. No coat hangers for her; she wanted a pill, a charm, a secret recipe. Now she dreaded the visit to the doctor, the false cheerfulness of the nurses, the disapproval in the doctor's eyes, his rough hand as he probed her.

She wasn't looking at the road when Cecelia suddenly hit the brakes. Lorraine was thrown forward, slamming her stomach hard against the glove compartment. She found herself staring at the back end of a car, just inches from their front bumper. For a moment she couldn't get her breath.

Cecelia was totally unnerved, quivering and panting.

101

She pulled the car over to the side of the road and gripped Lorraine's shoulder. "Are you all right, honey?"

Lorraine lifted her blouse, revealing the beginning of an ugly purple bruise across her round belly.

"Oh, my God," whispered Cecelia. "We'd better hurry to the doctor."

As they continued on, Lorraine felt a rush of hope. She held her breath and closed her eyes; it seemed to her that something inside her was cramping and shifting. "Please, please," she kept thinking.

But after the doctor finished his examination, he stood up straight and looked directly at her until she had to meet his eyes. "The baby is fine," he said. "You're not going to lose it."

Lorraine was dressed in a pink and white suit and matching hat, ready to go out, when Denis strolled in wearing faded blue jeans with a hole in the knee.

"Hey, where are you going?" he asked.

"The D.A.R. luncheon. I told you about it." She looked exasperated, and her face darkened. "Denis, I hope you're not going out in public dressed that way."

She had already criticized my outfit, which happened to be a pair of Connie's gym shorts and a long-sleeved sweatshirt. She told me it wasn't appropriate to wear shorts while waiting on customers, especially in November. "I'll change," I said, but I hadn't done it yet.

"You look gorgeous," Denis said to Lorraine in a mollifying way, giving her a peck on the cheek. "I was hoping to take you out to lunch."

She put her hands on her hips and heaved a big sigh. "Why didn't you call? You can't just come by here and expect me to be available. I'm tied up all day. After the luncheon, Jo Penny wants to go shopping."

"All right," Denis said, his hands raised in mock surrender. "Maybe next Saturday."

After she had gone, Denis went to the kitchen and came back with a beer. He tipped it back in his mouth and then handed it to me. The cold bottle felt good in my hand; I took a long swallow.

He stood over the dining room table, shuffling through the day's mail. "There's nothing interesting there," I said.

He picked up a brochure for a dating service in Reedsboro. "Did Lorraine ask for this?"

"I don't know. I need to get the dusting done." I picked up a rag and walked out of the room.

He followed me, standing in the doorway to watch while I swiped at the furniture. He cleared his throat. "I know it's a tough time for you, kid."

I kept wiping at the same place on a tabletop. "Yeah. I guess so."

"Look, let's go look around some more. There are some places…"

"What for? She's not here."

"You can't be sure. Come on, it won't hurt to look."

He's bored, I thought. *He doesn't want to be alone.* "I can't leave the shop," I said.

"Just for thirty minutes? Come on, I'll write a note and tape it to the door."

He grabbed a piece of paper from the kitchen and scrawled in big letters: "RIGHT BACK."

As usual, Denis had to move a stack of stuff from his front

seat before I got in the car. This time there was a stack of library books, including *Watership Down* and *You Can Profit from a Monetary Crisis*. He tossed them on the floor in the back, and I sat gingerly, taking care not to step on the sticky mass of Sugar Babies that had melted and congealed on the floorboard next to a cluster of old styrofoam cups. I thought about Lorraine's meticulously clean car. I wished I were alone in Connie's room, away from both of them.

"I knew you would come," he said, smiling at me as we backed out the driveway.

I was suddenly conscious of my bare legs, and I tugged at the hem of my shorts. "How did you know?"

"The law of inertia."

"What does that mean?"

"It means that behavior is very predictable."

"Connie wasn't predictable," I said.

He turned the car right, heading away from town. "So you're still thinking she's on the West Coast?"

I nodded.

"Your mother thinks so, too."

I looked at him in astonishment. "Lorraine has talked about her?"

"She didn't want to at first, but I kept asking questions. Finally, she broke down and cried. She thought Connie would be back by now."

"She cried?" I was shocked; it took me a moment to register this information. "Does she *want* Connie back?"

"Well," he hesitated. "Of course. She wants her to straighten up and change her ways, but she's worried about her."

"She acts like Connie never existed..."

"She doesn't know what else to do. She doesn't want to get the police involved, she's afraid it would become public."

"She didn't think about that when she kicked her out."

"Your mother has a temper, but after some time, she gets over things. God knows, it's happened enough with me."

"Even if she's over it, Connie's still gone."

"I can help you find her," he said.

You've said that before, I thought, but said nothing.

"You've heard me mention Don Taylor, the guy I hired to do my construction work?"

I nodded.

"Well, it turns out his brother is a private detective. Has an office in Reedsboro."

I had never heard anyone mention a detective outside a TV show. "Connie wouldn't like it."

"She wouldn't know. It's not like he would be following her around. All he needs to do is find her address."

"I don't know…"

"Do you really want to find her?"

"It would cost a lot of money…"

"Don't worry about that. Don says he can get me a good deal. And he says his brother knows what he's doing. In just a week or two, maybe, we'll know exactly where she is."

A week or two. A time within reach, specific enough to hold a real hope. "Okay," I said. "That would be great." I felt like I had been trapped in a deep hole for weeks, and he was handing me a rope and a light. "Thank you."

We were on a small two-lane road, a place I had never seen before. A sign said we were entering the next county. "There's something I want to tell you," I said.

He glanced at me. "Shoot."

"I got a job. I took Connie's job."

He gave a low whistle. "Your mother won't be happy about that."

"Will you tell her it's all right?"

"Well, I don't know," he said, teasing. "Maybe you shouldn't be working in a place like that, where all the boys can come in and flirt with you. Won't what's-his-name be jealous?"

I hadn't seen or heard from Joseph since the day he had come to the shop, but through Jo Penny and talk at school, I knew he was dating Marlene. I tried not to think about it. "He doesn't have anything to say about this," I said stiffly. "Will you back me up when I tell Lorraine about the job?"

"I'll give it my best shot."

I felt a surge of hope and an unfamiliar sense of freedom. "Lorraine is a bitch."

Denis flashed a grin at me. "Now, now," he said mildly. "It's not easy to be a mother on your own, Lily. Don't be too hard on her."

"She's hard on us," I said bitterly, turning away toward the window. I stared out at a stripped tobacco field. Then I felt his hand on my shoulder.

"Come here," he said. He pulled me toward him, and I let myself sink down until I was lying across the seat with my head on his lap. He kept driving fast; my head bounced as we hit bumps in the road. He stroked the edges of my ears. It didn't seem right, but it didn't seem wrong, either. My heart was beating hard, and I was embarrassed because he could see how fast I was breathing. He kept rubbing my ears and then my shoulder until, gradually, I relaxed.

I was nearly dozing when I felt something hard beneath my cheek, and I realized it was him. He was petting me in long strokes, his hand moving from my shoulder down to my waist and over the curve of my shorts and on down to the bare side of my thigh. I was sleepy, too sleepy to move, even when I felt his fingers tickling over the cups of my bra. "Okay?" he whispered.

I kept my eyes closed.

He slipped his hand under my sweatshirt, reached around my back and unhooked my bra. Then my bare breast was in his hand. *I'm smaller than Lorraine,* I thought. He pinched my nipple lightly between his fingers. After a while he took his hand away, and I felt the car make a turn. I was afraid he would start touching me again and I was afraid he wouldn't. The car jostled through bumps and ruts; I knew we must be on a dirt road. I stirred a little, as if just waking up. "Where are we?"

"Shh." He stopped the car and turned off the ignition. His fingers fumbled beneath me as he unzipped his pants. I lifted my head a little to give him room. Then I looked and saw it, his dick, poking out through his fist. It was shorter than I would have thought, but thick and hard. He took his hand away and told me to touch it. I reached out gingerly and tapped it; it swayed like a balloon tied to a string. He asked me to kiss it, and I did. He told me to put it in my mouth, and after a minute he told me to stop. He said we should get in the back seat where there was more room.

Connie can never know about this, I thought. I sat up and opened the door and climbed into the back. He lay on top of me; I was surprised he didn't feel heavier. Candy wrappers crackled around our feet. He's not my father, I kept thinking. He's not even married to my mother.

I panicked when I woke to the sound of Lorraine's high heels in the hall. When Denis had brought me home, I stumbled to my room to sleep. I felt sticky and sore between my legs. Lorraine tapped on my door and opened it at the same time.

"Lily?"

I pulled the covers up over my chest, hoping to cover my

smell. "Ma'am?"

She opened the door wider. "What are you doing in bed? Are you sick?"

"I have a stomachache."

"What have you been eating? Did you have junk for lunch?" She walked toward me. I clutched the covers at my chin and held my breath.

"You're shivering," she said. "Do you have a fever?" She pressed her hand against my forehead. Her hand was cool; I could feel the edge of her nails. "You do feel warm," she said.

"I'm all right. Or I don't know, maybe I am sick. I just want to sleep."

She stood up straight and stepped away. "I need a nap, too. Jo Penny dragged me all over the county looking for a new sofa for her sunroom. I swear to God, there's not a thing wrong with the one she has that wouldn't be fixed by new slipcovers, but she won't listen to me."

At the doorway, she turned. "Did we make any good sales today?"

"No."

She sighed as she walked away. "That's too bad."

11

Lorraine and I were in the dining room arranging a display of glass ashtrays she had labeled "Early American." Since I had come home from school, our conversation had been careful and polite. As I took the ashtrays from a box, they flashed spectrums in the mirrors on the wall. The light caught Lorraine's eye. She looked up and saw herself reflected in a large oval of glass. She touched her hair.

"I look pretty good for my age, don't you think?"

"Uh huh," I said. When it was necessary to look at her, I did so in quick glances that avoided her eyes. I had been doing exactly what she told me to do.

"I've got good cheekbones, and the color's still bright in my hair." She lifted a wavy strand from the crown of her head and let it fall. "Some blondes fade or turn dark, but I haven't. A lot of girls pay good money to get this color from a bottle."

She lifted her skirt and extended one of her legs, flexing it so the calf looked round and firm. "And I have great legs, don't I?" When I didn't answer immediately, she looked up at me.

"They're nice, Mother."

"If we went out together, we could almost pass as sisters, don't you think?"

"Sure."

"I'm still in my prime, Lily. I'll be damned if I'll sit around and wait for the phone to ring. If Denis is waiting to hear from me, then I hope he's not holding his breath. He thinks he can call ten minutes before he decides to go out, and I'll come running. Well, one of these days he might find that I am

109

permanently unavailable."

I kept polishing ashtrays and stacking them on the table. She hadn't heard from Denis, but I had. I thought he might avoid me after our ride, at least for a while, but he came around the very next day when Lorraine had her hair appointment. He said I had seduced him, and I believed it, though it seemed to me that we had struck a bargain, just as my whole life I had seen Lorraine bargaining. She often told us nothing was free. A thought came that I didn't want: This was a twofer, a two-for-one deal. I was making Lorraine pay for kicking out Connie while paying Denis for the hope of finding her. This entered my mind in the most fleeting way. Mostly I thought the thing with Denis had just happened, the way I might trip and suddenly find myself sprawling in a forbidden room.

Lorraine sighed. She went to the telephone in the kitchen and dialed.

"Jo? Hey, what are you doing?"

There was a pause. "Look, I'm sorry I haven't called you lately. Things have been so damned busy here, but, listen, I'm going stir crazy. What do you say we go to Reedsboro tonight?" Another pause. "I don't care where, as long as the scenery is good, if you know what I mean. I've had it with Denis." Her lighter made its clicking sound and then snapped shut as she lit her cigarette. "No, I mean it. If he calls tonight, I don't want to be here."

She came back into the dining room looking noticeably more cheerful. "JP knows a place in Reedsboro where they play oldies, all the good records when we were coming along. She's picking me up after supper." She looked at me pointedly. "You have homework to do tonight, don't you?"

"Yes ma'am." It was true, including a book report I hadn't started.

She hummed around me, fussing with the ashtrays I had already arranged on the side table. "This is too many," she said, putting some back in the box. "They need to look unique."

~⁓~

A picture of Lorraine at seventeen, a story: She's sitting outside on the front porch, her chin on her knees. Her hair is longer and a lighter blonde, gleaming on her shoulders in a soft curve. Her hands dangle over her knees; she's not smiling. While her friends lounge at the Carlington Country Club and go to end-of-summer parties, she's stuck in the house with Cecelia and Connie, who both grow more difficult and demanding every day.

Without consulting Cecelia, she arranges for a friend to pick her up on a Saturday night. She takes a bath and curls her hair. As she sits at her vanity putting on her makeup, Cecelia comes in and stands with her hands on her hips. "Why are you getting fixed up?"

"I'm going out." She draws a bow of red lipstick on her mouth. "You can't make me stay here."

"What about your daughter?" Cecelia asks.

"She'll go to sleep soon. You'll be here—you're always here."

They are still arguing when a horn blows in the driveway. Cecelia's chest is heaving; her face turns red all the way down to her neck. "You are not leaving this house."

With Cecelia shouting behind her, Lorraine grabs her pocketbook, runs out of the house, and throws herself into Cindy Stevens' convertible, where Cindy waits with a shiny new fifth of bourbon in a discreet brown bag.

Riding in Cindy's car gives her a feeling of joy, an exhilaration she hasn't felt since she flew with her father. Everything feels easy, anything feels possible. She isn't about to spoil her evening by dwelling on the unpleasant business with her mother. They head for a bar just outside of town called Club 91, a place with pool tables, a jukebox and a small dance floor. Most of the regulars are older than Lorraine's crowd, but the manager isn't particular about the age of his patrons, especially young girls who might be good for business.

The club isn't crowded when she and Cindy arrive, but by the time they order their second glasses of Coke to mix with the bourbon, there's noise and heat all around them. A homely man walks up and asks Lorraine to dance. She shakes her head, and she and Cindy giggle as he shuffles back to his table. A guy Cindy knows taps her shoulder, and she puts her drink down and lets him lead her away. Lorraine doesn't mind being left alone at the bar; she feels beautiful and invincible and free.

A man comes in and stands at the door, surveying the dancers and pool players. He is good looking in a classic way, tall and dark with broad shoulders. His hair is trimmed very short, but not quite military. He sees Lorraine and smiles. She smiles back. She smiles because he's beautiful and she's beautiful and it's so wonderful to be away from home.

He makes his way over to the bar and asks her to dance to a fast song. She gets up and walks to the dance floor with him, glad for a chance to move. He's good. And she's great. She isn't always a good dancer—she can be stiff and self-conscious—but in her current mood, every movement feels just right.

When it's over, he invites her to join him for a drink. "Or would you like to dance again?" he asks politely.

She doesn't care. She honestly doesn't care. He's older, he's tall and good looking, but none of it matters. Looking back on it later, she realizes that he is drawn to her then, at least in part, by her indifference.

"If you keep my glass filled up," she says lazily, "we'll get along just fine."

He takes her elbow and leads her to a table. Cindy, who is still dancing, winks as they pass. Lorraine lifts her chin and smiles.

He doesn't ask what she wants to drink, and she likes that. Someone puts a glass half-filled with tonic in front of her, and he pours gin to the top. She takes a sip; it's pretty good. She finds her cigarettes and lays the pack on the table.

His name is Jack, he tells her. There's nothing shy or uncertain about him; he looks straight into her eyes. She looks back. His eyes are the blue of marbles, a striking color with his dark hair. He asks where she's from.

"Everybody here is from around here," she says. "Aren't you?"

He takes one of her cigarettes and lights it before handing it to her. "I've been living in Turkey."

She pretends to look him over again. "You don't look Turkish."

It turns out that he works for the tobacco company in a job that requires occasional trips overseas. She doesn't know exactly where Turkey is, but the name makes her think of turbans and women in veils.

"What about you?" he asks. "How do you spend your days?"

"Oh, I shouldn't tell you." She looks up at him from lowered lashes. "In fact, you probably don't want to be seen with me."

"Why wouldn't I want to be seen with you?"

"Because I'm ruined in Carlington. I'm a bad girl."

"I find that hard to believe."

She looks at her nails, noticing a place where her polish is chipped. "I have a baby at home," she said.

He lifts his eyebrows. "So where's the daddy?"

She shrugs. "Don't know. Maybe somewhere in California."

113

Jack reaches for a cigarette for himself. He lights it, turning his head to blow the smoke away from her. "I've got a kid at home, too."

There's no ring, but she should have known. "So is your wife still in Turkey?"

He nods, avoiding her eyes. "I got married young. Too young."

She fakes a yawn. "Save your violin stories for somebody else."

He laughs, showing his even white teeth. "It doesn't bother you to be talking to an old married guy?"

"How old?"

She guesses that he's thirty; he tells her twenty-eight. He guesses she's twenty-two. She lies and tells him eighteen. She's flattered by his interest, and she doesn't mind, at first, that he's married. He's cute and fun, and she's much too smart to fall for a married man.

When Cindy signals that she's ready to go, Jack asks if he can come along. "Why not," Lorraine says. By then, she's a bit drunk and hazy, right where she wants to be. The three of them pile into Cindy's convertible, Jack in the back seat. He leans forward behind Lorraine and smoothes her hair when it blows in the wind.

Cindy drives them to a small house in the country that is rented by an older girl named Sandra. By then it's nearly midnight, and it occurs to Lorraine that Cecelia might do something stupid like call the police. Lorraine goes to the bedroom to use the telephone. Cecelia answers on the first ring. "Don't wait up. I'll be home in the morning," Lorraine says, and she hangs up.

Cindy and Sandra have turned on the hi-fi in the living room, and they are dancing. Jack sits in a chair, but he stands when Lorraine walks in. "I missed you," he says, and they dance, too. Lorraine likes the way he smiles at her, the way he hardly looks at Cindy and Sandra, only her.

When they get tired of dancing, Sandra pours drinks. After that, Lorraine begins to lose track of time. At some point, somebody plays "That'll Be the Day," and Cindy cries because Buddy Holly is dead, and then she passes out on the sofa. Sandra throws sheets and a pillow at Lorraine and announces that she's going to bed. Jack takes the linens and spreads them on the floor.

"I'm not sleeping with you," Lorraine slurs. "This isn't even our first date."

Jack tells her to lie down and close her eyes. She lies on her stomach, snuggling against the pillow, and then Jack's lying close beside her, his arm draped across her shoulders.

The next morning she's the first to wake up, and she's surprised and touched to find Jack's arm is still around her. He didn't let go of her all night.

At nine o'clock, Lorraine and Jo Penny stroll, with studied nonchalance, into the Black Velvet Inn. They had a drink at home before they came, and another in the car on the way over; both of them are feeling especially pretty. The bar is a large, dimly lit room with black shag carpet surrounding a circular dance floor. "Can't Buy Me Love" blares out of large speakers, but only a few people are there and no one is dancing. Lorraine starts to head for a table; Jo Penny catches her sleeve and pulls her toward the bar.

They arrange themselves on the bar stools, taking care to smooth down their short skirts. Lorraine smiles to herself, seeing how long and shapely her legs look next to Jo Penny's knobby knees. They light their cigarettes and order drinks to go with the bottles they've brought—soda for Lorraine's Scotch, Coke for Jo Penny's rum.

Lorraine sits up straight and glances around discreetly at the other patrons. Two tables are occupied by couples, and another by three women who look like secretaries having an extended happy hour. A fat man with long, greasy hair sits on the other side of the bar. All dullards and losers; the place is dead. Damn, Lorraine thinks, knowing she will be blamed. After their first drink at home, Jo Penny changed her mind about going out, saying she was tired, and it was Monday, and why didn't they just stay in and watch TV, but Lorraine had insisted. Now she smiles at Jo Penny with determined cheerfulness. "You look great, honey. I love your outfit," she says, though she has never liked the dress, which is low-cut and emblazoned with bright green and black horizontal stripes.

"I told you no one would be here tonight," Jo Penny says, loud enough for everyone in the room to hear.

"Shh," Lorraine says. "It's still early."

Jo Penny sighs. "If you didn't want to talk to Denis, you could just stay at home and not answer the phone."

"I have to answer calls for my business," Lorraine says. "You wouldn't believe how many people call after hours, and sometimes they ask for the strangest things…"

"Oh. My. God." Jo Penny is staring over Lorraine's shoulder. "You've got to see what just walked in."

Pretending to reach for a swizzle stick, Lorraine turns and sees a man walking toward the bar. He is fit, with tanned arms and thick brown hair. His gray pants and dark blue knit shirt are casual but expensive looking. A tuft of chest hair shows at his open collar. "He looks like Tom Jones," Jo Penny says.

No, he doesn't, Lorraine thinks. He looks like Jack. Slightly

116

older, not quite as handsome, but there's a resemblance.

The man walks up to the bar, and the bartender smiles broadly. "Good evening, Mr. Tedrow. What will you have tonight?" The man sits on Lorraine's side, leaving three empty stools between them. He orders a club soda.

"Talk to him," Jo Penny whispers, but too loudly.

Lorraine is mortified, but the man gives no sign of having heard. She gives Jo Penny a scathing look. "Let's just pretend like we're normal people," she says under her breath.

Jo Penny begins a monologue on her day at the store, where clothes had been left in mangled piles after a big weekend sale, and a parade of difficult customers had dropped by to demand reduced prices even though the sale was over. Lorraine pretends to listen while she poses, offering her best smiles and most attractive laughs. She tilts her head and hopes the bar lights are flattering. "I Saw Her Standing There" plays, and she moves her shoulders to the music, taking quick peeks at Tedrow. Yes, he is watching her. She's sure of it. But minutes go by, and he makes no move to speak. She orders another club soda.

Halfway through the third drink, she decides he must be shy. He just needs a little encouragement to get him going. When Jo Penny finally pauses to take a breath, she turns to Tedrow and gives him her most dazzling smile. "Excuse me," she says. "I'm sorry to disturb you, but I'm curious...do you own this place?"

The man looks startled. "No, I'm afraid not."

"Oh, I thought maybe you did, the way the bartender spoke to you. It just so happens that I own a business myself." She laughs. "It's a fun little hobby."

"Is that right?"

"Yes, I have a crystal and antique shop in Carlington." Jo Penny starts to say something, but Lorraine quickly cuts in.

"Perhaps you've seen it?"

He shakes his head. Lorraine tells him more about the shop, and he listens politely. After a few minutes, she realizes she's talking too much, and interrupts herself in mid-sentence. "Oh, I've been rude, babbling on like this, not even introducing you," she says. "This is my friend, Jo Penny Medcastle. Jo Penny, this is Mr. ... Tedrow?"

Jo Penny gives him a little wave. Tedrow nods, but he doesn't offer his first name. He's just shy, Lorraine tells herself again. Her glass is empty, but he doesn't seem to notice.

"Hey, we were thinking about maybe going somewhere else," she says, giving Jo Penny a meaningful look intended to mean *go along with this.* "Somewhere a little nicer, maybe."

"Well, there are lots of places around here," Tedrow says.

"We don't know the area very well," Lorraine says, ignoring Jo Penny's smirk. "Why don't you come with us?" She keeps her voice light, as if she might be joking. Men have always extended this kind of invitation to *her*; surely he will be flattered.

He shakes his head. "No. Thanks. As a matter of fact, I need to be going."

He finishes his drink in a swallow, gives her a tight smile, then reaches for his wallet to pay. The bartender comes immediately to settle the check, and out of the corner of her eye, Lorraine sees him grin and exchange a knowing look with Tedrow. The full measure of her humiliation hits her then, and she feels a blaze of hatred toward them both.

"Guess we weren't his type," Jo Penny says after Tedrow is gone. "He's out of our league, darlin'. I couldn't believe it when you started talking to him. How much have you had to drink? It made me think of the time..."

Jo Penny keeps talking, but Lorraine stops listening. He might be out of *your* league, she thinks. So often she has turned heads, much better looking heads than Tedrow's. Even in Atlanta, a city full of beautiful women, men had noticed her: Becky's married neighbor. The cab driver who passed others with raised hands to stop for her. And the one she would always remember, the tall man dressed in a nice suit who stopped on the sidewalk and stared when he saw her walking down Peachtree. She was wearing a simple summer dress and no makeup other than a little lipstick, and this man looked at her as if she were a goddess. As she walked by, he said in a low drawl, just loud enough for her to hear, "Ma'am, you are a sight to behold."

She was only twenty-three, maybe twenty-four then. It was definitely after Jack, but not so long ago, not *that* many years. Men are so often out of reach except when they want something, and then you can have them on their knees, just because you smiled, or sometimes just because you're there, breathing. It's the closest thing to grace she has ever known.

Jo Penny is still talking, but Lorraine slides off the stool. "I need to go to the ladies' room." The room spins around her, the people sitting at tables seem to be floating toward her with alarming speed as she walks across the floor. Ten minutes earlier she had felt charming and vivacious, now she feels drunk and ugly. She keeps a close eye on the black carpet beneath her feet so she won't stumble.

The bathroom is a dump. The lighting is harsh, the concrete floor has damp spots on it. Scraps of toilet paper litter the floor, but there isn't any paper in the stalls. She digs around in her purse until she finds some tissue and then gingerly relieves herself, trying to minimize contact with the toilet seat. When she finishes, she goes to the sink to wash her hands and apply fresh lipstick.

She leans over the sink with the lipstick tube poised toward her mouth. Then, almost against her will, she looks at her face in the mirror. The glare of yellow light shows every pore in her skin, every incipient wrinkle. The lines around her eyes and mouth, lines she had thought of as tiny, hardly noticeable at all, look long and deep. Her eyes are small and dull.

She never looks this way in her own house, in her own mirrors, in the normal shadowy lights of home. "This is not how I am." She speaks aloud. When she starts to cry, she stumbles back inside a stall, closes the door and leans against it.

She's not sure how long she's in there before she hears the door open. She knows it's Jo Penny; she can smell her Avon perfume.

"Lorraine? Are you in here?" shouts Jo Penny.

"Yes." Lorraine strains to make her voice sound natural; she isn't about to let anybody catch her crying.

"What's taking so long? Did you fall in?" Jo Penny laughs raucously.

"No. My stomach's upset."

"Well, take a Rolaids and come on out. There's another guy at the bar, almost as cute as the one who got away. And this one seems friendlier."

"I'll be out in a minute," Lorraine says. But as soon as Jo Penny leaves, she lights a cigarette.

Two girls come in, clomping around on platform shoes, talking in young, throaty voices. They are laughing. They're laughing, and she is old. She is over thirty and she has nobody. Her own children hate her. She listens to the sound of the girls peeing in the other stalls. Everybody hates her, nobody understands her except Denis. He's not perfect, sometimes he's awful, but he *knows* her; he recognizes who she really is. The two toilets flush at the same time, covering the sound of her sniffling. Denis is a remarkable man, really. After all, he is

120

a published writer, and he has a good head for business. He's smarter than all the hicks around here. She hears water running in the sink, and the girls are chatting in front of the mirror. "Your hair looks good tonight," one of them says.

"No, it doesn't," the other says vehemently. "It looks like shit." There is the prolonged hissing of spray and the click of a metal cap as it snaps back into place. Lorraine hears their shoes clatter toward the door, then the brief noise of the music outside as the door opens, then nothing. She is left in silence and a cloud of hairspray.

The smell sickens her; she already has a headache from crying. She leaves the stall and goes to the sink to wash her face and repair her makeup. She does these things automatically, without really looking, so she won't see herself in the mirror.

Jo Penny is sitting next to a balding man with long sideburns who is wearing a yellow turtleneck sweater with a plaid jacket. As Lorraine watches, Jo Penny leans forward to take a sip of her drink, showing off her small suggestion of a cleavage. Her new friend wears the alert, elated expression of a man who's sure he's going to score.

Lorraine walks up to Jo Penny and taps her on the shoulder. "Let's go."

Jo Penny looks up and smiles. "Lorraine! This is Eddie. He's waiting for his friend Ray."

"I'm ready to go home," Lorraine says.

"But Eddie has invited us for a drink at his place, just as soon..." Jo Penny begins to protest.

"I want to go now."

Jo Penny sulks all the way home, but Lorraine doesn't care. Jo Penny is a slut who would sleep with anybody. I've sunk low in my life, Lorraine thinks, but I won't sink that low again. She wonders if Denis will be at home when she calls him.

12

On Thanksgiving afternoon, I heard a door slam downstairs followed by a series of strange thumps. When I went to look, there was a tall white pine tree standing in the foyer, twisting and shivering, dripping water from the rain outside. For a second I had the illusion the tree was moving by itself, then I saw a pair of red flannel sleeves tangled among the branches, and I heard Denis grunting from behind. He walked the tree slowly toward the staircase, scratching the hardwood floor and causing little showers of pine needles to fall in his wake.

Lorraine came in from the kitchen, holding a cup of coffee. "What in the world…Denis, why is a tree in my house?"

He and I were alone together almost every day. He was spending more time with Lorraine, too, just hanging around to chat and help with chores. As soon as she became occupied with a task or left to run an errand, he turned to me. I didn't like to think about what we were doing, but he made me laugh, he made me feel less alone, and he made me believe we could find Connie. My body seemed like such a paltry offering in return, but he treated it like something he would die for. When Lorraine went to sleep early, he would scoop me up and carry me to my bed. His hands trembled over me as we lay down, his breathing was quick and hard. I tried to keep my own breaths shallow so I could hear beyond the closed door, which didn't lock. It was as if I had two selves: one warm and liquid, the surface Denis touched, and the other tense and anxious, constantly alert for any sound in the hall.

"I brought cranberries, too," Denis said. With a final grunt, he laid the tree on its side. His face was shiny from the rain and cold; bits of pine litter had settled on his shoulders. He grinned at Lorraine like a kid who had brought home an art project.

She forced a smile. "It's lovely of you to bring a tree, Denis, but I don't know where it will go."

We hadn't bothered with a real tree for years; Lorraine assembled a small pink and silver tree for the dining room table and declared the room decorated.

Denis gestured toward a space between the staircase and a collection of floor lamps. "What about here?" I could smell his sweat mingled with pine resin.

Lorraine held her cup with both hands. "Honey, it's a nice tree, but it's so…big. This time of year, I need every bit of sales space."

Since their most recent reunion, she had been more deferential and easier to please. Now that Denis was courting both of us, we all seemed to exist in a weird state of harmony. Softened by guilt and the satisfaction of revenge, I was more civil to Lorraine. She was happy because Denis seemed less restless. He seemed to draw a new, even higher level of energy through me, I could see that, and his generosity knew no bounds. He had been saying yes to everything Lorraine wanted: restaurant meals, help around the house, a stream of compliments. "I really think this is the year," she had confided to me again, stroking her bare finger where the ring would go.

"You've got to allow space for this, Lo," Denis said. "Studies show that shoppers buy twenty percent more when there's a tree."

He dashed out the door, then returned carrying a large round tree stand. With an enormous effort, he lifted the tree from the floor and heaved it into the stand. "Come on, you two. Hold it up so I can lock this thing in."

When Lorraine and I had the tree balanced between us, he got down on his hands and knees and stuck his head under the branches. We struggled to hold the tree upright while he secured it. Lorraine complained that the branches were scratching her. "I'm allergic to pine," she said.

"Just a minute, Sugar." Denis's elbow kicked through the greenery as he tightened screws. Finally he crawled out from beneath the tree, and we all stepped back to look at it. It was asymmetrical—one side was fuller than the other—but I liked it, especially the smell, which made me think of times Connie and I had spent in the woods.

"It's a beauty," Denis said with satisfaction. "Who's going to help decorate?"

"I can't," Lorraine said. "I promised Jo Penny I would go over and help her paint her dining room. That girl will make a huge mess if someone's not there to stop her."

"She's painting her dining room on Thanksgiving Day?" Denis said, giving me a quick glance.

"It gives her an excuse not to host their family dinner. They're all going to her sister's. And guess what," she turned to me. "Marlene has invited a *date.* That Joseph boy who was calling you."

"I feel sorry for him," Denis said. "Marlene's family will put him through the wringer."

They will love Joseph, I thought. He would pull out Marlene's chair for her as they sat down to eat, and he would help clear the dishes when they were done. I could hear Jo Penny already: "He's so polite, Lorraine, such a perfect gentleman!" She would probably want Marlene to follow him to college and marry him as soon as they graduated. I felt depressed, as if it had already happened.

"We'll be fine here," Denis said. "Lily will help me with the

125

tree, won't you?"

I watched Lorraine's face, looking for any hint of suspicion. Denis used to stay with Connie and me while Lorraine was out, and even as we got older, it wasn't unusual to find him watching TV or puttering around the kitchen when she wasn't at home. I could see Lorraine was giving no thought to our being alone now.

"Well, that's fine," she said, "but we don't have any decorations."

"Sure we do." Denis pointed to a display of crystal ornaments. "You can sell those right off the tree. We'll make some more, and I brought a few of my own. Just hold on a sec."

He jogged outside and came back holding a battered shoe box. "Look at these," he said proudly, setting the box down and plucking out a pair of wooden hula girls, topless except for leis decorated to look like Christmas wreaths. "Exquisite, n'est- pas?"

Lorraine rolled her eyes. "Denis…"

"Go on and let Lily and me handle it."

"All right," she said, shaking her head in an indulgent "boys will be boys" way. "Do you have dinner under control?"

"You bet. A veritable feast will be ready when you return, Madam."

"That's 'mademoiselle,'" she said coyly, picking up her pocketbook and heading toward the door.

"*Oui, bien sur*," he said, giving her a mock bow. "*Ma belle mademoiselle.*"

After the door shut behind her, he and I were left alone in the silent house. I looked down, feeling dread and anticipation. "You've been like Santa Claus today," I said.

He sat in an armchair and beckoned to me. "Come and sit on my lap, little girl."

An hour later we were in the kitchen sharing a can of beer while Denis cooked dinner and I strung popcorn and cranberries. He bopped around the kitchen, throwing things in the air, whistling and making up little ditties. "Hey, lady, I love getting laid," he crooned in his best imitation of Frank Sinatra.

His singing irritated me, but I was relieved to be downstairs again, where all would look innocent if Lorraine came home early. He had wanted to linger in my room. "Give me five minutes, and I can do it again," he had said, but I finally convinced him to leave. Now I felt depressed and dirty; I wished I had taken time for a shower. I was awkward with the needle, slowly threading it through the popcorn kernels, occasionally pricking myself. "What are you making?" I asked, hoping to stop the singing.

"Veal parmesano," he said, attempting an Italian accent.

"For Thanksgiving?"

"Lorraine likes it better than turkey," he said.

"Oh." I loved a big fat turkey, I always had. A bright dot of blood bubbled up on my finger, and I thought of Connie with a guilty start. Usually she was on my mind every minute, but I hadn't thought of her much in hours. She would be appalled that I was hanging out with Denis, let alone everything else. *I need to stop this.*

As if he could read my mind, Denis brushed his hand across my hair and sat down at the table. He took a swig from the beer can and handed it to me, but I waved it away.

"Any news from the detective?" I had been asking nearly every day, but now my voice had an edge.

"Oh, yeah," he said, snapping his fingers. "I meant to tell

127

you. I just talked to him again yesterday."

"What did he say?"

"He's working on it."

"Are you sure? I mean, did he tell you what he's actually doing?"

He shook his head. "He says it will take some time. We need to be patient." He coughed into his hand. "Meanwhile, it's not cheap."

It should have been obvious to me he was lying, that there was no detective, but I trusted him. I felt grateful and beholden, exactly as he intended. "This string is nearly finished," I said. I poked my needle into a kernel that splintered into crumbs, causing another hard jab into my finger. "Ouch. Shit."

Denis laughed. "Give me that," he said, taking the strand. I watched as he plucked another kernel from the bowl and expertly speared it with the needle. The needle looked strange in his thick, stubby fingers, but he used it as if he sewed every day. He saw me looking. "I sew my own buttons," he said. "You learn things like that when you're a bachelor."

"Are you planning to marry Lorraine?" I blurted out the question, but it didn't feel strange to ask; it didn't feel like it had anything to do with me.

He threw a piece of popcorn in the air and caught it neatly in his mouth before answering. "Definitely," he said. "One of these days. There's no hurry, is there?"

"Connie used to say that marriage is an instrument of repression."

He smiled a little. "That sounds like the kind of bullshit those crazy kidnappers fed to Patty Hearst."

"Well, she wasn't married. She was living with her boyfriend when they kidnapped her." The media couldn't get enough of the Hearsts, constantly reporting new revelations while

Patty met with her lawyers in jail, preparing for her trial. "The papers didn't print that at first because Patty's father told them to keep it quiet."

"Yeah, she was with that candy-ass professor." He stretched out the popcorn string and held it between his hands, admiring his work.

"Steve Weed," I said, for once feeling as if I knew as much as he did.

"The one who ran around screaming and did nothing while they dragged his girlfriend away."

"They beat him up. What could he do?"

He tossed the string down on the table. "I wouldn't let anyone take you away."

"That's easy to say."

"You know, you look a little like Patty Hearst," he said. There was a silence, and he kept staring at me. "My God, you do something to me," he said softly. He grabbed my hand. "Come on."

"Where?"

"Don't ask any questions, and nobody will get hurt," he said in a mock-gangster voice. He led me out of the kitchen and started toward the stairs, but I stopped. "We don't know when Lorraine will be back."

"Shh, it's okay." He kept my hand firmly and led me to my room. Without letting go, he went to my bureau and used his other hand to rummage through a drawer. "What are you doing?" I asked.

He pulled out a scarf, a dark blue swatch I never wore. He placed it over my eyes and quickly tied it behind my head. "It's too tight," I said, reaching up to adjust it, but he caught my hand and pulled me toward the bed.

"I've kidnapped you," he said. "You're mine."

He took off my clothes quickly, nearly ripping my underpants. I could have told him to stop, I could have taken off the blindfold and pushed him away, but I lay there, even knowing that Lorraine could be back any minute. "Relax," he murmured. He played with me, touching me here and there, knowing each touch gave me a small shock since I couldn't see. His breath skimmed across my neck and my breasts. Then he was suddenly inside me, again.

I wanted him to hurry, but I had already learned that the second time took longer. The clock on my night table hummed in a low, mechanical murmur. I kept listening for the sound of Lorraine's car in the driveway. If caught, what could I say? "He blindfolded me, Lorraine. I couldn't see where I was going, and I don't even know who's lying here under your boyfriend. She's someone else, not me." I *was* like Patty—trapped with Lorraine, dependent on Denis—but with my own earned guilt. I wondered what Patty would do if someone locked her in the same room with her kidnappers and her parents. Who would she be? If Lorraine and Connie walked in now and saw me in bed with Denis, who was I?

Denis rolled over on his back and threw back his head. "That was fun," he panted.

A sound came from the hallway, a small but clearly audible creak. I ripped off the scarf and sat up, waiting for Lorraine to burst through the door.

Denis looked exasperated. "What's wrong, Sweetie?"

I listened. There was nothing; it had been a random house noise. "We can't keep this up," I whispered.

It wasn't the first time I had said it. He answered the way he always did. "Why not?"

"Jo Penny told me the sweetest thing today," Lorraine said at dinner. "When her family has Thanksgiving, instead of saying a traditional blessing, they all hold hands and everybody names something they're thankful for. Why don't we do that, too?" She looked at us brightly. Denis had opened a bottle of champagne, and each sip seemed to make her feel more sentimental.

"Sure, why not," Denis said.

"Okay," I said, trying to look agreeable. Denis and I were set to tell her about the job at Earl's, so it was in my best interest to be pleasant.

Lorraine extended her arms, and we joined hands. She closed her eyes and spoke. "Dear Lord, we thank you for good food, good health and prosperity. We pray that inflation goes down, and...for world peace."

After a brief silence, Denis crossed himself and said, "Ditto."

"That's not what I had in mind," Lorraine said dryly. "Lily?"

I closed my eyes and groped for words that would sound right. "I'm thankful to have a house to live in...and food...and for the earth...and the sunshine," I ended lamely. It had been cold and rainy all day.

Lorraine looked surprised. "Why, Lily, that was lovely. And what a nice meal you have prepared, Denis," she said, surveying the dishes around her.

Denis and I exchanged a quick look. "You need some more bubbly, Lo," he said.

"No, I'm fine..." But before she could say more, he went to the kitchen and brought back the bottle wrapped in a towel. With a flourish, he filled her glass, then his own. "How about some for Lily?"

"No, no, thanks," I said. "I don't care for any."

There was a brief silence. I took a breath. "There's something else I'm thankful for." I tried to sound casual, but my voice came out unnaturally high.

Lorraine, helping herself to a slice of veal, smiled expectantly. "What is it?"

"I got a job," I said.

Her smile vanished. "Doing what?"

"Waitressing. At Earl's. I'm supposed to start tomorrow night." I held my breath.

She closed her eyes and shook her head. "No, Lily. Not that horrible place."

"It's not horrible," I said.

She opened her eyes. "You already have a job. Right here in the shop."

"She'll keep on working here, Lo," Denis said. "You're not losing anything."

"You hush, I'm not talking to you." She narrowed her eyes at him before turning back to me. "It didn't do your sister any good to work there, Lily. In fact, her attitude got even worse."

"You've always wanted me to go to college," I said. "If I work, I can save a lot of money during the next couple of years."

She leaned back, considering. "That's true."

"Of course it's true," Denis said. "The job will be good for her, Lo."

"How will you get back and forth? I will not be your taxi, and I won't have you begging for rides or walking around at night like your sister did. After dealing with the shop and customers and working like a slave all day, I need my sleep. I absolutely cannot…"

"I can take her to work and pick her up," Denis broke in. "Hell, you know I stay up late anyway. I might as well do something constructive."

"What about writing your book?" Lorraine shot back. "That's what you're supposed to be doing when you're up half the night."

"It won't hurt me to take a little break," he said mildly.

Lorraine sighed. "Well, if you really want to bother with it." She picked up her napkin and dabbed at her mouth. "I don't feel good about this, Lily, but it looks like you have it all worked out."

Connie wakes to the sound of Mrs. Brooks singing about Jesus. Out the front window, she has a direct view of the upper branches of a maple tree. It makes her feel as if she's living in a tree house. Looking down in the yard, she sees Mrs. Brooks flitting from one bird feeder to another, pouring seeds, singing about the Lord in a high lilting voice. She is wearing the same black dress she seems to wear every day. It has cuffs that have probably been white at one time, but now they are distinctly yellow. When her job is done, Mrs. Brooks goes back inside.

Connie leaves the window and goes to her new radio, which she bought as soon as she moved into the apartment. The radio sits on the floor, plugged into the only electrical outlet in the room. She twists the volume knob, letting "Tangled Up in Blue" fill the room.

With a newly acquired tidiness, she makes her bed, which means pulling up the covers and smoothing them around the mattress on the floor. It is this mattress and a single wooden chair that allow Mrs. Brooks to say the apartment is furnished. Other than her knapsack, there is nothing else in the room except a few groceries, a styrofoam cooler she bought at a 7-11 store, and a spoon and a plastic bowl she stole from Blue Jay's. She pours herself a bowl of raisin bran and takes it to the window.

She thinks of things she wants to tell me, but she doesn't miss me. All of her life she has heard people—characters in books, people on TV—talk about somebody they miss. Recently she overheard a customer talking about how she missed her old town. Connie didn't believe her. She didn't believe any of them. Words like that remind her of commercials where some idiot actor pretends to be in anguish over a clogged-up sink. She keeps most of her desires low; she has never missed anybody.

She is satisfied, for now, to be in this small bare room on top of a garage. No strangers will come knocking on the door looking for bargains. She has everything she needs. Once a week she goes to a store to buy cereal, a box of graham crackers, a jar of peanut butter, a box of raisins and a bag of ice. The cooler is big enough to hold a carton of milk and a six-pack of beer. The rest of her food comes from the restaurant. She's pleased with her savings, though she doesn't yet have as much as she wants.

Looking out the window, she can see the patchy grass in the yard, the sandy driveway leading to the road, and on the other side, a back view of Blue Jay's. Two large dumpsters stand in the parking lot near the back doors. The breeze blowing through the window brings in the smell of stale beer and fried food. She looks at her watch. Still two hours before she's due at work.

A movement in the yard catches her eye, and she sees a dog prowling around Mrs. Brooks's garbage cans. It is thin and mean looking, with spiky yellow fur and a black face. It has no collar. Thinking she will shoo it away, she gets up and goes outside. The dog is gnawing on something she can't see. When she begins walking down the stairs, he looks up. His body stiffens, making his ribs stick out, and he bares his teeth.

Moving very slowly, she makes her way to the last step.

She stoops down, thinking he might come to her if she's at eye level. But the instant she moves toward the ground, the dog cringes and dashes away. He stops at a distance, turns toward her and gives a low growl.

"You thought I was going to throw a rock, didn't you?" she says softly.

The dog steps back, but doesn't run. Connie goes upstairs and pours a large mound of raisin bran and a splash of milk into her dirty bowl. When she takes it outside, the dog is still there, skulking around a tree. She moves carefully out into the yard and he turns to run. "Wait," she says. She puts the bowl on the ground and walks a few yards away.

The dog sniffs the air and takes a few steps toward the bowl. His nose twitches frantically, but his eyes stay on Connie. He sidles closer until he finally reaches it. With one last glance at her, he dips his nose into the cereal, lifting his head to chew. He finishes the rest quickly, then licks the bowl so hard that it slides around in the dirt. She steps toward him, humming softly. The dog holds his ground for a moment, then turns and trots away. Later she sees him sniffing around the dumpsters near Blue Jay's.

13

As soon as I punched in a time card at Earl's, I felt something like stage fright. My experience working in the shop, with its slow pace and familiar routines, meant nothing. I had no idea what to do. I lingered by the kitchen door, trying to look indifferent.

Already the main room was noisy and crowded with kids, mostly from school, a few in their twenties. The place had a festive Friday-afternoon feeling, and I realized everyone had come to escape Thanksgiving weekend at home. Two boys tossed a Frisbee to each other across the length of the room. A girl wearing a tie-dyed shirt sprawled on a bean bag and gave out long, high-pitched yodels. The jukebox played "Born to Run" at a bone-jarring volume.

Sherry was dashing back and forth between tables and booths, joking with people, but looking frazzled. It was easy to imagine Connie in the same situation, but unsmiling and completely in command. She once told me that sullen waitresses get better tips. "People want to please you," she said.

A table filled up with a gang of girls, seven of them. I recognized them as seniors, though they looked older. They all wore high heels with tight pants, and some of them had stringy hair and bad teeth. Beneath their makeup, their faces were mean and calculating. These were the kind of girls who had boyfriends in jail. I felt an automatic superiority before it occurred to me that they would probably consider their mothers' boyfriends to be off limits.

Sherry noticed me loitering and impatiently motioned

137

toward the girls' table. I took a deep breath and approached them, stumbling over a Frisbee along the way. I kicked it aside. "What are you having?" I shouted over the noise.

"A ginger ale," said one girl, pulling out a flask and a pack of cigarettes. "And give me a burger, too."

The next order came from a witchy-looking brunette with a scar on her cheek. As she began muttering at me, I realized I had forgotten to bring anything to write on. My face went warm. "Uh, need a pad. Right back."

"Fuckin' dingbat," the brunette said, blowing smoke out of her nose.

It was tempting to leave; I knew no one would come after me if I slipped away. But I imagined Connie watching, her face wearing a resigned but self-satisfied expression, because she would have known all along I wouldn't make it here. I got the pad and finished the order.

The rest of the night was a blur: scribbling orders, carrying heavy trays and learning Fry-Boy's abbreviations: CB-AW (cheeseburger, all the way), w/oK (without ketchup), XCh (extra cheese). I ran back and forth between tables and the kitchen, desperately trying to keep orders straight, holding my trays in a death-grip to avoid dropping them. Several times kids from school shouted at me, "Hey, Lily, I didn't know you worked here." I just nodded and tried to remember who ordered plain and who got cheese.

Things were going reasonably well, I thought, until I tried pouring a beer. The flow from the tap dissolved into a heap of thick, white foam, leaving only an inch of actual beer in the bottom of the mug. I wished I could ask Denis what to do.

Sherry came up behind me and looked at the mug with disdain. "You idiot. Nobody wants a big head on their beer."

"I never said I was a beer expert," I said.

Earl appeared from the kitchen and strolled over to us. She was wearing a red bandana around her hair and her usual overalls. In the midst of all the noise and chaos, she looked serene.

"This girl can't pour," Sherry said to her.

Earl glanced at my mug, then at Sherry. "Two of your tables over there need to be cleared."

She waited until Sherry huffed away, then picked up a clean mug. "Here, let me give you a lesson." She showed me how to tilt the glass under the tap to minimize the foam. "There's a certain Zen to it; you'll know when you have it right." I didn't know anything about Zen, but she smiled at me, and I knew why Connie had liked her.

I turned to serve the beer, but suddenly stopped when newcomers at the front door caught my eye. Joseph had just walked in with Marlene. The two of them looked good together, her shiny white-blondness a pretty contrast against his darkness. Right behind them was Carl Dalton, and Carl's girlfriend, Ginny Belski, who had just moved to town a few months earlier. Carl was short and knotty looking, known to be a good wrestler. He and Joseph had hung out together as long as I could remember.

Please let them go to Sherry, I quickly prayed, but they shuffled over to my section. I delayed as long as I could, then ambled over to their booth, doing my best to look professional and bored.

Marlene and Ginny had each done their hair exactly the same way, pulled back in high ponytails with little corkscrew curls dangling in front of their ears. Marlene leaned on one elbow, showing off a row of silver bangles. She looked surprised to see me, then pleased; she scooted over closer to Joseph. He looked away and fidgeted with his car keys.

"Mom told me you started working here," Marlene said.

"Yep." As I handed out menus, Joseph studied his as if he had never seen one before. Carl's eyes darted over to him. Ginny, oblivious, smiled at me pleasantly.

"You ready to order?" I asked.

"I know what I want," Marlene said. "You'll buy me a cheeseburger, won't you, Joey?" She brushed his arm with her bracelets.

"Yes," he said, still frowning at the menu.

"And a beer," she added.

Joseph looked up, clearly disturbed. "You're not eighteen."

"Oh, I'm just kidding," she said in a baby-talk voice. "Let me have a Co' Cola."

"I'd like a salad with Thousand Island," Ginny said.

"I just want water," Joseph said, meeting my eyes briefly before looking away.

"Hey, come on," Marlene said. "You're a growing boy."

Joseph said nothing. I turned to Carl. "Can't make up my mind," he said. "Just a sec."

I stood there tapping my foot while Carl pondered the menu. A gummy stew of sweat and deodorant was collecting in my armpits. The jukebox finished a song and suddenly went silent.

"Where's your sister?" Marlene asked, though I knew Jo Penny had told her everything. "I haven't seen her around lately."

"She moved," I said. "To the West Coast."

Marlene raised her eyebrows. "By herself?"

"She went to meet her fiancé." The words slipped out; I didn't know where they came from. Marlene's brows arched even higher. "Lorraine doesn't know," I added hastily.

"She's *engaged?*" Marlene said with exaggerated surprise. She leaned toward Ginny. "You never knew Connie, did you?

Strange girl." She looked at me. "No offense. You know what I mean." I turned to take Carl's order as if I hadn't heard her.

When Fry-Boy told me their food was ready, I took the plates to a work table in the kitchen. As I loaded their tray, I noticed a small greenish spider making its way across the table. Without thinking, I crushed it with my thumb. I looked around for a way to dispose of it. The smell of Marlene's cheeseburger wafted up from the tray. I lifted the top half of her bun and flicked the spider carcass underneath a soggy scrap of lettuce. After reassembling the hamburger, I added some complimentary chips on the side.

I took the tray out to their table and served all the plates as if I had been doing it all my life. "Does anyone need another Coke?" I asked pleasantly. "I hope you enjoy your meal."

Later, when they got up to leave, Joseph lagged behind the others. He turned and gave me a long, questioning look. I thought of the time he had almost kissed me and wondered what it would have been like. Better than with Denis, more than likely; his kisses were too hard and sloppy. Looking at Joseph's honest, love-struck eyes, everything seemed clear to me. Tonight I had proven I could do Connie's job. I was strong enough to hold her place, for now. I needed to stay away from Denis, but I had to keep my distance from Joseph, too, in case Connie came back. I turned away from him.

When I went to clean the table, I saw that Marlene had eaten every bite of her burger. There was a quarter by Carl's place, and a dollar by Joseph's. I put the money in my pocket and went to take the next order.

The pace slowed as it got later and the crowd thinned out. Sometime around ten o'clock Fry-Boy threw a final hamburger on the grill, then settled in a chair with a joint. He told me he was working on a screenplay about some kids who live in a clothes-optional commune and grow their own marijuana. "It'll be great," he said in a strangled voice, trying to hold down his smoke. He extended a tiny scrap of a roach toward me.

I shook my head. "Gotta get back to work."

I cleared a table, took a drink order, and returned to the dining room with a tray of beers. As I served them, I heard a loud wolf whistle. I looked up to see Denis sitting in a booth grinning at me.

Without smiling back I began wiping off a table. Sherry slouched over to him. "The kitchen's closed," she said, "but I can bring you a drink."

"I want Lily to wait on me." Denis's voice boomed out, making the kids at a nearby table stop talking and stare at him. I could have crawled under the table, but I kept wiping as if I hadn't heard anything. Sherry came over and tapped me on the shoulder. "Hey," she said. "Some old guy over there is asking for you."

I walked over to him slowly, scowling. "You're too early," I said.

He looked puzzled, then hurt. "Sorry. I'll be waiting outside." He got up and walked out.

Earl, who had disappeared for part of the night, came in again and showed me the routine for closing: wipe off every table, ball up the dish rags and throw them in the dirty laundry box, swing the chairs up on the tables, sweep the floor. I was tired. My legs were aching, I couldn't think anymore, and I was worried I had hurt Denis. I overlooked some of the chairs and forgot where to return the broom. "You don't catch on as fast as your sister," Sherry said.

I waited for her to leave before I went out and got in Denis's car. "Hi," I said, trying not to sound exhausted.

"How did it go?"

"Okay," I said.

He tipped a beer bottle to his mouth, then handed it to me and started the engine. I clutched the cold bottle and took a long swallow. The motion of the car soothed me; after the hours of running and serving and thinking too hard, it felt good to be a passenger. I took another drink and handed it back to him.

"I'm sorry if I embarrassed you, Lily."

I was startled, then moved. Rarely had anyone apologized to me about anything. "I'm sorry I was a jerk," I said. "It's just that nobody your age ever comes into Earl's."

"So you think I'm old."

I sighed. "If you start coming in and asking for me, they're going to talk about us. People will think…"

He reached over and put his hand on my knee. "Lily, you shouldn't care about what other people think."

"Lorraine says all that matters is what other people think. You say it doesn't matter at all. I'm confused."

He laughed, and I had to laugh, too. As we pulled into the driveway, I looked up and saw that Lorraine's room was dark. "She's been asleep for a couple of hours," Denis said.

He followed me into the house. I stopped in the foyer and looked at him. "I'm really tired. I guess I'll go on to bed."

He reached out and smoothed my hair. "Why don't I tuck you in?"

It felt good, his fingers massaging my scalp. I wanted to lie down and fall asleep while he stroked my hair and my ears, and that's all I wanted. We went upstairs and tiptoed past Lorraine's door. When we got to my room, I closed the door behind us; I winced when it creaked.

He took me by the shoulders and guided me toward the bed. "Stop worrying," he whispered. "She won't wake up." He kissed me on the ear, on my neck.

I was tired down to my bones; I smelled like grease and onions. He used a rubber, as he usually did. He had shown me how to squeeze the air out of the tip and roll it on him. When it was over, he stayed next to me until I fell asleep. That was kind of nice.

Lorraine always meets Jack at Club 91, but they leave almost immediately to be alone. They make love in his car. Once or twice Jack pays for a hotel, even though Lorraine must be home by midnight. Once on a warm and balmy evening, they lie down on the edge of the golf course at the Carlington Country Club.

It's fine until she begins to need him. She hates being that way, needy. She can't stand herself when she asks him to repeat the things he had once told her without prompting: Yes, he loves her; yes, he will leave his wife. He just wants his baby boy to get a bit older, he doesn't want to leave until his son knows him. Each time she hears this, she feels satisfied. But then they fight about something trivial, and she needs to hear it all again.

Gradually, so gradually that it could have been her imagination, Jack becomes more distant. It's suddenly difficult for him to get away from his wife in the evenings. He becomes more preoccupied with his job. He looks away too often, and he talks too much about his boring problems at work when she wants him to look at *her*, to talk about *them*. She begins to suspect there is someone else, and then she knows it. She suspects everyone except his wife, April, a woman he describes

144

as dowdy and nagging.

One night at the Club, Jack finally confesses. "April would get everything. She would wipe me out. Don't you see? It would cost too much."

Lorraine is relieved to hear the truth; she feels strangely calm. "I'm going home now," she says. "Cindy can give me a ride."

For nearly three weeks, she stays at home every night. She helps Cecelia with chores, she dutifully strolls Connie around the driveway. She thinks about Jack all the time, but she tells herself she won't give in to him again.

But the routine begins to feel endless. Longing sets in again and a growing panic. What if her life goes on the same way forever? What if nothing ever happens to her again? Jack is probably seeing someone else already, somebody prettier and perkier, somebody without a baby. These thoughts are intolerable. When the next Saturday comes, she finds herself in the bathroom carefully rolling her hair. She tells herself she just needs to have some fun.

When Jack walks into the Club, she's sitting at the bar, the same seat where he had seen her the first time. She senses him before she sees him, and she doesn't acknowledge him. He doesn't approach her right away; he goes to a table across the room. She knows she looks especially good that night, she knows he's watching her. She can feel his desire like a hot hand on her back. When he finally crosses the room, she feels him behind her before he speaks, before his hand touches her shoulder, before he says, "I've got to talk to you."

Everyone in the bar watches as the two of them walk out, and within hours it's all over Carlington that they are back together. The whole town has been monitoring the affair. As Lorraine leaves with Jack, she knows that people will talk about her, even Cindy and Sandra and others who have been her friends. But there she is in Jack's car, sitting beside him in the dark, listening to him say how much he has missed her. He drives down a dirt road and stops, and then he begins kissing her as if she can save his life. It is the most anyone has ever wanted her; she's sure of that. When she can't stand it anymore, when she must have him or die, she pulls up her skirt and straddles him.

They agree to meet again the next night, but someone calls Cecelia. When Lorraine tries to leave the house, all the doors are locked from the inside, and the keys are in Cecelia's pocket. Lorraine flies from one door to another. She even goes to a window and fumbles with a latch, but Cecelia pulls her away. When Lorraine realizes she is truly trapped, she goes to her room. She cries, she throws things, she beats on the walls. She knows Jack won't wait long for her, and she is right.

As I began to work at Earl's several nights a week, my responsibilities at home increased, too. Lorraine went on rampages of house cleaning, especially on the upper floors. Instead of sleeping late on Sundays, she woke me up early to help me with chores that left us both exhausted. "I'm sick of looking at dirt and clutter," she kept saying. "What would people say if they saw this?"

"But nobody ever comes up here except Denis," I said.

"And it's a shame," she retorted. "I would love to really open up the house. Wouldn't it be nice to have a big event here?"

Not a party, I noticed; an "event," like a wedding reception. We scrubbed every inch of the bedrooms and bathrooms, including the baseboards, windowsills and closet shelves. Though it was nearly winter, she insisted that we wash the windows. We knocked down cobwebs, cleaned out cupboards, and even rinsed the driveway with a hose.

One side effect of these campaigns is that I was no longer allowed to leave clothes on my bedroom floor, which is where Connie and I had always put them. One morning I was in my room surveying the scatter of jeans and T-shirts on the floor, trying to figure out which ones to wash and which ones to ball up in a drawer, when Lorraine burst in. "I'm washing all of the sheets," she announced.

I continued picking up clothes while she shook my pillow out of its case and let it drop to the floor. She started to peel back the top sheet, then stopped. From the corner of my eye, I saw her lean down and pluck something off the bed. She suddenly became very still, staring at an object pinched between her thumb and forefinger. I looked closer; it was a strand of red hair. Too light and too short to be mine. She gazed at the hair in a puzzled way, as if she had found a seashell in the mountains.

I snatched the remaining clothes from the floor, whistling nervously between my teeth. She slowly gathered the sheets and walked out.

When she called me to her room a few minutes later, I was ready. "Coming." I wouldn't lie; it felt too late for that. I deserved to be caught. Already I was thinking about what I would take with me, though I had no idea where I would go. My knees were shaking when I went to her doorway.

She was lying on top of her bedspread still wearing her jeans and tennis shoes. Her face looked pale; every line showed. "I've got a headache." She pressed her hand against her forehead. "I need to rest for a while."

"Okay," I said, though she hadn't asked me to agree to anything.

She turned her head away, toward the window. "Will you

put the sheets on the line when the washer stops? And close the door behind you."

Out in the hallway, a dust mop was propped against the wall near a small pile of debris. I grabbed the mop and finished the rest of the floor, then went on to do all the other hardwood floors in the house. When the washer stopped, I stuffed the wet sheets in a laundry basket and took them outside to the clothesline in the back. I was pinning the last sheet when Denis's car pulled up in the driveway. I went out to meet him as he bounded toward the house. "You shouldn't come in," I said.

"Why?"

"Lorraine's in bed with a headache."

He glanced up toward the second floor. "That's too bad." He put his hand on my hip and drew me toward him. "Maybe you and I could take a little nap."

I pulled away.

He looked at my face closely. "What's wrong?"

"She found one of your hairs in my bed."

To my surprise, he laughed. "You know, Lily, no one has hair that's a uniform color. Even people with dark hair have lighter ones. One little strand doesn't prove anything unless she plans to perform an analysis under a microscope."

I shrugged and looked down. "There's no way I'm taking you to my room today."

"Then come for a drive."

I shook my head. "If I leave, it will make things worse." I took a breath and looked up at him. "And…I don't want to. Not right now."

"Okay, all right," he said. "You don't have to be belligerent."

"I've got to go," I said.

Lorraine never came out of her room the rest of the day or evening, but she was up early the next morning. "All that sleep did me good," she said, without looking at me.

When I came home from school, she was standing on a ladder in the parlor, spraying a light fixture on the ceiling and polishing it with a rag.

14

Connie hated birthday parties, even simple cake-and-ice cream events at home, but real parties were the worst. As small children, we had been forced to wear dresses with bows and attend Marlene's annual celebrations, where we were expected to mingle with whiney and vicious little girls who eyed us as they whispered to each other behind cupped hands. Connie and I always sneaked away from the crowd to scavenge through Marlene's closet and drawers, hoping to find cash or interesting toys. One time, when forced to play pin-the-tail-on-the-donkey, Connie managed to stab three of the little guests before Jo Penny intervened. When Jo Penny said she must leave, I went too.

Still, Connie and I had always recognized each other's birthdays with little surprises that couldn't have been from anyone else: homemade pictures and poems, odd-shaped stones, necklaces made from painted noodles. As we got older, we gave each other books. We swiped them from the library so we could save all our money for buying a car. Connie said no one else was reading in Carlington anyway, it didn't matter. She gave me things I had never heard of: *Notes from Underground, The Aristos, The Fire Next Time*, everything by Kurt Vonnegut. I gave her Sylvia Plath, Wallace Stevens and *Rolling Stone* magazines—anything she mentioned that I could find. Once we surprised each other with the same gift, a copy of *The Catcher in the Rye*. Lorraine said if she caught us reading one more time when customers needed help, she would burn every book in the house.

I woke up on the last day of November thinking about these things and wondering what Connie was reading now. It was my birthday. No matter where she was or what she was doing, she would remember; it was unthinkable to turn sixteen without her. I felt a new surge of bitterness toward Lorraine for kicking her out.

I got up as usual. Lorraine slept until it was time to drive me to school, then woke up groggy and out of sorts. "God, I have the worst crick in my neck," she said when she came into the kitchen for coffee. I knew she would remember my birthday eventually, but I took satisfaction in having another reason to feel wronged. "I'll be outside," I said. I gathered up my books and went out to read in the car.

A few minutes later Lorraine came tripping out on high heels, wrapped in her long raincoat, coffee cup in hand. "All ready?" she asked, as if she had been waiting for me. I didn't look up from my book.

She started the car and backed out of the driveway. On the road, a heavy silence grew and hardened between us. Lorraine switched on the radio. The station played "Love Will Keep Us Together," there was no escaping it, then the deejay launched into his regular "On This Day in History" feature.

"Why, Lily, my goodness, I'm not awake yet...it's your birthday!" Lorraine exclaimed. "'Sweet sixteen and never been kissed.' That's what they always say." She paused, and I saw her swallow. "How would you like to celebrate? We should do something special."

"We don't need to do anything."

"You can take the afternoon off from the shop. Would you like to have a friend over? What about Marlene?"

"Thanks, but I don't think so."

We went quiet again, and I was glad to get to school, where

I blended in enough to go through the day invisibly. I was an above-average mediocre student; it was the best way not to be noticed. Lorraine gushed over the papers I brought home and pronounced them "outstanding," but they were just okay. Notes on my report card said the same thing year after year: "Lily is a good student."

That afternoon Lorraine told me Denis was coming over. "For your birthday. He's planning a special dinner."

"That means we'll be eating at ten o'clock," I grumbled. If he had bothered to ask, I would have told him that a long dinner with him and Lorraine was not my idea of a treat.

I had kept my distance from Denis since Lorraine found the hair, but he kept inviting himself to my room. I said it was too risky. I had managed to hold him off, but he was getting more insistent. The night before, after Lorraine had gone to bed, he tried to get me to go to the back porch with him.

"Even if she gets up to go to the john, she won't hear us," he said. "There's that nice big couch. It would be romantic out there, under the stars..."

"It would be freezing cold," I said. "Do you have any news?"

He had looked blank.

"From the detective?"

"Oh, yeah." He rubbed the back of his neck, avoiding my eyes. "I checked in with him yesterday. He's still working on it. That's all he would say."

I didn't believe half of what Denis told me. Still, when he said I was a beautiful angel and other absurdities, it was nice to hear, and it felt good to say Connie's name when Lorraine and everyone at school treated her like an unmentionable disease. I could say almost anything to Denis; that was worth a lot, even

153

when he wasn't really listening.

"I want to kill myself," I said when he told me there was no news.

He ran his fingers through my hair and stroked my neck. "I think about you all the time. I miss you when we're not together."

"I know what that's like."

"You mean your sister. Don't you ever miss me?"

"Not really."

He laughed. "You've gotten feisty since Connie left. It's kind of sexy."

The truth is, I knew I would miss him if I didn't have him; he felt like all I had. But my attraction had very little to do with anything physical. In some ways he had become less appealing to me. He had grown his hair out longer and bought new clothes lately—"my groovy new threads" he called them, half mocking himself, half fishing for compliments. Bell-bottom jeans and a tight polyester shirt made him look older and silly. His belly hung over his peace-sign belt buckle. He had looked a lot better to me when I thought he might find Connie.

As I had predicted, my birthday dinner began late. Denis arrived with bags of groceries around seven, then began preparations in a leisurely way. He wanted me to stay in the kitchen to keep him company, but I had the convenient excuse of homework. Lorraine disappeared into her room with a glass of ice and a pint of Scotch. So Denis worked on his own, creating piles of dirty dishes and giving Lorraine far too much time to drink.

When he called us to dinner, I went downstairs right away and automatically stood at my chair, waiting until Lorraine was seated, as we had been taught. Denis came bursting out of the kitchen looking sweaty and red in the face. "Where's your mother? I don't want things to get cold. Lorraine?" he shouted.

There was no answer. He went to the staircase and called her again.

"I'm coming," she called down gaily.

"She's looped," Denis said matter-of-factly when he came back to the dining room.

"I know."

"I've got something to tell you," he said in a low voice.

"I'm on my way!" Lorraine called again, closer this time.

"After dinner, let's get together."

"We can't," I said. "Not in my room."

Lorraine appeared in the doorway and stopped so we could take her in. She was wearing a green satin evening gown. Her cleavage swelled hugely out of the low-cut neckline. The satin strained across her stomach and hips, not in a flattering way.

Denis gave a wolf whistle. "You didn't tell us the dress was formal tonight." He glanced at me.

Lorraine's face was flushed, her eyes were shining. "This is a dress I bought ten years ago. Can you believe it still fits?"

She slinked into the dining room unsteadily and stopped at her place, at the head of the table. She gave Denis a pointed look, and he took the hint and went to pull out her chair. Behind her back, he looked at me and rolled his eyes. I ducked my head. Lorraine was far from sober, but she was quite capable of noticing any glances between us. Denis made a move as if to help me with my chair, but I hastily sat down.

Lorraine turned and reached for a pack of Lucky Strikes on the buffet. "It's too bright in here," she said. "Denis, why don't you light the candles?"

"Excellent idea, Lo. If you ladies can be patient, I'll be back in just moment." He turned off the lights and went into the kitchen. We were left in total darkness.

"Denis, I will not sit in the dark," Lorraine called.

There was no answer. Her breathing sounded ragged. "Denis…" she called again.

The kitchen door opened and he appeared carrying an oversized casserole dish crowned with sixteen burning candles. The mirrors on the walls filled with flames, and our faces popped out of the dark like pale moons.

"What in God's name have you set on fire?" Lorraine asked.

Denis set the dish down in front of me with a flourish. The candlelight jumped around on his smiling face, giving him a maniacal look. "Lily's not crazy about cake, so I made a pepperoni casserole *en flambé*."

"You don't like cake, Lily?" Lorraine peered at me as if I were someone she was trying to remember, then she turned her attention to the casserole dish. "What's that on top?"

"About two pounds of ze finest *fromage*," Denis said, pinching his fingers together.

Lorraine's bracelets jangled. "Denis, you know I don't touch cheese. It's too fattening…"

Denis rubbed his hands together. "Blow 'em out, Lily, and make a wish."

"We should sing first," Lorraine said with a noticeable slur.

I shook my head. "No. Thank you, but I don't…"

"Hap-py birth-day to you…" Lorraine began in a loud, scratchy voice.

My shoulders slumped. "Mother, don't…" But Denis had joined in, and their voices drowned me out. When they finished, Lorraine leaned forward, showing nearly all of her breasts, and applauded enthusiastically. I stared down at the table.

"Make a wish, Lily!" Denis boomed.

"I wish *I* could make a wish," Lorraine said. "There's about a thousand things I need."

I closed my eyes, filled with regret, again, that I hadn't left with Connie. God, help me get out of here, I prayed. I opened my eyes and blew fiercely over the candles, leaving thin trails of smoke in the air.

"Watch it, you're getting wax on the table," Lorraine said.

Denis got up to turn on the lights, but Lorraine stopped him. "Let's keep candlelight," she said, motioning to the candelabra in the middle of the table. "It's so much nicer, don't you think?"

I lit the candles while Denis cut the casserole and served. Lorraine lit a cigarette; I could see she was past the stage of being hungry.

"When I was sixteen," she said, "boys were calling me all the time. I was the only blonde on the cheerleading squad. I'll never forget Homecoming during my junior year. Have I ever told you about it?"

"Yes," I said. The flames on the candles shivered in the room's draft. A pool of grease gleamed on my plate. I imagined taking a candle and tilting it against the edge of the tablecloth, waiting patiently until the fabric flared and then turned into a full-fledged fire, shooting up to the ceiling…

"My dress was gorgeous," Lorraine said. "Mother called it pink, but it was a deeper color, really a rose. Dark rose with lace around the neckline. People tried to tell me that rose wasn't my color, but I didn't listen. I've never been one to care…"

"This is a special night," Denis interrupted. "Lily is of age to get her license."

I felt betrayed; he knew I didn't like this subject. Lorraine stopped and blinked; her head wobbled. "But she hasn't taken driver's education yet."

"She doesn't need to. I can teach her. Hell, you don't need

to know much to pass the test."

"Well, she doesn't have anything to drive, and that's not going to change. We're not in a position now…"

"It's okay," I said, hoping to stop her.

Lorraine took a gulp of her drink then set it down emphatically. "Lily, you had better tell me if you ever get in any trouble with a boy. Let me know right away so we can do something about it. Not that any boys are calling you now, but they will if you just show a modicum of personality."

"For God's sake, lay off her," Denis said. "You don't need to encourage her to obsess over boys."

There was a small silence. I couldn't look at either of them.

Lorraine cleared her throat. "I didn't get you a birthday present, Lily. I know you need clothes, but it's so close to Christmas, I thought I'd just wait."

I stood and shoved my chair against the table. "It never entered my mind you'd get me a present. May I please be excused?" Without waiting for an answer, I strode out of the room.

I was nearly asleep when I heard my door open quietly, and Denis came in.

I sat up and whispered, "You can't be in here."

"Lorraine went to bed and passed out," he whispered back, turning on the lamp on my night table. "She's dead to the world."

"Well, I was sleeping, too. Please, Denis, you need to…"

"You better stay awake, Sleepyhead," he sang in my ear. "Because I have a birthday present for you."

"Denis, I'm really tired…"

"I don't think you're too tired for this."

He pulled a slip of paper out of his pocket and handed it to me. It was an address in Reedsboro: 2101 Firehouse Street, #2. I stared at it without really reading the words. "What is this?"

"Someone you know lives there."

I looked at him sharply; he nodded, barely suppressing a huge grin.

"But this is in Reedsboro," I said.

"That's where she is."

I searched his face again and saw he wasn't joking. I stopped breathing. "Are you sure?"

He tucked a strand of hair behind my ear. "She's renting a garage apartment, working at a diner called Blue Jay's."

She didn't go without me. "How did the detective find her?"

"Elementary, Watson. It's a matter of public record that she got a parking ticket. Said ticket includes her address."

"But she doesn't have a car…how do we know it's her? It could be another Connie Stokes."

"After I went to the courthouse, I drove to her place and talked to the landlady. It's her."

" *You* went to the courthouse? But…"

"The detective was being too slow. I took matters in my own hands."

Then I was sure he had lied about the detective, but I didn't care. "Do you have a number? Can I call her?"

"She doesn't have a phone. But you could try to reach her at work."

I shook my head. "I need to go there. Will you help me?"

"You know I will," he said, reaching down to take off his shoes. "We always need to help each other, Lily."

I did what he told me to do. I took off my clothes, I kissed him, I got on my knees on the floor while he stood in front of me. My head was buzzing with his news. *She didn't really leave me.* I was aware of the transactions between his body and mine, but in a background kind of way, like a TV playing in the next room.

Afterwards, he lay down next to me and held me. We talked about a plan for going to her apartment. "I'm so happy," I said.

He held me tighter. "Me, too, Sweetie." He asked if I wanted him to wait until I fell asleep, and I said no, it was okay.

After he left, I got dressed and grabbed my cigarettes from their hiding place in the closet, and slipped up to the third floor ballroom. A stream of cold air leaked beneath the double doors that led to the balcony. I opened the doors and went out.

Connie and I had always liked the privacy and height of the balcony, its nearness to the stars at night. When we couldn't go to the woods, this is where we came. Until now, I hadn't wanted to be here alone, but now that I knew she was so close, it felt okay. I sat down next to the railing and looked out as I smoked. The bypass was dark and silent; this late, there wasn't much traffic. From down the road, a bright security light glowed over the front door of the church. A line from a barely remembered song came to me: *Praise God from whom all blessings flow.* God had answered my prayers, I knew that with certainty. Thank you, I whispered, feeling a familiar guilt and a new sense of not deserving.

Connie and I had sometimes speculated about God out here, especially when we were little girls. We heard someone refer to the "heavenly bodies," so we had deduced that when people died, their souls floated upward and turned into stars. We were fuzzy on the mechanics of this process, but the basic concept seemed right.

Only the year before, I sat in this same spot and felt a

similar gratitude. Connie and Lorraine had just been through an especially ugly fight. I don't remember what it was about, but it ended when Connie called Lorraine a fascist lunatic and Lorraine screamed that Connie was ruining her life. When the shouting stopped, I went to my room and got something I had been saving for Connie, a present. I went to find her, but she had disappeared. I searched all over the house, but she didn't seem to be anywhere. Finally I came up to the ballroom and saw the doors that led outside were slightly open. I went and stood at the crack. She was sitting cross-legged near the rail, her back to me. A tall bottle of bourbon stood beside her.

Even though I hadn't made a sound, I knew she felt me behind her. "It's freezing out here," I said.

"'Icicles filled the long window/With barbaric glass,'" she said without turning around. "Come on out."

I closed the doors behind me. "Are you drinking?"

"'O thin men of Haddam,/Why do you imagine golden birds?'" she recited. "'Do you not see how the blackbird/Walks around the feet/Of the women around you?'"

She was in her Wallace Stevens phase then. She seemed to memorize his poems as quickly as she could read them. I sat down beside her, placing my package in the space between us. She pressed her arms against her stomach. "I don't feel anything yet," she said.

"I'm sorry it was a shitty night," I said.

She looked straight in front of her, through the wooden rails. "Smell the air."

I sniffed. "It's cold."

"There's snow in it." She handed me the bottle. "Have some."

"What if Lorraine sees this is missing?" I asked.

"She has half-open bottles all over the house. She'll never know."

161

I tipped the bottle against my mouth. It tasted terrible, like hot pennies. I forced myself to swallow, knowing I'd drink more. I picked up the package. "I have something for you."

She took it from me and shook it a little before peeling off the wrapping and opening the box. "Look at this," she said.

It was a key chain made from a white rabbit's foot. I had lifted it from the drug store downtown. The first sight of it had sent a chill through me, the small shock of seeing a limb separated from a body, but Connie had picked it up in the store and looked at it for a long time. "You can use it when you have car keys," I said. "And carry it for good luck, too. There's a longer chain with it."

Connie unclasped the chain and put it around her neck. She fumbled until she hooked it again and the foot lay against her old green sweater. She reached up and touched it. "I like it," she said.

We both took another long swallow from the bottle. It wasn't bad; at least I was feeling warmer. I saw that Connie was shivering, so I moved over until we were huddled close together. I thought she might wriggle away, but she didn't move. We looked out at the sky, which seemed close enough to touch. There wasn't much of a moon you could see, just a glow behind a patch of clouds. The air was so sharp that it stung my nose to breathe.

"Sometimes I've wanted to die," Connie said.

If she had said it in sober daylight, I would have been sad and upset. But sitting up there in the dark, close to the clouds, bourbon swirling in my head, I was just glad she told me. "Do you want to now?"

She shook her head.

I tried to remember the last time she had mentioned the gods; it had been several years. I asked a question that had been

162

on my mind. "Do you think there's a God?"

She jerked her head toward the sky. "Do you know how many planets there are? Billions. Gazillions. We happen to be the right distance from the sun, just at a point where we don't burn up or freeze. It's luck. We started out as a germ in a swamp, and we just got here by damned accident."

Later I thought about this and argued with her in my head, but at the time, I just made a joke. "Well, it's definitely true of you and me," I said, giggling. "Oops Number One and Oops Number Two."

She snickered and bumped me with her shoulder.

"If it's all about luck, I guess it's a good thing you have your rabbit's foot," I said.

"Damned straight," she said.

We drank some more and sat in companionable silence. I was thinking we should go back inside before Lorraine started looking for us when Connie spoke. Her voice was low, not much more than a breath. "I love you."

It wasn't a word we used in our family, none of us. The warmth in my throat seemed to seep into every part of me. I knew to stay still, that any move might ruin it.

"Look," she said, and then, as if she had made it happen, it was snowing. The flakes began small but quickly became as large as quarters, decorating our hair and shoulders. We stuck out our tongues to catch it. It was snowing, and it was going to snow, and it wasn't cold at all.

But now, shivering alone, sticky between my legs, I looked out at a clear sky with hard, bright stars. I smoked one last cigarette and went back to my bed, knowing I wouldn't sleep much until I saw her.

15

After Lorraine dropped me off at school, I walked up the steps to the main entrance and leaned against the brick wall, holding my books against my chest. I nodded at kids as they streamed in, but peered over their heads as if I were looking for someone. As the crowd dwindled, I looked at my watch, then walked briskly down the steps and to the parking lot. The last bell rang. Many times Connie had asked me to skip school with her, but I said it was too risky. Now I felt like a burglar fleeing a house. I carried my math and English books and a paper sack with my regular ham-and-cheese sandwich.

Denis and I had agreed to meet at the first corner down the street, but it hadn't occurred to me that I would need to stand there while cars drove by: ladies headed to the grocery store, people on their way to work. Some of them would recognize me as Lorraine's daughter. I sat down next to a tree, huddled in my coat, and riffled through my English book, pretending to look for a particular page. The passersby might wonder what I was doing there, but my experience with Lorraine had shown that if you looked busy, you could get away with just about anything.

The day was cold and bright. The wind blew in urgent gusts, making me feel jumpier. I had gone to bed elated, but woke up worried. What if Denis was wrong? He hadn't actually seen Connie. If she were in my place, she would be thinking, "Don't count on it."

The Mustang chugged into view, loud and smoky. I scrambled up from my place by the tree and dashed to get in.

Denis's hair was damp, and he was wearing a shirt with a collar. "Hi, Sugar Britches," he said.

I threw my stuff in his back seat. "You're late. A million people have seen me. Why are you dressed up?"

He did a U-turn and headed away from the school. "I have a lunch meeting with a contractor at noon."

"That doesn't give me much time," I said, dismayed.

"You were in a hurry to see your sister, Honey. If it has to be today, we won't have much time with her."

We. I cleared my throat. "I'd like to see her alone."

"Well, sure, okay," he said, though I could see he was annoyed. "I'll drop you off and find a cup of coffee somewhere."

He drove us to a part of Reedsboro I had never seen before. We passed seedy stores and restaurants, a few old houses. As we made a turn, I spotted Blue Jay's. It was a compact building of metal and fake bricks, with narrow windows and a glassed-in box on the side where people entered. A sign on the roof featured faded blue birds perched on a giant coffee cup. I asked Denis to let me out.

"She's not working now," he said. "I called before we left and checked. She lives a couple of blocks away."

I thought of all the lies he had told through the years, all the times he had made pronouncements that were wrong. "I'll walk," I said. "She might run if she sees your car."

"Okay, I'll walk with you."

"No. Denis…"

He held up a hand. "Okay, okay, I'll hang out here and get coffee." He gave me directions, describing a garage apartment next to a small brick house. He spoke in a leisurely and overly-detailed way; I just wanted to go. When he started repeating himself, I opened the door and scrambled out. "Got it," I said. "See you back here by eleven."

166

I jogged through Blue Jay's parking lot, inhaling the stench from the dumpsters, scattering paper cups littered in my path. Just beyond there was a hedge Denis had mentioned and a vacant lot. Hamburger wrappers stirred in the breeze among scrubby yellow grass. On the other side of the lot, I came to a narrow street lined with small, prim houses fronted by tidy yards. Puddles gleamed in the street from a recent rain. Smoke floated from some of the chimneys. Except for the twittering of birds, all was quiet.

I stopped, breathing hard. This was not a place where Connie would be. I started walking again, slowly at first, then running. The cold stung my eyes. I didn't feel like I was going toward anything, but away. If she wasn't here, I wouldn't go back to Denis. I would run until I found a highway, and I would stick out my thumb and it wouldn't matter who picked me up.

Near the end of the street, I spotted a small brick house with a garage. An old lady wearing a stiff black dress stood in the yard, her back to me. The air carried a quavering, high-pitched sound that seemed to come from nowhere. I slowed down and walked closer until I could read the house number: 2101. The lady, who hadn't noticed me, stood on her toes and raised a rusty watering can toward a tree. I realized she was singing.

It seemed unlikely this woman would know Connie. I didn't want to speak to her; I didn't want to speak to anyone who wasn't Connie, especially someone trilling in her yard like a five-year-old. But there was a room over the garage, a contained area that included a door and a window. Without making a sound, I crept up to a fat shrub on the edge of the yard. I stayed behind it, peering through the branches.

"What a fe-rend we have in Jesus," the lady sang. She was pouring grain out of the watering can to fill a series of bird feeders that hung from low branches of her trees. She flitted from one feeder to another, making quick, birdlike motions herself. When she had emptied the can, she went into the house, her song trailing behind her.

The garage was a two-story building with peeling paint. A red Volkswagen, battered looking but clean, was parked on the ground level. A set of rickety stairs ran along the side of the building leading to a small landing on the second floor. The upstairs window was cracked open. Through the opening, a tiny wisp of smoke wafted out.

I left the cover of the bush and went and stood beneath the window, watching as another puff floated. Staring up at the ledge, I called her name. My voice was low and hoarse. I cleared my throat and called again, louder.

Before my mouth had closed, there was a storm of barking. The enormous head of a dog appeared at the window. His face was fringed with spiky yellow fur; his barks were deep and outraged.

The door opened at the top of the stairs, and a thin girl with black hair came out and stood at the landing. It took me a second to see it was Connie; she had dyed her hair. The dark shade made her look paler. She was wearing a baggy gray sweater that nearly reached her knees; no pants or shoes. We looked at each other in stunned silence. Behind her, the dog barked harder and louder.

She turned and murmured something; the dog was immediately silent. Then she looked at me. "Is anybody with you?"

"No."

She jerked her head toward the door and disappeared inside. I made my way up the steps, forcing myself to walk slowly when I wanted to run to her.

The apartment was all one room with a scuffed wooden floor. Connie was at the far wall, crouched beside the dog with her hand wrapped around his collar. When I stepped through the doorway, he gave a low, mean growl. Connie rubbed his ears.

"What's his name?" My voice sounded strange and shaky.

"She's a girl."

We had always wanted a dog; for years we had begged and wheedled Lorraine with no success. I put my hand out and took another step toward the two of them. The growling turned into an ugly snarl. Connie put her arm around the dog's neck, as if to shield her from me. "She won't let anybody else touch her."

I backed away and sat down on the floor. I reached for the top button of my coat, then let my hands fall to my lap. "Nice place," I said. There was a sink and a stove in one corner and a small curtained area that I guessed must be the bathroom. The mattress on the floor was made up with a brown blanket that I had never seen before. Two magazine pictures of Janis Joplin were taped on the wall. I scanned the room, studying every object, and she watched me. We both knew I was looking for some sign of myself. "You don't seem glad to see me," I said. "Are you mad because I didn't come with you?"

"I was at first."

"But not anymore?"

She shrugged. "There's no reason for you to leave home. You've got a good deal there. Lorraine likes you, everyone likes you. You can finish school and marry Joseph, and everything will be hunky dory."

"I'm not speaking to Joseph," I said.

She reached for her cigarettes. "How did you find me?"

"Denis…" I hesitated, glancing away from her. "He tracked you down. It's okay. Lorraine doesn't know anything."

"This is none of Denis's business. Why was he looking for me?"

"I asked him to. He's been really…nice since you left. I

169

wanted to find you, Con."

She picked up a lighter from the top of a small styrofoam cooler and flicked it. I tried not to look at her hair, which, in its strangeness, seemed deeply disturbing. Instead I focused on her legs, with their familiar bony knees.

"So how are you?" I asked.

"Fine," she said, exhaling out of the side of her mouth, toward the window. She hadn't offered me the cigarettes, but, tentatively, I reached over and took one. There was a silence as I lit up.

"I've got a job," she said after a moment. "I'm making pretty good money."

"Blue Jay's," I said. "I just saw it."

Her face darkened; I should have pretended I didn't know. "I have a job, too," I said.

She raised her eyebrows.

"Your old job. At Earl's. I'm holding it in case you want to come back." Before she could respond, I rushed on. "I have your last check. Earl told me to give it to you." I slipped the envelope out of my pocket and extended it to her.

"Thanks," she said, quickly plucking it from my hand. She got up and went over to the cooler. "Do you want a beer?"

"Sure."

She opened two cans and gave one to me.

"I like your hair," I said.

"Yeah? I did it myself." She glanced at me. "You look exactly the same."

All of my questions, everything I wanted to say, suddenly seemed impossible. "I don't have much time," I said. "Denis is picking me up at Blue Jay's at eleven."

"I have to go to work anyway." She got up abruptly and went to a corner of the room and started changing into her

170

waitress uniform, black pants and a red top. She slipped on the pants, then glanced at me before turning her back to take off her sweater. I quickly looked away, feeling slapped. She picked up her keys and went over to stroke the dog, which was lying down with her head between her paws.

"I don't want to be at home," I said. "I'd rather be with you."

She stopped petting the dog. "You could have come with me," she said evenly. "Even if Lorraine had called the cops, we could have gotten away."

"Con...Look, I'm skipping school, I'm working at Earl's."

"I'm impressed," she said flatly.

I felt a surge of anger. "I'm doing things I've never done in my life," I said, "and you're still here doing the same things except now you have a stupid dog instead of me."

There was a long silence while we stared at each other. To my relief, she finally smiled. "You've gone and gotten uppity on me."

"Are you still going to California?" I asked.

She nodded.

"When?"

"Soon. I want to get one more paycheck and buy some supplies, then I'm ready."

"I've been saving money. We could combine what we have, and then we'd have more than enough."

She didn't say anything; I could see she was thinking. "I've got to get going." She filled the dog's bowl with water, then headed for the door. "Come on," she said without looking at me. I followed her out. She began striding across the yard at a fast pace. I caught up with her. "Is that your car in the garage?"

She stopped to look back at it; the sight made her smile. "Yep. Just bought it last week and got it registered and everything."

"That's great."

We began walking again, and everything began to feel normal, as if we walked to work together every day. She told me she had found a park nearby with trails in the woods; she liked to take her dog there. "I named her Lola," she said.

As we got to the edge of Blue Jay's parking lot, I suddenly stopped and touched her arm. "I messed up. You're right; I should have left with you." I waited until her eyes met mine. "I'm ready to go now. Whenever you are."

"You really would come?"

"Yes." I gripped her arm. She looked at the ground, chewing on her lip, thinking. "Could you be ready soon?"

"Any time."

"How are you going to get here?"

I thought for a moment. "Can you pick me up? At Earl's?"

She nodded slowly. "That would work. What time?"

"Four o'clock. On Saturday?"

"Okay." She nodded and said it again: "Okay." She glanced toward the diner. "I don't want to see Denis. I'll go in through the back door."

"I hate to say goodbye," I said. We were standing close, face to face. Her eyes turned soft, and she reached out as if she would pat me on the shoulder. I took her hand and pressed it to my cheek. Her fingers were cold; she brushed them lightly against my skin, smoothing back a strand of my hair. "I'll see you on Saturday," she said. She took a step backward, holding my gaze for a moment before turning and going toward the back of the restaurant.

I watched her until she disappeared. Through the cold air, I felt the sun on my face, warm where she had touched me. I closed my eyes and sent a prayer up: Thank you, thank you, thank you.

I went through the front entrance of Blue Jay's and looked

172

around. Compared to Earl's, the place was bare and unadorned: a long counter lined with worn stools, dingy oilcloth on the tables. There was no music, only the sound of clattering dishes and the low rumble of men chatting at the counter. I spotted Denis sitting at a booth reading a newspaper. I walked over and stood next to him, smiling broadly. "Ready?"

"Hi there," he said, setting aside his paper. "How did that go?"

"Great. You did it. You found her."

"Hey, was there ever any doubt? Sit down and tell me about it."

I shifted nervously. "We'd better leave. You need to get back, don't you?"

He looked at his watch. "We have a few minutes."

"I'd really rather go…"

"It'll only take a sec," he said, signaling the waitress. Reluctantly, I sat and watched the waitress refill his coffee. He settled back into the booth. "Well, how is Connie? Is she still thinking about going out West?"

"No, I think she's given up on that," I said, meeting his eyes briefly to make it convincing. "She seems pretty happy where she is now."

I saw that he wasn't really listening, but staring at me with a smitten look he got sometimes. "Did she say you look beautiful?" he asked softly in a tone that was meant to be teasing. He reached across the table and took my hand.

Just then Connie came out of the kitchen. I didn't see her—I was facing the other way—but I saw Denis's expression change and he quickly removed his hand.

"You didn't tell me Connie was here," he said. "Hey, Connie," he waved at her.

I turned and saw her. She had stopped where she was on the other side of the dining room, holding a tray full of steaming plates. She was looking directly at us, but I couldn't see her face clearly. I started shaking my head, but she had already turned away. She strode back to the kitchen, taking the tray with her. The swinging door flapped behind her.

"She saw you holding my hand," I said grimly.

"No, she didn't," Denis said, but I could tell he didn't believe it.

My head began to ache, and I felt as if I might vomit. "Let's get out of here."

"It's not a big deal," Denis said, fumbling through his pockets for money to pay. "If she mentions it, you can tell her we were just kidding around."

But I knew it wouldn't matter what I said. If by some weird, unimaginable reversal, Connie had been at the table with Denis and I had seen him holding her hand, she could convince me that it didn't mean anything. But Connie had always had more faith in her own perceptions than I did in mine. In that one glance toward our table, I knew she had seen everything.

16

Connie scoops up her tips and clocks out of Blue Jay's at two-thirty, glad to walk away from her last shift. Her Volkswagen is already packed with her knapsack and the cooler, everything she owns except the dog. A new road atlas is tucked between the front seats.

The instant she saw what was going on between Denis and me, she knew she would leave on her own. I broke her trust again. She doesn't try to justify it; it's simple cause and effect. I have formed yet another outside attachment, this one particularly loathsome. There are consequences.

It is raining and sleeting, and as she drives away from the restaurant, a light snow begins to fall. She turns on the radio, looking for music, but she finds the news instead. Squeaky Fromme got sentenced to life in prison. The grim voice of the newscaster reports that Miss Fromme threw an apple at the prosecuting attorney. Connie laughs. The day before it had been Sara Jane Moore pleading guilty to the same thing, a bungled shot at President Ford. Connie wonders if she will meet anyone in California who knows Charles Manson. It seems likely. She thinks he's creepy, but smart. She would like to ask him the trick to making people loyal.

Patches of fog drift and roll in slow motion across the road. Snow flies into the windshield and melts against the thin warmth of the car's defroster. She loves snow; she sees it as a good omen.

She drives to her apartment and goes inside to get Lola, who immediately stands at attention and wags her tail. When they come out, Mrs. Brooks is dashing around the front yard scattering birdseed in the snow. An old yellow sweater is draped over her shoulders and a second sweater—white with a floral pattern—is wrapped around her head. She moves nimbly, pausing now and then to fling seeds into the icy bushes.

Connie walks toward her car with her head down, hoping Mrs. Brooks won't notice her, but Lola is alarmed by the snow. Her spiky fur bristles, and she runs ahead, barking and growling.

Mrs. Brooks squints toward them and shouts across the yard. "You're not going out in this weather, are you?"

"Yep," Connie says. "The Lord calls." She opens the passenger door of her car, and the dog bounds in, shaking her fur and showering the car with melted snow.

Mrs. Brooks nods vaguely. "Well, do be careful."

Connie waves and gets behind the wheel. By the time the next rent check is due, she plans to be in California.

The snow turns to sleet again, sounding like tiny rocks hitting the car. Lola pants against the window, smearing the pane with her nose. The low roar of the defroster fades into a murmur, and Connie wonders if it's working. She takes off her glasses and rubs the lenses on the edge of her shirt, then she wipes the windshield with her hand. Through the fog, she sees ice gleaming in the trees. She turns on the radio, then snaps it off when there's nothing except commercials and the loud babble of disc jockeys. It is quiet except for the motor's exertions as she shifts gears, the tapping of sleet on the windshield, the breath of the dog. A cardinal forages on the ground by the road, blood-red against the snow. She sits up straighter and grips the steering wheel tightly. This is it, she thinks, I'm splitting for good. But driving away doesn't feel as gratifying as she had expected. She doesn't want to think of me, but my face comes to her mind anyway, the way she always sees me: age five, before I started school, with messy curls and questioning brown eyes. The whole world was the two of us then; no one could have told us it would be any other way.

Even though it's not the direct route, she decides to drive through Carlington one more time. She tells herself it's a sort of thumbing-her-nose joy ride; she knows no one will be out in this weather.

By the time she gets to town, an early twilight has set in. The windshield is wet and cloudy; the defroster has definitely stopped working. She reaches up and wipes the glass with her hand. The streets look empty, as she expected. "Sissy asses," she mutters to the dog. She feels proud of her driving ability and contempt for the less skilled.

Up ahead, a pickup truck has stopped in the middle of the road, blocked by a tree that has fallen across its path. The driver, an old farmer who doesn't bother with the niceties of turn signals or hazard lights, curses and jumps out of the vehicle. He's not that far from his son's house; he sets off in the falling sleet to fetch a chainsaw.

The Volkswagen barrels ahead. Connie leans forward to peer through the windshield. When she wipes it with her sleeve, the back of the truck suddenly looms through the fog.

In normal weather, it would work out; she isn't going that fast. She could stop in time with only the mildest squeal of brakes. Now a quick stop isn't an option. She slams on the brake, but there's nothing beneath her, no friction between the tires and the road. The car spins around, a red pinwheel in the fog, then it flies off the road into a ditch.

The predicted storm blew through town, beginning with rain during the night. I stayed awake, listening to it beat against my window as I finalized plans in my head. "It will work," Connie had said. "I'll be there." She had been that definite, hadn't she? A knot of doubt formed in my chest. I tried to distract myself by imagining California, but my mind kept jumping back to the diner, to Connie's stiff back as she walked away.

When I dozed off, I saw her standing on the floor of an ocean, her hair undulating like black seaweed, her eyes staring straight ahead. I swam toward her, splashing frantically. When I got near, she pushed off and swam away. I clawed through the resistant water, trying to follow. It was hard to see; the ocean was murky and snow was falling. I spotted a sunken ship, an old red boat lying on its side. The only entrance was a porthole with broken glass. I scraped through the jagged edges and searched in the darkness inside. She wasn't there.

In the morning, Lorraine called me at seven o'clock. "We have a lot to do today," she said through my door. I was already awake, thinking of my own to-do list. I needed to pack my things while pretending to get ready for work. I would also need to go through my drawers and closets to make sure I didn't leave anything incriminating like old journals or a stray note from Denis.

The dream had left something like a hangover, an edge of undefined worry. I would just tell Connie the truth, I decided as I brushed my teeth. It would be a relief, really, to spill the whole story and make her understand I did what I had to do with Denis to find her. Once we were together again and on the road, it wouldn't make any difference at all. I would tell her it had been easy to leave home. Now I had no hesitation about running away. Every day without Connie, every day of sitting between Denis and Lorraine at the table while trying to choke down food…it had all become unbearable.

When we were together now, Lorraine and I had no

178

memory. We made a point of looking each other in the eye sometimes, for a second or two, but in a polite, unfocused way. I had to forget I had been naked with Denis the night before. She had to forget all the little things that told her this was happening. Looking back, I see it was a necessary amnesia, but also a fragile one. I had to go.

When I went downstairs, Lorraine was in the dining room hanging newly washed curtains. She was dressed in old pants and a flannel shirt, but her face was made up with the fruits of a recent cosmetics spree. Sunset pink rouge blazed on her cheeks, and false lashes perched oddly on her lids. She greeted me curtly, and I had just started helping her when the bell on the front door tinkled and Denis's baritone flowed in: "Hidey ho, hidey hi, gonna get me a piece of the sky!" He paused and called out, "Where are you guys?"

"In here," Lorraine called. "You're just in time to cook us breakfast."

"I can dig it," he said, strolling into the room. He had continued to grow his hair out, and each day the wild, springy frizz looked more like a wig. "What do you girls want?"

Lorraine was standing on a stepladder, reaching up to attach the curtain to the rod. I stood below her, gripping a heavy bunch of the material to keep it off the floor. Neither of us answered.

"Eggs? Pancakes? Nothing is too good for the Stokes ladies."

"You're the cook," Lorraine said.

He served scrambled eggs and toast on Cecelia's china. We sat at the table and began eating in silence. The room echoed a dim, gray light from outside, where freezing rain continued to fall.

"Probably won't get many shoppers today in this weather," Denis said.

"They say it might turn to snow," Lorraine said.

"It won't amount to anything," I said quickly. Lorraine was skittish about driving in sleet or snow, and it was crucial that she let me go to work. "We never get much."

Lorraine folded her pink-streaked napkin next to her plate. "Business is down anyway. I haven't even seen Mrs. Dellwood in ages, or her mother, either. They used to shop here all the time."

"They'll be back," I said. "We're not lucky enough to be rid of them."

"Denis, do you think I should raise prices again?" Lorraine asked.

He looked at her oddly. "You know what I think. All of your stuff is priced too low."

"You're right," she sighed. "This inflation...we just need to stop and re-tag everything. It will take most of a day, but I suppose we must do it."

Denis put down his fork. "Do you know we had this conversation two nights ago? With the same precise words?"

Lorraine and I looked at him blankly.

"Verbatim. You said Mrs. Dellwood and her mother haven't been in, Lily said they would come back. Then you talked about prices."

"I think you are mistaken, Denis," Lorraine said. "Have we had this conversation, Lily?"

"I don't know," I said, but then I knew he was right. I looked down at the cold eggs on my plate. In a few hours, I would be gone.

After lunch, the rain turned to sleet. I knew Connie wouldn't let the weather stop her. Us. I thought about the long drive ahead, just the two of us, anonymous on the road except to each other. I paced around my room, looked out the window, sat on the bed, then got up and looked out again. My room was a mess; the bed was unmade, everything I had worn during the past week was scattered on the floor. The house was quiet. Denis was watching football on TV and Lorraine was taking a nap. I went to the window again and knelt. Cold air leaked through the edges of the glass. The sleet sounded sharp and whispery at the same time, a background for a single sentence: Please let her come to me.

⚮

"It's time to go," I said to Lorraine. "Are you ready?"

She and Denis were in the parlor sitting on either end of a couch, Raggedy Ann dolls displayed in a row between them. Denis was reading the paper, and Lorraine was rubbing lotion on her hands. Lately, she had been driving me to work. She said Denis shouldn't always be the one hauling me around. Now she raised her chin toward me. "Honey, you can't go to work today. There's sleet all over the roads, it's too dangerous."

Everything seemed to stop; I felt like howling. If Connie showed up and I wasn't there, she wouldn't wait. "Earl is counting on me. I might get fired." I tried to sound calm, but my voice shook.

"Better to get fired than wreck the car, Lily," Lorraine said. "I won't take the risk." The lines around her eyes seemed deeper than usual; she looked tired.

Denis folded the sports section and tossed it aside. "You forget my New England roots. I love driving on ice."

"Denis, you're not immune to accidents. It's crazy to go out there. No one will be at Earl's anyway."

He shook his head as if she didn't understand anything. "Every kid in town is heading to Earl's now. In weather like

181

this, they're all looking for a party."

She tipped the lotion over her left hand and squeezed it; nothing came out. "I don't see why you and Lily need to be there."

"I won't be," Denis said. "I'm coming right back."

"Please, I've got to go," I said.

She slammed her lotion on the table and stood. "You'll do what you want anyway. Please, don't let me stop you." She strode out of the room, her heels clattering.

I won't be seeing her again, I thought. Not for a long time. I couldn't think "never." She would miss me, I realized. I would never hear it, but she would.

Denis seemed unperturbed. "Ready to go?"

"Just a sec." I ran to my room and got my backpack. We both put on our coats and walked outside. It was only three thirty, but the air had a gloom like the beginning of twilight. Ice hung from the trees; sleet pelted my face.

"What's this?" Denis asked, tugging on the strap of my backpack as we made our way to the car.

"This?" I said, my voice a little too high. "Sherry needs to borrow some books for school."

There were books in the pack, a collection of poetry, *The Drifters*, *On the Road*, things I could read to Connie as she drove. Otherwise, there wasn't much: some underwear, two T-shirts, and a small billfold that contained all of my money.

"Watch this," he said. On the bypass, he deliberately made the car skid, then expertly brought it under control again. "This is nothing," he said, as we sped past several cars abandoned by the side of the road. "Southerners don't know shit about winter driving, that's the problem."

"Watch out, there's a big branch in the road."

He whipped around the limb just in time. "The town bureaucrats will probably call off school on Monday. If they do, maybe we can slip away and get some quiet time together."

"Yeah," I nodded.

"Are you okay?" he asked.

"I'm fine."

I was caught between what I was supposed to feel about him and what was really there. He wanted me to be with him without thinking, one moment at a time, and sometimes I had been able to do that. Some of the guilt I should have been feeling all along washed through me, but not because I had been too free with my body, a capricious collection of parts that didn't really seem to belong to me anyway. I was about to do something Lorraine had never been able to do: I could leave him. Soon he and Lorraine would be alone together, really, for the first time. My disappearance would hit both of them hard, but I couldn't imagine them coming together in their grief. I wondered if they would break up for good.

When the car stopped in front of Earl's, I looked around quickly; no sign of a Volkswagen. Ten minutes before she was due. The ride had left me dizzy and slightly queasy. I snatched up my backpack and started to open the door. "Thanks for bringing me here."

"Don't I get a kiss?" Denis asked, pretending to pout.

His nose was red from the cold, his blue eyes were shining. He was like a kid, always wanting someone to play with, always looking for the next pleasure. I felt a pang of regret and gratitude. If I had been living alone with Lorraine, things would have been harder, that was for sure. I scanned the parking lot to make sure no one was around, then I put my arms around him and kissed him for a long time before pulling away.

His eyes went soft. "Hey, that was nice. Let's do that again."

"I need to go."

"Lily, I'm crazy about you."

"Maybe you're just crazy." I hoped he would laugh, but he didn't even smile. I kissed him quickly on the cheek and got out of the car.

I loitered at the side entrance to Earl's until I was sure he had driven away. Then I went to the front of the building and stood to wait for Connie.

17

An oversized clock hung over the gas pumps across the street with a sign that said, "Time to fill up!" People bundled up in heavy coats scurried into the convenience store to buy milk and bread. I stood on the sidewalk in front of Earl's, visible from the parking lot but far enough from the front door to avoid the few kids who came in and out. Snow and sleet continued to fall steadily, pelting Earl's roof and blowing into my face.

Cars chugged by slowly on the main road. I craned my neck to examine each one, looking for a red Volkswagen under coats of snow and ice. I took off my backpack so I could stand against the building to get shelter from a narrow strip of awning. My eyes burned in the cold.

I made a rule: no checking the time until I counted slowly to three hundred and recited, silently, the big soliloquy from *Macbeth*, the only thing I knew by heart because we had just memorized it in English class. *Tomorrow and tomorrow and tomorrow creeps in this petty pace...* I hadn't minded the assignment; the lines sounded like a poem Connie would like. I counted and recited and looked at the clock. The wind kept nudging the hood of my coat off my head. I tried to smoke, but the brief comfort wasn't worth the misery of exposing my bare hands; it hadn't occurred to me to wear gloves. After one or two puffs, I threw each cigarette into the parking lot and jammed my hands back into my pockets. Only twenty minutes passed before I knew she wasn't coming. I continued to stand there, letting a cigarette burn down to my numb fingers. I was

185

colder than I had ever been in my life.

A red VW appeared on the road. It pulled into the store's lot across the street and stopped, idling. *She's here,* I thought. *She doesn't want to be seen at Earl's.* I grabbed my backpack and sprinted to the edge of the street, needles of sleet biting into my face. As she got out of the car, I waved and shouted, almost laughing, "Hey!"

A woman wearing a brown raincoat looked around. Her head was covered in tight rows of pink foam curlers. She peered at me through the sleet.

I turned around and trudged back to my post at Earl's. I watched the woman in curlers leave the store with a brown paper bag and drive away in her Volkswagen. I hated her. The clock at the gas pumps said four thirty-five.

I thought of a time when Connie and I had been walking in downtown Reedsboro, and she had found a picture of Patty Hearst, a dirt-smeared flyer dropped on the sidewalk. Patty was still on the lam then. The paper showed a blurry picture of her wearing a beret and holding a gun; the headline said "Patty is Free." Connie had wiped off the flyer and carried it like a treasure, taping it on the wall above her bed as soon as we got home. Lorraine shook her head when she saw it. "That Hearst girl is associating with a bunch of hoodlums and the entire FBI is searching for her. I would hardly call that free."

Connie had shrugged. "She could go back to her family if she wanted to."

We would be together if that's what she wanted… The early twilight deepened. People stopped coming to buy bread. Someone inside the restaurant flipped a switch, and then I was standing in a purple field of black lights. I didn't want to go into Earl's and I didn't want to go home. The neon sign began flashing in the window. I recalled all the times Connie had

186

kept me waiting. She had always come, finally. Usually she had. *Out, out brief candle!* The neon sprinkled monotonous pink reflections across the wet parking lot. I stopped feeling the cold. I stopped counting. I stopped looking at the clock. Tears mixed with the ice on my cheeks. Connie and I had talked about suicide sometimes, just as we had talked about earthquakes and guerrilla war and whether to pierce our ears. We argued over the best methods. I always said pills, but Connie said a gun would be better. I didn't have a gun, I didn't know anyone who had a gun. My shoulders ached under the weight of my backpack. The sleet had stopped falling, and the wind was quiet. Denis will pick me up early if I call him, I thought.

Twin beams of light brushed across the parking lot, and a big Cadillac sedan drove up, thumping along oddly because of thick metal chains wrapped around its tires. The car was bigger and newer than the vehicles typically driven by Earl's customers. Without any real interest, I wondered who owned it. The driver's door opened and Joseph got out.

He was wearing a dark blue overcoat, gloves and heavy boots. A wool scarf was tied around his neck. He looked thoroughly warm and dry.

I watched him close his door and lock it carefully. He started toward the entrance, then he saw me. "Hello," I said.

He took a step toward me, but stopped. His face was closed and wary. The black lights bathed him in a lavender glow, making him look exotic. "What are you doing out here?"

"My ride didn't come."

He ran his fingers through his hair and looked away. I knew he wouldn't want to offer anything I might turn down. "Would you mind taking me somewhere?" I asked.

"Home?"

I shook my head. "Just for a ride."

"Sure. Okay. We'll have to take it slow with the chains on the car."

I followed him to the passenger side. He unlocked the car, took my backpack and stowed it behind the front seats. He held the door open for me. "This is my dad's car," he said. "Well, really it's the church's car. They let the pastors use it."

I got in, dripping on his seat and floor mats. "I'm getting everything wet."

"It's okay," he said, not quite convincingly.

The car smelled like cookies and grape juice, the same smells I remembered from Sunday school. The heat had been running, and as soon as Joseph started the engine, he switched it on again. Warm air blew out of the vents, but I couldn't feel it; it was as if my body wouldn't recognize anything other than cold. In the same distant way, it was good to be with Joseph in his big barricaded car, but I didn't feel glad or nervous or anything beyond relief to be sitting down in a place where getting warm might be possible. Joseph sat very straight, both hands gripping the steering wheel, and I could tell he was trying to think of something to say. I rummaged in my coat pocket and pulled out my cigarettes.

"I didn't know you smoked," he said.

"I don't. Not usually."

He cleared his throat. "My dad doesn't allow smoking in his car."

"Okay," I said, putting the cigarettes away.

"Would you like a Lifesaver?" He offered me a roll, which had already been neatly opened. I took a green one and slipped it in my mouth. "Where's Marlene tonight?"

"I don't know," he said. "I haven't been seeing much of her lately." He glanced over at me. "She's not really my type."

"What is your type?" I asked.

He shook his head. Then, "I think you know."

I turned away from him and stared out the window. *He still likes me.* We passed a row of shabby houses that glistened in their new coat of ice. Abandoned cars were parked at odd angles along the shoulder of the road, either unable or afraid to make it further, but his car plodded past them. I felt safer than I did in my own bed. "It's pretty out there," I said.

"It's clearing up," he said.

We looked out at the moon. It was nearly full, floating among wispy clouds.

"Is there any place in particular you want to go?" he asked.

"It doesn't matter."

"I want to show you something."

He headed outside town, a place out in the country where I had ridden with Connie sometimes. We bumped along slowly in the chains, finding nothing to talk about. The radio was on low playing a song that sounded kind of like rock music, but it was about Jesus. I didn't wonder where we were going; it was enough to feel the car's heat blowing at me. When we were beyond any landmarks I recognized, he braked, and even though we hadn't seen another car since we left town, he flicked on his turn signal and turned onto a wide gravel road.

"Where are we?" I asked.

"This is my uncle's property. His widow lives about a mile down at the end of this driveway, but we're not going that far." Thick groves of trees stood on either side of the road. Farther down there was an opening on the right, and he turned. The narrow road ran down a steep hill, and in the distance ahead, I could see a broad white field.

"This is far as I should go," Joseph said. He stopped the car and cut off the motor, but left the headlights burning. "Look."

Tucked into the woods, we were surrounded by icy trees,

sculptures of brilliant silvery light, as if all the diamonds in the world had been collected and draped on these pines and hardwoods. I saw that what I had mistaken for a field was actually a body of water glazed with ice. It was so beautiful it didn't look real. I thought of stories Connie and I made up when we were little, about princesses who lived in ice castles and used ice daggers to ward off enemy attacks. I looked out; this is the place I had imagined.

"When I was a kid, I used to come out here to swim in the summer and sled in the winter," Joseph said. "The lake is deep; we had a rope swing..." He paused. "I think this is the prettiest place God ever made."

"It's nice," I said.

He nodded, but looked down and gave a small sigh. Outside, a gust blew through, causing the ice to shimmer. I heard him swallow.

"When I came to Earl's...I was hoping you would be there. There's something I want to tell you."

I looked at him, waiting. His face is so perfect, I thought. His nose and jaw were strong, like a man's, but his mouth was full and soft looking. I wanted to touch it.

"Evans," he began, then cleared his throat. "The Christian school up in Virginia called James Evans?"

I nodded even though I had never heard of it.

"Well, they gave me a football scholarship." He looked down modestly, but I could hear the pride in his voice. "It's all-expenses-paid. Just found out this week, and...I know it doesn't make sense, but I wanted you to know."

"That's nice," I said. "I mean, that's really great." He was so earnest and normal and *good*. I loved him; I had always loved him.

We both looked out over the lake again. From outside, we could hear the sounds of the ice: tree branches creaking, a crash as a limb broke. He took my hand tentatively, then gripped it when he felt the cold. He raised my fingers to his mouth and blew on them. Then, gently and with some regret, I thought, he returned my hand to me.

"I guess we'd better head back," he said. "Your folks don't know where you are…I don't want them to worry."

"I don't want to go home."

"Why not?"

"I don't really have folks, not the way you do." I was playing on his sympathies, but I would have said anything to stay there with him. "My mother and her boyfriend fight a lot."

He looked embarrassed and disturbed. "Sometimes I argue with my brothers," he said. "I've never heard my parents fight."

There was nothing about my life he could understand. A house, crammed with merchandise and secret sex, a crazy mother, a lost sister. Even if I told him in the plainest and most precise words, which I would never do, none of it would translate. Looking at his clear, chiseled face again, his dark and innocent eyes, I felt a sudden longing and envy: I wanted to *be* him.

"You're such a sweet girl, Lily. I hate to hear you have trouble at home."

I leaned over and kissed him. His mouth felt as warm and soft as I had imagined, better than I had imagined. He drew back, then pulled me close again and pressed his lips against my cheek. He felt strange in my arms, so lean and compact after Denis's soft body. When our mouths met again, he stopped being careful. We kissed long and hard, we kissed until I felt dizzy. I sank back on the car's wide seat until he was partly on top of me, one foot on the floorboard. I watched his face, his closed eyes, his quick breathing. I wondered if I would ever see Connie again, and I wanted to stop thinking about her.

191

I unzipped my coat, and he helped me pull it off. He threw it in the back seat. The gesture seemed unlike him; I was sure it was the first time he had put away an article of clothing without folding or hanging it. I tugged my sweater up to leave my stomach bare. "I want to feel you against my skin," I said.

We moved close together again, his hand warm on my naked waist. We kept kissing. I wriggled down until his fingers brushed my breast through my sweater, then he was touching my bra and beneath my bra. He drew back and whispered, "We shouldn't do this."

"I know," I said, feeling a raw and single-minded desire I had never felt with Denis. When I slipped the sweater over my head, he did fold it carefully over the top of the seat, but he was breathing hard, and his hands shook. Then there was only my jeans, and they didn't last long. When the time came, he entered me slowly and carefully, as if he were afraid of hurting me, but then he lunged, doing what he had do because of something stronger than himself that couldn't wait. And then it was over.

We lay together quietly, my head near his chest. His heart was beating fast, as if he were running, but it was over and there was nowhere to go. The windows around us had fogged up, covering the splendor outside. This had been my power over him, I thought, all these years. And now it was all used up.

"Are you okay?" he whispered. "I didn't hurt you, did I?"

"I'm fine."

"I'd better take you home."

He seemed more ill at ease than he had before; we groped around for topics of conversation. He mentioned that Evans wasn't really far away, that it would be easy to drive back to Carlington on weekends. He asked me where I wanted to go to college. I said I didn't know, but already I was wondering what Evans was like and imagining parties after his football games. Lorraine would be ecstatic that I was dating; I would have to find a way to deal with Denis.

In my driveway, Joseph left the motor running. He offered to walk me to the door, but didn't insist when I said no. He said he would call.

"Okay," I said. I smiled at him; we didn't kiss good night.

Maybe it should have been obvious to me then, but it wasn't. I didn't know he wouldn't call the next day or even the day after that. It was nearly a week before I heard from him, and then he wasn't calling to make a date. He said we had fallen into temptation. He said he didn't think it was safe to see each other, not after what had happened. He said he was sorry.

Connie and Lola sit in the shadows on the end of Earl's front porch, huddled on a low bench next to a wire sculpture of a cat and a stack of empty flower pots. Connie can't think of anywhere else to go, but she can't make herself knock on the door. She and Lola are wet and cold; her arm aches, her feet are soaking wet. There's a light in the front window. Inside she hears the faint strains of music, a song she doesn't recognize. After a while the music stops and the light blinks off. The front door opens and Earl appears.

She is wearing a dark purple poncho and a knit cap, and her car keys are in her hand. Connie watches as she pauses at the top of the steps and looks out toward the street. The air is crazy with sleet; it swirls and hisses in the air around a streetlight. Tree branches shine like glass. Connie follows Earl's gaze: She is looking at the tracks in the icy front yard. There are two distinct sets, one made by Connie and the other dotted marks pressed by Lola. Connie sees Earl frown as she traces their route to the far end of the porch. She whirls around and peers in their direction. "Who's there?" she says. Her voice is strong and no-nonsense.

Lola gives a small bark, and Connie stands.

"It's me. And my dog."

"Connie?"

"I wrecked my car." Connie's words come out hoarsely, in a puff of white mist. She clears her throat. "Just outside of town on Ashe Road."

Earl's eyebrows shoot up. "How did you get here?"

"We walked." She holds one arm at the elbow and tries not to shiver.

Earl takes a step toward her. "Are you okay?"

"Yeah. I'm bleeding a little, but –"

"Come in." Earl turns to open the door.

Connie doesn't move. "I've got the dog…"

"There's a good dry place for her in the utility room," Earl says. "I'll put a pile of towels on the floor." She enters the house. Lola shakes off, and she and Connie follow.

Earl lets Lola sniff her hand, pets her, then gently takes her collar. "Go on," Connie says, and Lola goes willingly with Earl to the back of the house. Connie glances around. The entrance hall opens into a room with several windows and almost no furniture. A partially painted canvas stands on an easel in a corner. On one side of the room the baseboard is lined with a long row of books. A stereo sits on a low shelf flanked by two large speakers. There are no chairs and no TV, only a large yellow bean bag and a set of Indian-print cushions layered together like a hand of cards.

"Come back here," Earl calls, and Connie follows the sound of her voice to a bathroom.

"Which arm?" Earl asks.

194

Connie rolls up her sleeve, showing several dark bruises and a large, ugly cut above her elbow.

"You might need stitches. I'll take you to the emergency room."

Connie shakes her head almost violently.

"Okay," Earl says. She rummages around in the medicine cabinet and in a drawer next to the sink. She brings out a bottle, a box of bandages and a fistful of cotton balls. Connie sits on the closed toilet seat, clenched inside against the pain she expects.

"This will definitely sting," Earl says, but it's okay, Connie has felt worse.

"You need to get out of those wet things," Earl says. "I'll get some clothes for you."

Connie goes into Earl's bedroom and changes into flannel pajama pants, a sweatshirt and long, soft socks. She walks out as Earl is hanging up a telephone. From the kitchen, she can hear the sound of a kettle beginning to boil.

"I called a guy I know over at Peterson's Body Shop," Earl said. "They do a good job on my van. They said they'll tow your car first thing in the morning. Do you want to get an estimate?"

Connie shakes her head. "It's totaled."

Earl nods. "Do you want some tea?"

They go into the kitchen, and she pours steaming water over a bag in a mug. She stirs in a spoonful of honey and milk.

"Give it a couple of minutes," Earl says, handing her the drink.

Lorraine is a coffee drinker; Connie has never tasted hot tea before. The mug warms her hands. When she sips it, it is spicy and sweet and slips down her throat like liquid flowers. She wants to say thanks, but the words won't come. "You were on your way out," she says.

"To work. But I called; they're not expecting me now."

You don't need to stay here because of me, Connie thinks. But she says nothing.

"Fry-Boy told me Lily didn't show up tonight, either," Earl says, looking at Connie closely.

"She's probably somewhere with a boyfriend," Connie says.

" 'A' boyfriend?" Earl asks.

Connie doesn't answer; she doesn't want to think about Denis or Lorraine or me right now. Her arm has begun to hurt again. Her cup is empty. It's strange being in Earl's house; she has been so alone for weeks now. Forever. Before she quite realizes it, her face is wet and her shoulders are heaving, and then Earl's arms are around her.

Connie's crying is like a storm; there's no stopping it until it has run its course. Tissues appear as she needs them. When she can speak, she says, "I don't know what this is. I don't know where it came from."

Earl strokes her hair, and the touch sends a current through Connie's arms and legs. "Some things get buried in a place so far inside," Earl says. "When they come to light, they don't have a name anymore." Her hand continues to brush softly against Connie's head. Connie almost stops breathing; she has never felt anything so purely good.

Connie finds herself being led into Earl's room and gently folded into her double bed. She closes her eyes and allows this to happen. The tips of Earl's fingers brush her own fingers, stroking them one by one. Then her neck, her face, then Earl's mouth is on her mouth.

Earl draws back briefly. "I'll stop if you don't like it," she says.

"No," Connie says. "It's all right."

18

December 25 broke warm and rainy, the worst possible combination for Christmas. I had stayed in my room for days, missing the last week of school before the holiday break. Lorraine decided I had flu, and I didn't argue. She kept bringing me crackers and ginger ale, which was all I wanted. Anything more than that, and sleeping and peeing, felt way beyond me.

Connie was gone in a new way; the silence around her absence had thickened. I was glad to be alone now, lying awake through the nights and sleeping through the days. The light that filtered through my curtains went through its cycles of dim, bright, dark, but it all seemed the same. When Lorraine checked on me, I sat up briefly and took what she offered before rolling over and going back to sleep. She told Denis I was contagious and kept him away from me. When I heard her shooing him down the stairs, I nearly cried with gratitude. I didn't want to see anybody except maybe Joseph, and even that felt more like the habit of desire rather than the actual thing. If I could stop wanting anything, I would be okay.

Lorraine had told me I must get up this morning and participate in gift-opening. A heaviness settled on me, the weight of the present combined with the weight of every Christmas past. Holidays brought out the worst in Lorraine, triggering a toxic mix of stress and melancholy. Even during years when we seemed to have enough money, she had always given us the same warning: "This will be a small Christmas, girls. Don't expect much." One year, when things had seemed particularly grim, Connie and I had celebrated the solstice. We dragged a small bush from the woods, sneaked it up to the ballroom, and set it up in a pot of dirt. We stole a box of Lorraine's tampons and glued glitter on the unwrapped cylinders before using their strings to hang them. Connie lit candles, and I found two small black masks left over from a Halloween. We put on the masks and danced around the bush. "Bona Saturnalia!" Connie had called out, with as much joy as I ever heard in her voice. I repeated the words, louder, nearly delirious to be communing with Connie and the gods. At the time it hadn't felt wrong, but now I knew this little celebration would be enough to get us shunned from any church in Carlington.

I heard Lorraine's door open, and Denis's footsteps sounded in the hallway. The night before, he and Lorraine had gone to a holiday party at the Carlington Country Club. They had returned late, with much slurred conversation and giggling. I had curled up and pressed my pillow over my ears to shut out the noise. Now I lay still, wondering if Denis would try to visit. But he thumped down the stairs, and I gradually relaxed into a doze.

When I woke up, it was after eleven. I got dressed slowly. After all the time in bed, I felt woozy and almost nauseated. I took deep breaths. I washed my face, combed the tangles out of my hair and went downstairs.

From the parlor, there was a crackling sound. When I went to look, a fire was blazing in the stone fireplace in the east parlor, the one Lorraine always said didn't work. I went toward it, then backed away from the heat.

"Ho, ho, ho," Denis said, appearing in the doorway. He was wearing his red flannel shirt. A patch of flour was smeared across the thigh of his jeans.

"Denis, it's a hundred degrees in here," I said, realizing I sounded like Lorraine. A yeasty smell hung in the air, sweet and overpowering. My stomach felt swimmy.

"Can't have Christmas without a fire," he said. He gave me a searching look. "How are you feeling?" He came over and touched my shoulder, but I moved away.

"Not the greatest."

"I miss you," he said in a low voice.

"It's good you've been able to party with Lorraine," I said lightly.

He looked surprised and more than a little pleased. "Hey now, don't be jealous. You know I have to keep your mother happy."

I turned away and made a show of sniffing the air. "What's cooking?"

"You'll find out. Have you looked to see if Santa came?"

The last time I had been downstairs, only a couple of packages had been under the Christmas tree. Now there were half a dozen more, boxes of all sizes wrapped in fancy reds and silvers and greens. The sight made me want to go back to bed. "Nobody was *that* good this year."

He gave a little laugh. "Don't sell yourself short. Besides, if presents depended on goodness, nobody would ever get anything. Go ahead and shake them."

"I don't really…"

"Go ahead," he insisted.

I went over to the packages and picked up those that had my name on them. From him, there were three for me and three for Lorraine. I dutifully shook mine one by one. The first was a record album; I couldn't tell about the other two. One was in a medium-sized box, and the other was very small. Looking at the small package, I remembered Lorraine's hopes for this Christmas. I scanned her packages. She also had a small box. I looked at Denis, but he had already turned back toward the kitchen. *I have to keep your mother happy.* I wondered if he would tell me before giving her a ring.

"Go wake up your mother," he called over his shoulder. "Everything's almost ready."

As I started up the stairs, I heard Lorraine's door burst open. "Merry Christmas," she called brightly as she came down. She was dressed in red slacks and a matching red sweater with a holly print around the V-neck. Her face was fully made up, and her hair had been curled and sprayed. It felt jarring to see her so perky in the morning, especially the morning after a party. I leaned against the banister, feeling dizzy. I need to eat, I thought.

"Merry Christmas," Lorraine said again, more pointedly.

"Merry Christmas," I echoed.

Denis came out and whistled when he saw her. He escorted her to the parlor, and I heard her exclaim over the fire. "I made my deluxe coffee cake," he told her. When we sat down to eat the cake, he poured her a cup of coffee, adding a shot of bourbon. "What the hell," he said. "It's Christmas."

She nuzzled against him and kissed his cheek, and I knew they had come home last night and had sex. Something stabbed in my chest. I stared at my slab of cake; it looked too rich and gooey, I didn't want it. Lorraine and Denis chatted about the party the evening before. "We had such a great time, Lily," Lorraine said.

He had gotten her a ring; I was suddenly certain. She must be sure, too, or she wouldn't be in such a good mood.

"Hey, let's get to the main event," Denis said, wiping his face. I could see he was excited. Lorraine immediately put down her coffee, even though she had just started her second cup.

"Come on," Denis said, urging us toward the Christmas

tree. He pulled up a chair for Lorraine—a throne-like armchair on sale for thirty-nine dollars—and I sat on the floor.

We had gone through this gift-opening ritual in the same way for years, both before and after Denis. This year was different—Connie was gone—and the three of us thought about it at the same time. We fell quiet. Lorraine's smile wavered, and she looked down. Denis and I glanced at each other, then quickly looked away. I imagined Connie as a transparent spirit, wearing a white nightgown and hovering above us near the ceiling. She was gazing down on our cozy scene with no expression on her face. Bona saturnalia, I told her silently.

Denis clapped his hands. "Okay," he said, "You two get started, but you have to open my gifts last."

As always, Lorraine and I exchanged gifts that were wrong for each other. She gave me a bright pink sweater with tiny yellow smiley faces around the cuffs and neckline. Fortunately, it was too small. When I managed to squeeze into it, she looked miffed. "I don't know why it doesn't fit," she said accusingly.

"She's a bigger girl than you think," Denis said lightly.

My gift for Lorraine went equally flat, a granny dress in a floral pattern. When I had picked it out, I thought it would make her feel young and stylish, but when she held it up – with an expression of obvious distaste—it just looked frumpy.

"Thank you, Lily," she said stiffly. "That's very nice."

Meanwhile, Denis was ripping happily into his packages: an expensive cashmere sweater from Lorraine ("You'll need it for Jo Penny's Super Bowl party," she said) and a large, fancy beer mug from me. Giving him a mug seemed absurd, since he always drank from a can or bottle, but Lorraine had insisted he needed it. Still, he acted pleased: "This is great," he kept saying.

"Now," he said, rubbing his hands. "It's Santa time. Wait, hold on." He dashed away to the kitchen and came back with a beer. He poured it into the new mug and took a long swallow. "Now," he said again.

"Lorraine, you open yours first."

I watched her face. She wore a small, close-mouthed smile that meant she was trying to suppress a larger feeling. She opened her packages slowly, beginning with the largest. It was a silk suit, a jacket and short skirt in a burnt orange color. She gasped, genuinely pleased. "This is gorgeous! Did you pick this out by yourself?"

"Well, Jo Penny helped a little. But when I saw it, I knew it was you."

"I love it."

"Go ahead and open the others."

"Okay," she said, taking a visible breath.

She reached for a rectangular package that turned out to be a new leather billfold. Inside, Denis had inserted a photo of himself standing on a boat. She made a fuss over this gift, too, but I could see that her mind wasn't really on it. He handed her the last package, the small one.

"Should we be alone when I open this?" she asked coyly.

"No, no," Denis said. "Lily should be here, too."

Lorraine's hands shook a little as she picked at the wrapping. Slowly, she put the paper aside and held up a small jewelry box, covered in light blue velvet. "Oh, my," she breathed. "What is it?"

The room went still as she fumbled with the box; the clocks ticking on the mantle sounded loud. She opened the lid. For a second she looked puzzled, as if there was some mistake. Then she tried to smile, but the corners of her mouth turned down.

"It's a brooch," Denis said. "A real antique, see. Those sapphires are from Sri Lanka. Don't you think it will look great with the suit?"

"Yes," Lorraine said faintly. She tried to smile, but it

didn't work.

Denis looked bewildered. *Dumb ass,* I thought. The brooch was pretty, the kind of thing Lorraine loved, but of course that wasn't the point. There was a silence. Lorraine stared away from us, the jewelry box still clutched in her hand.

"Well, Lily," Denis said, speaking too loudly to cover the awkwardness. "You need to open your stash."

The first gift was a Blood, Sweat & Tears album that I had been wanting. The second was a bottle of perfume, something called Nightshade. Denis often commented that I smelled like the food at Earl's. As I opened the package, Lorraine leaned forward in her chair, craning her neck to look. "Don't you think she's a little young for that?"

He shook his head. "Every girl needs a signature fragrance, Lo."

I dabbed a drop on my wrist and sniffed at it: spice and flowers and something musky. It was way too strong. "Thank you."

"You're not done yet," he said.

I picked up the small box and had a sudden fear that it would be a ring. Even an innocent ring—say, a signet or a cheap birthstone—would be horrible. I pulled off the lid and found, resting on a small cottony pad, a silver key.

I picked up the key and examined it. "What's this?"

I looked at Lorraine, but I could see she didn't know, either. Denis was grinning broadly. "Follow me," he said. "You, too," he said to Lorraine, and he put his arm around her. I followed them to the front door.

"Where are we going?"

"You'll see."

We stepped outside onto the front porch. The early morning rain had dwindled to a barely perceptible spitting. A strange car sat in the driveway, a curvy four-door with a flat front and double headlights on each side. Surrounded by mist, the car looked like a contraption that might appear in a horror movie, both menacing and alluring at the same time. It was painted the dark purple color of an eggplant.

"Denis, whose car…?" asked Lorraine, but we both understood at the same time. My mouth dropped open.

"Come on, take a look at it," Denis said, rushing ahead. I followed him slowly, and Lorraine trailed behind me.

"For a Corvair, it's practically brand new," Denis said, slapping his hand on the hood. "Only ninety-eight thousand miles." He looked at me expectantly. I tried to smile.

"Denis, you know she doesn't have her license yet," said Lorraine, trying to sound calm but not succeeding.

"I know, I know. Don't freak out, Lo. I got a good deal, so I wanted to go ahead and give it to her. She's sixteen, you know. There's no reason she shouldn't be driving."

If I learned to drive, I could look for Connie on my own. That was my first thought before I remembered she didn't want to be found. My second thought was escape, but I suspected this gift might somehow tie me tighter to Denis. I wanted to refuse it; I wanted to leap behind the wheel and take off. I could see in Lorraine's face that it would cause trouble.

Denis opened the driver's door and started the engine. "Get in on the other side, and I'll show you all the features, Lily."

I gingerly sat in the passenger seat. "This is great," I said softly, but I was watching Lorraine as she strode quickly back to the house. Her back was heaving.

In loud, babbling sentences, Denis was using terms such as "power glide automatic" and "in-dash ignition." He turned on the engine. "Listen to that."

"Lorraine isn't happy about this," I said.

"She'll be all right. Come on, you get behind the wheel now."

He left the motor running while we switched seats. I suddenly felt tired. Walking around the car and sitting down in the driver's seat seemed to take all the energy I had.

Denis reached over and tickled my neck. "Your own wheels, Lily. When you get your license, you can come over to my place."

"Yeah, no one would ever notice this bright purple car in front of your apartment."

"There's a good parking space away from the street, no one will see."

"What makes you think I won't take off on my own?"

"Because you're a scaredy-cat." He looked me in the eye, and I had to look away. "Go on, get driving," he said.

The engine ran in a low, noisy growl, like mumbled threats. In the rearview mirror I saw a gathering cloud of exhaust. I thought of a time Connie and I had gone deep into the woods and found a creek. It ran between steep banks, and the water swirled around rocks as big as our heads. Connie took only a moment to gauge the distance before leaping across to the other side. "Come on," she had said. "You can do it." But I couldn't. She had showed me it was possible, but only possible for her. She had pleaded with me, then yelled, then finally she left, determined to explore further. I had turned around and found my way home.

I lifted my hands to the steering wheel. They were shaking so hard I could barely get a grip. I let them fall in my lap again. "I can't do this right now."

Denis sighed. He reached over and stroked my hair and ran his finger down the side of my face. "It'll just take a little practice."

When we went back inside, the house was quiet, too quiet, and I knew immediately that Lorraine was shut away in her room. Hoping to appease her, I looked around to see what needed to be done. Chairs were out of place, and wrapping paper was scattered in bunches around the tree. I found a bag and began picking up the paper. Denis started toward the kitchen, but then Lorraine called him from her room. Her voice was softer than usual and very controlled.

"Uh oh," Denis murmured. He hurried up to her room, and I heard her snap, "Close the door behind you."

I crept up to the top of the staircase and listened. It wasn't hard to hear. He was undermining her, he had no business getting that car without consulting her. "I have never been able to count on you," she said, almost sobbing. "And now you get this dangerous vehicle."

Denis's voice was lower, defensive but soothing. I could only hear snatches. "…just wanted us to have a nice Christmas." Lorraine's voice went lower, too, and I had to strain to hear: "Well, it's been the worst damned Christmas I can remember."

I went to my room and closed the door behind me. I turned on Connie's radio loud enough to drown any outside noise, and I went to sleep.

When I woke up, it was nearly dark outside. I cut off the radio. The house was quiet with the tense sort of silence that follows a big fight. I got up and looked out the window; the purple car glowed in the driveway, but Denis's was gone.

As I turned to get back in bed, I saw that a large scrap of paper had been slipped under my door. I picked up a note in Denis's big loopy handwriting: *Lily, I'm staying low until L. cools down. She has your car keys, it probably wouldn't be a good idea to ask for them right now. Hope to see you soon!! D.*

And there was a postscript, scrawled at the bottom of the page: *That boy Joseph came by, but I told him you weren't here. You don't want to see him, do you?*

19

After Christmas, we ate cereal in the morning and scrambled eggs at night. We both missed Denis's cooking. Lorraine never said she had broken up with him, but he didn't come over, and neither of us mentioned his name. We had never been alone so much, just the two of us. The walls of the house seemed taller, and the usual words between us sounded stagy, like lines we had rehearsed. We were polite, almost shy. I did my chores without being reminded, and Lorraine went out of her way to be agreeable. At first I dreaded meals, when the absences and silences were most obvious. Our conversation at the table was sparse and halting, but we came up with a ritual of flipping through the Carlington newspaper and reading little snippets aloud to each other, saving the Ann Landers column for last. We would critique the advice and laugh at the silly, hopeless people who wrote the letters. Something about Ann's stock phrase "wake up and smell the coffee" tickled both of us. One night we laughed until my stomach ached and tears ran down Lorraine's cheeks.

Earl's was closed between Christmas and New Year's, but I was scheduled to work the following week. Before I even asked, Lorraine said she would give me a ride.

When I clocked in, Earl was in the kitchen stirring an enormous pot of chili. She glanced up at me. "You've been getting calls here. From Denis. He wants to know your schedule."

"Oh." I busied myself rummaging around a drawer to find a pad and pen.

"I told him I don't take personal calls here unless it's an emergency. He said it was urgent that you call him."

"Okay. Thanks."

She turned and looked at me. "Lily, do you want him to know when you're working?"

Without meeting her eyes, I shook my head.

"Okay. He won't hear it from me."

When I finished my shift, Lorraine was outside in the car waiting for me. As I walked toward her, I saw Denis's car cruise by slowly, up on the road beyond the parking lot. It was the same stretch of road where I had spent hours looking for Connie's car. Denis's Mustang slowed down. I couldn't see him clearly, but I knew he was watching us. When Lorraine pulled out of the lot, he was gone.

"How was work?" Lorraine asked.

"Fine."

I was afraid he would be waiting for us when we got home, but the driveway was empty. Lorraine and I walked into the house silently.

I paused at the foot of the stairs. "Thanks for picking me up."

She same over and touched me on the shoulder. I jumped, surprised to find her so close. She smelled like tobacco and Arpège. Tottering on her high heels, she leaned over and kissed the top of my head. It was a sweet kiss, but awkward, like the first kiss between a boy and a girl. "Good night," she said.

As I got into bed, I could still feel the place where she had pressed her mouth. She had often tried to be affectionate before, but when Connie was here, it seemed like a betrayal to respond. Even now, I felt wary, knowing that Lorraine's powers could turn against me. I also felt protective of the secret I had been keeping, one I had barely let myself think about: My period was late. I wasn't sure exactly how late, but I should have had it in December, and there was no sign of it yet.

During the night I have two dreams. In the first one, Connie and I are in a shiny new convertible. She drives fast, and we pass everything on the road, even the transfer trucks. We never get anywhere; we are always going.

In the second one, faceless men burst into our house and tie us up. The one wearing black boots paces in front of Lorraine, Connie and me. "One stays with me, one is released," he says. "And one of them must die." He points at me. "You, I'll keep. But you must decide who is eliminated."

A woman comes in dressed in a white nurse's uniform. "Good news," she says without smiling. "The baby is out of surgery now. She must be named."

"Her name is Connie," I say, but no one hears me.

The nurse carries the baby to Lorraine. "Here," she says. A jagged line of blood runs across the baby's chest, and a tube dangles out of her thin arm, connected to nothing. The baby's eyes are huge and silvery gray, like pewter plates. She stares without blinking at Lorraine. Lorraine reaches out to take the baby, but the nurse steps back. "She's dead," the woman says. The baby's eyes never leave Lorraine's face.

When Lorraine tells Cecelia she's pregnant with a second child, she expects to be killed. She goes to her mother's bedroom, knocks on the door, blurts out the news and waits for her mother's hysteria. But Cecelia merely flushes, nods and retreats to the kitchen. She is still there, running water, banging pots and pans, long after Lorraine goes to bed. The next morning, there are seventeen loaves of banana bread on the kitchen counter, all neatly wrapped in foil.

Six weeks before my birth, Cecelia has a stroke and dies. At the funeral, Lorraine wears her nicest maternity outfit, a Navy blue dotted Swiss. A lot of people come to the church, almost as many as when her father died. But after the service is over, no one except the minister speaks to her. Lorraine waits in the car while Becky and her husband, Delmont, who have driven from Atlanta, receive condolences.

Back at the house, there are covered dishes—casseroles and biscuits and cakes and gelatin salads—waiting in the kitchen. A few of Becky's friends from high school come by to visit. Lorraine fixes herself a plate of food and takes it up to her room. She stays up there all evening, thinking about Jack.

When she had told him about the baby, he offered her money. He talked her into one lump sum. "Regular payments would be awkward, you see that, don't you?"

After Cecelia's death, Lorraine has nothing except the drafty, leaky house and the money from Jack. People say, "You're lucky to have a roof over your head." She knows no one will help her go against Cecelia's wish to keep the house in the family. She is stuck.

For a while, against all reason and every fact, she holds onto the hope that Jack will leave his wife and rescue her. She imagines getting married, fixing up the house together. They will fill it up with more babies, if that's what Jack wants. He calls her once, late one night, and even though he isn't entirely sober, it gives her hope.

She starts the shop by selling most of Cecelia's furniture, and she uses Jack's money to paint the front rooms and buy more inventory. She discovers she has a knack for finding pieces with potential, those that will fix up nicely and sell at a profit. But even as she negotiates prices and sands furniture and feeds the babies, she's waiting for Jack to realize he can't live without her. Hardly an hour passes that she doesn't think of him. When she looks at me as a baby, she feels him looking, too. She never dresses me, never combs my hair, without seeing me through Jack's eyes. She imagines driving to Jack's shiny new house in Durham. His wife isn't there, of course. Conveniently, April is out shopping or having lunch with friends. Lorraine takes me—the baby me—out of the car, carries me up their front porch and knocks. She watches Jack's face as he answers the door. He looks surprised and worried and glad to see her all at once. Then he looks down at me and sees his own eyes and his own olive skin, and he says…

Lorraine is never sure what he would say, and she's never sure where Connie is while this is happening. She skips over the details. But she continues to believe, without even knowing it herself, that I'm her only hope.

Once she gets crazy enough to try it. By then, Connie is five and I am four. Even as she bundles us up and puts us in the car, she knows she's out of her mind. She leaves town and gets on the highway toward Durham. After a couple of hours, she announces that we are close to "my friend Jack's house."

We never arrive. We must have been very close when she suddenly stops, takes a shuddering breath, and turns the car around to head back to the highway. When she gets home, exhausted from crying, parched from too many cigarettes, she parks the car in the driveway and puts her head down on the steering wheel and says, "Thank God."

Slowly, Jack becomes less real in Lorraine's head. Starting a business keeps her too busy to think much. She stays sane by doing all the things required to take care of two children and earn a living. At first, she sells just enough to survive, but not enough to get ahead. The shop drains her energy without giving much back, and we are a disappointment, too. The older Connie gets, the more unattractive and unpleasant she becomes. I'm too shy and have no gumption. We always need new dresses and new shoes, all three of us. We need, she needs. There is never enough of anything. After some time has passed, Lorraine decides that Jack had been right. Money is the only thing that matters after all.

⌒

For several mornings in a row, I threw up. Usually I managed to wait until Lorraine went downstairs, but sometimes I couldn't wait. She called through the bathroom door, "Lily, are you okay?"

"I'm fine," I said, trying not to sound strangled. "Just coughing."

"Come on down and eat some breakfast."

"Okay." I held my breath until I heard her walk away. My legs were shaking; I sat on the edge of the tub. I lifted my shirt and stared at my stomach. There was a small bulge there, barely perceptible, but distinct to me. I was terrified, but I also felt sure about several things. This was a girl, I wanted her badly, and Lorraine would try to take her away. I couldn't be certain about the father, though it seemed more likely to be Joseph. But it didn't matter, because this baby was mine. Desire flooded me, the fierce kind of wanting I had been trying to avoid since Connie stood me up. Wanting this baby was dangerous, I knew that. I thought about a girl in my class who had gotten pregnant. Rhonda Duncan, who was tall and gawky and not at all sexy. She had ended up going to a home for unwed mothers in Reedsboro where they put babies up for adoption. I suspected Lorraine would want it to be faster and easier than that. There was only one thing to do: I would have to run away.

When I stood, the floor seemed to sway beneath my feet. My stomach churned, my mouth filled with salt. I heaved into the toilet again until I had nothing left.

When I went downstairs, there was a hard-boiled egg and a plain piece of toast on the table. "Thanks," I said to Lorraine, who had already finished eating and was stubbing out a cigarette.

She told me she wanted me to sand two end tables when I had finished eating. "Would you like to work on the porch? It's nice out today."

I put on a sweater, grabbed some sandpaper and went outside to the front porch, where Lorraine had placed two small, square tables on spread-out pieces of newspaper. She was right: It was a warm day for January, almost balmy. After sanding for a few minutes, I was too hot in my sweater. I was taking it off when the front door opened and Lorraine came out.

"Hi," I said, quickly turning away. It probably wasn't necessary to hide my stomach yet, but my shirt was tight, and I thought I should be careful. I felt full of my secret, and possessive, like a lunatic hiding a hostage.

Lorraine smiled at me oddly, and I waited for her to say what she wanted, but she sat down on the glider. I felt her watching as I finished sanding one table and began the other. The only sound was the scratching of the paper against the wood and the windy noise of cars passing down on the road. Her stillness made me nervous; I was relieved when she finally spoke.

"Is there anything you want to tell me?"

"No, I don't think so." I kept scrubbing at the wood.

"Lily, I know you're pregnant."

215

I stopped working; the stiff sheet of sandpaper trembled in my hand.

Lorraine cleared her throat. She was sitting very straight on the edge of the glider. "I've always been afraid that you would make the same mistakes I did…"

"It's my baby," I said. "I want to keep it."

She nodded, as if she had expected this. "There's the question of the father," she began.

There was something in her voice, a certain restraint and caution. I knew she was thinking of Denis. I took a breath to speak, but she interrupted.

"Lily, I'm going to ask you something, and you need to tell me the truth."

Beneath a sickening wave of fear, I felt some relief. Now, finally, she would ask about Denis. It would be awful to confess, almost the worst thing I could imagine, yet it would also feel good to look her in the eye and say something true.

"The Satterfield boy was calling for a while. Joseph." She looked at me in a probing way. "Marlene told Jo Penny that someone saw you get in a car with him." She looked at me hard; I looked away. "Did you have a date with that boy without telling me?"

I paused, not sure I could actually call it a date, then nodded.

"Could he be…is he the father of this baby?"

I stared out at the bypass. A bright orange Corvette flew by, speeding. It was followed, at a much slower pace, by a beat-up old truck with no hubcaps, thumping along in a hobbled way. I wondered if the truck had a flat.

"Lily, I asked you something. Did you have sex with Joseph Satterfield?"

I nodded.

She sat back and smiled a little. "Well, I've been wanting a wedding for a long time. You've beat me to it. Of course, under the circumstances, it can't be a real wedding. You'll need to do it quickly and discreetly."

"Mother, I don't think Joseph wants to marry me."

She gave a little wave, as if shooing a fly, and smiled serenely. "The Satterfields are a good family. They'll do the right thing."

On my wedding day, I wore a white satin suit under my long winter coat, a fuzzy plaid thing with a belt. The day was bright and sunny, but the wind blew in long, cold blasts. After a morning of ironing and primping and watching Lorraine scurry around the house as she packed my clothes, I found myself in the driveway with her and Joseph, bracing against the gusts. My carefully sprayed hair divided into messy strands and whipped across my face.

Joseph spread a map over the hood of his car, and he and Lorraine leaned over it with their hands splayed against the edges to hold it down in the wind. They discussed the best way to drive to South Carolina, where state laws would allow us to get married quickly and privately. That was the phrase Lorraine had used with Reverend Satterfield: "quickly and privately."

I had imagined that Joseph would greet me by kissing me on the cheek, but he had stood stiffly at the door and politely declined to come in. He was wearing a dark blue shirt, gray pants, and shiny black shoes. His long bangs were gone. He had gotten a drastic haircut, leaving little more than stubble against his bare skull. As he and Lorraine discussed our route, we looked at each other in glancing ways, both of us testing shy smiles. I huddled in my coat, slashed by the wind, and realized we were getting married when we had never had an actual premeditated date.

Joseph carefully folded the map and put it in the glove compartment. He took my suitcase from Lorraine and placed it in the trunk of his car along with his own small bag, the type Lorraine called a valise. She was keeping up a continuous stream of chatter. "Lily, why don't you take your coat off? You'll get too hot in the car. You two need to be on your way. Joseph, do you have plenty of gas? You'll go through a long stretch where there's nowhere to stop."

I took off my coat, shivering in my thin suit. I knew Lorraine wanted Joseph to view me in my bridal splendor, but he took my coat without actually looking at me. He laid the coat over the suitcases and closed the trunk. He fidgeted with the lock, making sure it was closed properly.

Lorraine came over to me, her eyes shining. I could see she meant to kiss me, but I felt a stubborn resistance. I ducked my head, and she licked her fingers and tried to pat my hair in place. "I'll miss you," she said.

"We'll be back tomorrow afternoon," I said.

Joseph got in the car, and Lorraine opened the door for me. I turned and waved at her as Joseph backed out of the driveway, just to have something to do. She was already walking toward the house, on her way to call Jo Penny, I was sure. She still wasn't speaking to Denis. I chewed on my thumbnail and tried not to think of him.

Joseph drove with both hands on the wheel, his eyes straight ahead. The silence between us filled the car and grew. We were nearly outside the Carlington city limits before he spoke. "Are you warm enough?"

"Yes, I'm fine."

"I can turn on the heat if you need it," he said.

"I'm okay," I said, wishing I had kept my coat. I groped for some way to keep the conversation going. I gave him a quick, sideways look. The starkness of his haircut scared me; he looked like he was prepared for war. "You look nice," I said.

He reached up and scratched his neck, then gripped the wheel again. "My tie's in my suitcase. When we get to…the place, I'll put it on."

"Oh," I said. "Okay."

I looked down at my belly, where the slight pooch seemed to gleam under my satin skirt. Lorraine assured Reverend Satterfield that I had seen a doctor, then the next day she took me to one in Reedsboro, someone we didn't know. She stayed in the room while he examined me and confirmed that I was pregnant. She asked all the questions, and he addressed all of his comments to her. I felt relieved that I didn't have to speak, that I didn't have to do anything except cooperate. I willingly left everything in Lorraine's hands. She had even packed my bag for me, including a typed permission slip, signed by her and stamped by a notary public—required for girls under eighteen. She made a reservation for us in a South Carolina chapel and another reservation for us in a hotel. When we came back to Carlington, we would live in a trailer on Joseph's aunt's farm. Aunt Dayna had been married to Joseph's father's brother until he died. Joseph would earn our keep by helping around the farm on weekends and after school.

Lorraine had made all of these arrangements in a series of phone calls with Reverend Satterfield, who was, Lorraine had told me, "less than thrilled." She had asked to speak to Mrs. Satterfield, too, thinking she might be easier to deal with, but the Reverend said, "I make the decisions in our family." He pointed out repeatedly that Joseph would lose his scholarship and his future was ruined. Yet, as Lorraine had predicted, the Reverend never had any doubt that we had to get married, even if we couldn't do so in a church "under the circumstances," as he put it. Lorraine said a quick wedding out-of-state would be best anyway. "The Satterfields will come around," Lorraine kept assuring me. "They just need time to get used to the idea."

I had believed her. I had convinced myself that Joseph and I would bring our families together and become a normal married couple. We would take care of the baby and go to church and save money to buy a house, a place of our own where nothing was for sale. Now, gazing out at the flat, empty road, those ideas seemed far-fetched, like a poor child's hopes for a dazzling Christmas. I sneaked looks at the side of Joseph's face. His jaw was set as if it would never move again. I leaned toward the window and closed my eyes.

When I woke up, we were on a straight highway that went through the flattest land I had ever seen, marked with farmhouses and barren fields. We passed a billboard that featured a cartoon Mexican man who advertised tourist attractions at the state border. In a sleepy stupor, I gazed at a picture of the little man wearing a sombrero and riding a pig. "Sixty more miles," he announced. "You never *sausage* a place!"

"I was beginning to think you would sleep the whole way," Joseph said.

I was startled by his voice, which was quieter than I remembered, and not as deep. "I haven't been sleeping much at night," I said.

He nodded. "Me, either."

I wanted to say, look, this doesn't have to happen. We can turn around now. I took a breath and opened my mouth, but the words wouldn't come. "Could we listen to the radio?" I asked.

He reached down and switched it on. He fiddled with the dial until he came to organ music. A choir of nasal voices sang "Onward Christian Soldiers."

I shifted in my seat. "Do you think we can get Reedsboro?"

"We're pretty far away. Which station?"

I looked at him in surprise; there was only one station that everybody listened to. "W-RED?"

"What's the number?"

"You don't listen to RED?"

"We don't…" He paused. "At my church, we're not allowed to listen to that kind of music."

"Why not?"

"Well, it's…ungodly."

I sat with that for a minute. He must think I was ungodly for even mentioning it. "Lots of rock musicians are Christians," I said, though I wasn't sure it was true. Then I remembered something Connie had told me. "Especially the black people. A lot of them began singing in church when they were kids. Would you listen, at least one song? Let's see if I can get a good station…" I leaned down to twist the dial. "Here's something."

Behind a buzz of static, I recognized the jerky beat of "Get Up Off That Thing." I quickly tuned to a different station, but we were out in the middle of nowhere, and even the gospel music got lost in static.

I turned off the radio and threw us back into our silence. I was cold. My nose felt itchy, and then I had to sneeze. I gasped for air and pressed my hands over my nose and mouth, hoping to suppress it, but the sneeze came in a loud, wet explosion. Joseph pulled a neatly folded handkerchief out of his back pocket. He handed it to me.

"Thank you." I wiped my nose and slimy hands. I looked around, but there was nowhere to put the handkerchief. I held it in my lap. We passed a billboard that showed the cartoon man leading a monkey by a leash. "No Monkey Business, Joost Hanky Panky!" the sign said. Fifteen miles to the border.

I looked over at Joseph. "What are you thinking about?"

I didn't know I was going to ask the question until I

spoke, but I knew the answer I wanted. I wanted to hear that he wanted to marry me, that he wanted to be a father. I felt ashamed to want this, but there it was, a desire as embarrassing as the soggy handkerchief clutched in my hand.

"Jobs," he said. A muscle jumped in his jaw. "We won't have to worry about rent, but there's all the other expenses, especially after the baby comes. I can get a second job, and we need to find something for you, too."

"I'm working at Earl's."

"That's not a good place for a married girl to work. My dad says you'll need to quit that job."

I was conscious of my congested breathing. "I don't know what else I would do."

"My mother saw an ad in the newspaper for classes in word processing. That's the wave of the future, you know. People will stop typing on regular typewriters. They'll train you on how to type on a gadget where the words show up on a screen."

I knew how to type. There were always old typewriters around the shop, and Connie and I had tapped on them since we were little. "What about the baby?"

"Maybe my mother could keep it while you're in school. We'll come up with something."

We both heard the word "we;" his cheeks turned a mild shade of red. Seeing that little bit of color made me feel the best I had all day. So it's settled, I thought. I would be a wife, a mother and a word processor. I wadded up the handkerchief and stuck it between my seat and the car door.

Even in the twilight, I could see that the towns in South Carolina looked a lot like Carlington. The outskirts were dotted with shabby houses surrounded by broken vehicles and rusty appliances. The main streets were nicer, with large, well-groomed yards and empty pots on the front porches that would be filled with geraniums when summer came. It was as if we hadn't gone anywhere. Consulting Lorraine's handwritten directions, Joseph turned this way and that until we came to a building that looked like a cross between a church and a motel. A brightly lit sign said "Weddings, $15 and up."

Joseph parked in the front and turned off the engine. I waited for him to get out, but he sat staring at the wood-frame building, which glowed in the light of the sign.

"This isn't how I had imagined getting married," I said in a low voice.

Without looking at me, he nodded. He got out of the car and opened the trunk. I heard a bag slide out, then it thumped back in place. When he came back and opened the door for me, he was wearing a gray tie. He looked determined, like a man going into battle. He took my hand and squeezed it. "God is with us, Lily."

I wanted to believe him, but Connie wasn't here and wasn't coming back, and that's all I had ever asked from God. If Joseph knew about Denis, which he never would, he would probably say some sins are unforgivable, that my prayers were a waste of breath. Maybe God is with *you*, I thought, looking at Joseph's grim face, but I'm going straight to hell.

Inside the chapel, there was a cramped lobby where a portable TV sat blaring on a counter. A stooped man with milky eyes handed a form to each of us. "You're both eighteen, aren't you?" he asked indifferently, and I produced my notarized permission.

The man led us to a room furnished with two church pews and a lectern. His wife, a thin woman in a faded gray dress, served as the witness. Joseph and I stood in front of the pews, not touching. My nose was runny; I sniffed quietly, trying not to drip. The man muttered a rapid string of words followed by brief mumbles from Joseph, and then my own faint echoes. The wife nudged the two of us in front of a backdrop of a waterfall scene painted in colors never seen in nature. There was the flash of a camera, and we were married.

⌇

"Denis," I whispered into the telephone. I was lying on the bed in our tiny hotel room, still wearing my suit and the high-heeled pumps. From behind the bathroom door, I could hear the low rush of water as Joseph took a shower. I looked up at the ceiling, which had a large yellowish stain shaped like a spider.

"Hello? Who is this?" Denis boomed. Our connection was weak and buzzy; he sounded as far away as he really was.

"It's me," I whispered. "I've only got a second."

"Hi there, Sugar," he said, sounding surprised and immensely pleased. I had never felt anything like homesickness before, but hearing his Boston "sugar"—loud and warm and without the "r"—tears came to my eyes. I had told myself I was only calling so he wouldn't hear my news from someone else.

"Can I meet you somewhere?" he asked. "You could come over."

"I'm not at home."

"Where the hell are you?"

I raised my hips and shifted away from a sag in the mattress. This place, the Castanet Hotel, advertised a honeymoon suite, but Lorraine hadn't splurged. Besides the stained ceiling and spotted carpet, our room featured a humid, mildewy odor. Joseph had wrinkled his nose as soon as walked in. I had tried to be positive, pointing out we had a color TV and our own balcony.

226

"I'm in South Carolina," I said.

Immediately Denis knew I wasn't kidding. "Are you with Connie?"

I cleared my throat. "I'm with Joseph. Joseph Satterfield. We got married."

There was a pause, the longest silence I had ever heard from him. "What are you talking about?"

"I'm married," I whispered. From the bathroom, the pipes squeaked and moaned as Joseph turned off the shower. "I've got to go."

"Look, Lily... Tell me exactly where you are and I'll come get you."

I could picture him standing up, tugging at his belt with that look on his face that said he was about to fix something. "If I leave now..."

"Denis, I'm going to have a baby." Muffled noises came from the bathroom. I could hear Denis breathing.

"Are you sure? Have you been to a doctor?"

"I'm sure. I've got to hang up now."

"When are you coming back?"

The bathroom door opened, and Joseph came out wearing white gym shorts and a T-shirt, a towel slung around his neck. His stubble of hair gleamed in the fluorescent light.

"Tomorrow," I said, speaking in a normal, business-like voice. "I'll call you then, okay?" Before Denis could answer, I hung up. I put the phone back on the nightstand and sat up against a pillow. I smoothed my skirt and slid my hands behind my back to hide their trembling.

"Who was that?" Joseph asked.

"My... cousin," I said. "Marlene." It was the only name that would come to me quickly.

"You have a cousin named Marlene?"

"Yeah, isn't that weird?"

He opened his bag and pulled out a toothbrush, frowning. "I thought we had agreed, our parents had agreed, that we wouldn't tell anyone yet."

"She won't tell," I said quickly.

"Please don't call anyone else," he said. "Calls from motels cost a lot of money."

"I didn't think of that. I'm sorry."

He went into the bathroom and brushed his teeth. He came back and sat on the other end of the bed from me. "Are you ready to go to sleep?" he asked.

"Yes," I said, though I felt wide awake. I went to the bathroom and washed my face and brushed my teeth. When I came out, he was lying on the far side of the bed with his back to me, still wearing his shirt. I went to my suitcase and pulled out a nightgown, a flimsy thing of light blue, also picked out by Lorraine. I wondered if he might turn over and face me, but he didn't move. I put on the gown and stood next to the bed uncertainly. "Are you ready for me to cut off the light?"

"Yes," he said.

I flicked off the overhead light and got in bed under the covers.

Outside in the parking lot, a car horn blew, and a man's voice yelled something I couldn't make out. Then it was quiet except for occasional footsteps and shouting in the hall. I reached over and touched the back of his head with the tip of my finger. "Your hair is gone," I said.

"It's better if you don't touch me, Lily."

"Honey." I tried out the word. "We're married now."

"It's still not right." He turned over and lay on his back. "Not until after the baby comes. I promised my father."

Maybe that would be okay, I thought. Maybe that would

be fine. "Is it all right if I just lie next to you sometimes?"

Through the darkness between us, I saw him shake his head. "That won't work."

21

I stood in the tiny bathroom of our trailer holding a long mess of curls in one hand and a pair of sharp scissors in the other. Joseph had asked me to cut my hair. He said I didn't have to if I didn't want to, but he said it would be pleasing to God, because long hair is a vanity that tempts sin. I pulled the hair away from my scalp and snipped. It fell at my feet.

My haircuts had always been few and far apart. Lorraine took Connie and me to the beauty parlor before Christmas, Easter and Labor Day. Connie always got hers whacked off above her ears; I got a trim. We dreaded these visits, being eyed by the ladies who sat in a row under the dryers, the ones who always seemed to be there, their carefully rolled permanents stuck under big plastic bubbles. When we were little, they were some of the same women who came to our house and riffled through our things and left hastily, as if they didn't want to be seen. As we got older and Lorraine was restored to grace in Carlington, they were friendlier. At the beauty parlor they bought us little bottles of Cokes from the machine in the corner and cooed over me. "Look at those long curls," they would say to me, ignoring Connie. They lifted the ends of my hair and inspected them the same way they looked at trinkets in the shop.

I picked up a long strand from the back of my head, opened the scissors wide, and cut. This wouldn't take long; it would go faster than I had imagined.

Once Connie gave me a haircut. We had been down by a creek playing Huckleberry Finn, and both of us needed to be boys. She had taken me upstairs to the bathroom and set me on the edge of the bathtub. She was careful, she actually did a pretty good job. We swept up all the hair when she was done. But Lorraine whipped her with a switch until the back of her legs bled. I kept saying it was okay, it would grow back. I had liked it short. It made me more like Connie.

As I clutched the unruly curls now, I felt as if I were holding the past, who I used to be. How many times had I sat still with tears in my eyes while Lorraine pulled at my scalp, trying to comb out the tangles? How many times had Denis run his hands through this same hair, buried his face in it? He said he loved the way it brushed his body when I leaned over him. My hair had always brought trouble; it felt right to let it go.

I cut until there was nothing below my ears, then I combed it down in front and cut bangs. One side was longer than the other. I cut some more, making it worse. When I took the scissors away, I had cut too far above my eyebrows. *Shit.* I lay the scissors on the edge of the sink. In the wavy mirror I saw a skinned chicken with big, startled eyes.

I walked out to get a broom just as Joseph came out of the kitchen, buttoning a freshly ironed plaid shirt. He ironed a shirt every morning before school, I had discovered. He stopped when he saw me. "You did it."

My head felt too light. "I look weird."

He shook his head. "No, you...you look good."

"I didn't get it even." He was so handsome, with his dark eyes, his full mouth. He had no idea.

He squinted at the crooked line of my bangs. "Do you want me to try?"

Our bathroom was no bigger than a closet. We stood together in front of the sink. We both tried to take a step back, but there was nowhere to go; we were close enough to

232

slow dance. Joseph wet a comb and carefully ran it through my bangs. His fingers brushed my forehead. The cloth of his shirt carried the damp, warm smell left by the iron. He leaned closer and made a small snip with the scissors. His breath came faster. So did mine. *If he doesn't kiss me, I might die.* He snipped again, and brushed the piece down with his fingers. A small sound came from him, a strangled sigh, and he put the scissors down. "That's good enough," he mumbled. "It's fine the way it is."

He retreated to the kitchen, and I stood with my eyes closed, clutching the back of my bare neck. I waited long enough to give him a chance to come back, then I let my hand drop. I wandered into our room. His blankets were already rolled up and tucked against the wall next to his Bible. The neat bundle, stored at a deliberate distance from my mattress on the floor, made my chest ache.

We had been together for five days, days of unpacking and questions about where to put things and long spells of silence, but I had never felt more cherished. I felt it when he opened a jar for me, when he came home with wood to make a crib for the baby, when we sat together in church. We didn't go to his father's church; I didn't ask why, but I felt sure that Joseph was following instructions, and wondered if my presence at his church would be an embarrassment. On Sunday mornings we went down the road to an old country church that didn't seem to be any particular denomination. These outings felt like a date to me, especially when we shared a hymnbook. Both of us were too shy to sing out. We mouthed the words, hardly able to breathe because our hips were so close on the hard wooden bench. He was thinking about me the same way. I felt it when he was close, I saw it in his eyes, no matter how quickly he looked away. Denis had taught me about sex; Joseph was teaching me about desire.

My love extended to our old, dingy trailer. It was planted in a cracked cement foundation at the edge of a clearing surrounded by tall pines. The trailer was narrow and compact, just a place to sleep, a place to pee, and a cramped nook to cook and eat. I loved that we had only three rooms. I loved that we had almost no furniture, just a rusty kitchen table and two straight-back chairs that came with the place. I had never been so alone with anyone, even Connie.

I went to the kitchen to make breakfast. Joseph was sweeping up the hair in the bathroom.

"I can do that," I said.

"It's okay," he said. "I'm finished."

"I'll fix some breakfast," I said.

"Um…"

"Yes?"

"Please don't put any butter on my toast."

Day by day, I was learning what he liked. Two squeezed oranges in the mornings, milk at night, never any coffee or tea. We couldn't have desserts, or television or playing cards or a telephone–such things were immoral or too expensive. I wasn't allowed to wear makeup or paint my nails, which was all right with me.

I set the table for our breakfast, folding paper towels under our forks. The kitchen had a small, rusty refrigerator and an ancient stove with one working burner. The lack of equipment didn't matter, since I knew how to cook only a few dishes. I made eggs and warmed four pieces of bread in a pan. I wasn't hungry; my stomach felt unsettled. A touch of morning sickness, I thought. I'd feel better if I ate.

We sat at our rickety table. Joseph mumbled the blessing, and I echoed a faint "amen."

"I'll take you over to Aunt Dayna's this morning," he said. "My dad called her yesterday and told her you'd be coming over to help out."

We had driven to a phone booth one day to call the college, and we found out it was too late to take a word processing course this semester; I would need to wait until summer. Meanwhile, my job would be helping Aunt Dayna. "Exactly what does she want me to do?" I asked.

He put his fork down and rubbed the back of his neck. "Well, she wasn't really looking for help. But my dad talked her into giving you a try."

"If she doesn't want me there…"

"It's not you." He paused. "She can be…a little strange. She claims to be a psychic." He glanced at me as if checking my reaction. "You'll see the sign in her yard."

"So people actually come to her to get their fortunes told?"

He nodded.

"How does she do it?"

He shrugged. "She uses cards or something." He broke off a piece of toast. "She's not a Satterfield by blood. She was married to my father's brother."

He said this as if it explained everything. I wanted to ask more, but he opened a textbook and started skimming through it. "Do you have a history test today?" I wasn't officially unenrolled from school yet, but already it seemed distant as a foreign country.

He nodded.

"Are you ready for it?" It was a dumb question; he was always prepared for tests.

"Yes." He seemed to realize that something more was called for. "It's on the French Revolution."

"Oh, really?" I sounded too emphatic, as if I had a real

interest in the French Revolution.

"Mr. Kelly wants us to relate it to the protests against the war, but I don't see how it compares."

"Me either."

"The Revolution was fought for a real cause," he said in a burst of anger that surprised me. "Those people were starving. The hoodlums who protested against the war were spoiled college kids. They just wanted to rebel." He tore off a piece of toast almost savagely. "They were lucky to have all they had."

"I guess they were lucky to be in college at all," I said quietly.

He looked down at his plate without answering. I wanted to say we would find a way for him to go, even without a scholarship, but I knew he wouldn't want to talk about it. His father had a plan, and we were sticking to it.

"I've been meaning to ask you something," I said.

He looked up warily.

"Have you...have you thought about names? For the baby?"

He dabbed his mouth on his paper towel. "My folks have mentioned it."

"What did they say?"

"I'm a junior. For a boy, they like Joseph the third. Joseph Paul Satterfield III."

"I didn't know your middle name," I said.

"I don't know yours, either."

"I don't have one. It's just Lily. Or I guess now it's Stokes. Lily Stokes Satterfield." We smiled shyly at each other.

"What if...what about a girl?" I asked.

"I don't know. My parents didn't say anything about a girl's name."

"I'd like to name her Connie."

He looked down, and his face darkened.

236

"We could give her any middle name you want," I said.

"We don't have to decide right now." He got up from the table and pushed his chair in. "I need to get going."

Aunt Dayna lived just over the hill from us, close enough to walk, but Joseph insisted on driving me. As we rode over, he told me that her husband had died five years earlier. "She used to keep a good house, but now she takes care of a few chickens, and…that psychic stuff. You'll just need to help with the house and keep an eye on her."

Cleaning sounded okay, I knew how to do that, but I had my doubts about watching over someone who didn't even want me around.

Joseph pulled up in a gravel driveway. Her house was a wood-frame all on one floor, shaped like our trailer and not much bigger. The yard was a tidy square of scrubby grass and dirt. On one side there was a large garden surrounded by a tangle of wire. Three chickens of various colors milled about under a tree, pecking in the ground. A sign in the yard said "Madam Dayna, Past – Present – Future, $5."

As we got out of the car, a woman came out on the front porch and stood, a bit unsteadily. She was tall and thin. A scraggle of gray curls framed her wrinkled face.

"Morning, Aunt Dayna," Joseph said.

She peered at me. Her eyes were dark and small, almost lost behind the bubbles of her cheeks.

"Hello," I said.

"Come closer, I won't bite." Her voice was sharp and clear; it sounded younger than she looked. I walked toward her until I was near enough to see the light gray hairs above her mouth.

She looked me up and down and nodded. "She's got a

pretty face, Joe. I see how you got in trouble."

He reddened and squinted toward the horizon, as if he were trying to gauge the weather. My training from Lorraine kicked in. "I hope I'll be a help to you."

She drew up to her full height, which was nearly as tall as Joseph. "I don't know why anybody thinks I need help."

After Joseph left and I followed her inside, it wasn't hard to see why I had been sent. A thin layer of dust seemed to cover everything in her small, cluttered house. A dirty bowl containing a crust of old food sat on the floor between two chairs in the living room. Loose dirt, like the leftover shavings of careless sweeping, trailed across the floors. In the kitchen, there was the strong smell of freshly burned toast.

I asked where she kept her rags and cleaners. Her face puckered. "Now don't move things around so I can't find them."

She came close and gave me another long assessment. I tried not to turn away. Staring at each other practically nose-to-nose didn't seem to embarrass her at all. "I'm going out to feed my chicks," she finally said.

I got busy, dusting all over the house and washing every dirty dish I could find. I was mopping the kitchen floor when I heard the front door slam. She came to the doorway and looked around. "Can't tell you've done much," she said.

I opened my mouth to speak, indignant, but then a wide grin broke out on her face, splitting her cheeks into deeper gullies. She brayed out a long laugh. "I'm just teasing you, girl," she said. "It's good. A damned sight better."

During the next couple of days I attacked all the floors and cleaned out her cabinets. After that, there wasn't much to do. We started staying outside together, puttering in the garden and taking care of the chickens.

Once a station wagon pulled up in her driveway, and a woman wearing sunglasses got out of the car. She had on a beige pantsuit with a matching pocketbook slung over her shoulder. Aunt Dayna stood up from the garden, rubbing her lower back. "Hey," she said. "I'll be right with you."

The two of them disappeared into the house. I pulled a few weeds in the garden, daydreaming about Joseph, picturing us playing with the baby. We needed a stroller; we needed a lot of things. I touched my stomach, which continued to feel crampy sometimes. Aunt Dayna told me it was normal, but she had never had any children. I had another appointment with the doctor later in the week. Joseph said he would drive me; I wouldn't need to call on Lorraine. I looked forward to being in the car with him and to having the entire trip to Reedsboro to sneak looks at the side of his face.

After about twenty minutes, the woman in the pantsuit came out of the house smiling to herself. She gave me a distracted nod, then she got in her car and drove away. Aunt Dayna came out and began pulling weeds with me.

We worked in silence for a while before I got the nerve to ask what was on my mind. "Can you tell me," I said, clearing my throat. "Will we have a boy or a girl?"

She stopped for a moment and looked in the distance, then she turned and pulled at a particularly stubborn clump of weeds, grunting a little as they finally gave and came out of the ground. She tossed the weeds over her shoulder and shook her head. "Honey, I really can't say."

Late in the afternoon, I left Aunt Dayna's and hurried back to the trailer, eager to be there when Joseph came home, but I felt uneasy as I walked up to our yard. The air was cold and very still, even the birds. Joseph was still gone; his car wasn't there. When I went inside, I felt too much by myself. My lower back ached, something I had been able to ignore most of the day. I wasn't hungry, but I rummaged around in the kitchen and found some hot dogs to fix for dinner. While I cut up a wedge of cabbage—I would mix it with mayonnaise for slaw—I turned on the little radio we kept in the kitchen and listened to the news.

The Patty Hearst trial had been going on for days. Before Joseph and I got married, I had watched the news every night and had scanned Denis's news magazines for articles about her. Now it was harder to keep up, but the pictures of her were burned in my mind. There was the school picture, where she looked like any average, pretty girl. I had watched the grainy tape of her robbing the bank in California, and I had to admit she seemed to be having a pretty good time. But she had been kept in a closet for almost two months; the kidnappers had told her no one cared. Bit by bit, through the trial, new information came out. She fell in love with one of her captors, a guy named Willie who, with others in the gang, had stayed in a burning house rather than surrender to the cops. People interviewed in articles kept saying "not credible," but when Patty's lawyer said her heart was broken, when she called herself an urban guerrilla, I believed her. When she said she had been brainwashed, I believed that, too.

Today there was no mention of her on the radio; I turned it off. As I started to warm rolls in the oven, there was a clatter of knocking at the door. My first thought was Aunt Dayna, and I went to let her in.

"Lily!" It was Denis. The sound of his voice shot through me, but I wasn't surprised. Without knowing it, I had been waiting for him to show up here.

Denis knocked and called my name again. I took a breath to speak, but nothing came out. I had never said no to him, I didn't know how. Joseph would be back anytime. I stared at the door, afraid Denis could somehow find a way through.

He knocked again, but stopped for a long minute. I thought he would go away.

"Lily." His voice was sure and determined. "Let me in."

I took a step toward the door. "Hello?" I said, as if I had just heard him.

"Hey!" He sounded relieved and maybe a little drunk. "Let me in, Baby."

I stood there, biting my lip. My hands were shaking. "I can't," I said, but it came out nearly a whisper, too low for him to hear.

"Come on." He sounded irritated. "I need to talk to you."

I went to the window and slowly lifted a corner of the shade. He stood with one hand pressed against the door, staring down. His stomach sagged over his jeans. Over the winter, his tan had faded, leaving his arm and neck blotchy. He didn't look good. He looked like he needed me.

I let the shade fall and went to the door. I put my hand on the handle and gripped it. "Denis, you can't be here. Joseph will be home soon."

"Just open the door, Honey." I could hear him breathing.

"I'll only stay a minute, I swear."

"Where is your car?"

"I parked way up the main road. No one will know I was here."

There was a long silence, then he said, "I love you."

Sometime after he and Lorraine first met, I had walked into the kitchen when they were kissing. She was arched back against the sink while he pressed against her, his hands moving over her body. He hadn't seen me; neither of them had. They had been totally absorbed in each other then, but that had changed, even before Connie left. He wouldn't be able to avoid Lorraine now. I wondered what would happen to them.

His voice came through the door again. "Are you there?"

"Yes."

"Haven't I been good to you? That boy...he's just a kid, he doesn't know you the way I do."

I was suddenly aware of the strong smell of something burning. The hot dog rolls. I ran to the kitchen, grabbed a potholder and jerked the rolls out of the oven. Smoke streamed out; they looked like black bricks. I set them down and waved my arm through the smoke. Denis was shouting. He must have heard me running away, and he was calling my name frantically and beating on the door again. I went back to the door and spoke loudly. "Denis, you have to leave."

Something thumped against the door. His hand, his foot?

"You've always been a coward, Lily." He sounded calm now and sober. "If you want me to go, tell me to my face. Look me in the eyes and say it."

I stood for a long moment, then I went to the window, acting on some decision I couldn't have named. I jerked on the shade. It flew up and curled in its roll. Denis was standing with his hands in his pockets; he spoke toward the door, something

I couldn't hear. I put my hands under the thin metal that crossed the window. At first it wouldn't budge. I kept pushing up, and finally it moved. I lifted the window.

At the sound, he whirled toward me and looked up. The trailer stood crooked but tall on its foundation. The window was high above him, out of reach. "There you are," he said, almost smiling. "Come on now…" He stopped, and his face changed. "Your hair. Where is your hair?"

"I'm married," I said. "You need to go." I forced myself to keep looking at him, to let him take a good look at me, before I backed away and closed the window.

He banged on the door again and yelled my name, then I heard him sobbing. I sat huddled in a kitchen chair, shivering, smelling burned bread. My head hurt and my stomach hurt. After several long minutes, it was quiet outside, and when I checked, he had gone.

Sometime during the night I woke with sharp, squeezing pains in my stomach. Joseph was lying on his place on the floor; I could tell by his breathing he was in a good sleep. I rolled over, trying to get comfortable. I had felt milder pains earlier in the evening, while Joseph and I were eating our dinner. When we sat down, I thought I was hungry, but when I started eating our macaroni and cheese and green beans, my appetite disappeared. I forced myself to eat a decent portion anyway, and I didn't say anything to Joseph.

I slipped out of bed and went to the bathroom. Joseph had cleaned it again this morning; fumes of Ajax made my eyes water. While I sat and peed, vomit rose in my throat. I swallowed it back. As I stood, I glanced down in the toilet and saw a bright red streak on the discarded toilet paper. Blood red.

Was the baby bleeding? I curled my arms around my stomach and cradled it. "You're okay," I whispered, but I didn't sense any answer. I wondered if my period had somehow broken through. The pain felt like regular cramps. I went back to bed and tried to sleep, but after a while I had to get up again. This time there was more blood. I went to the kitchen and found a dishrag. I folded it into a pad and placed it in my underwear.

When it began to get light outside, Joseph got up quietly, trying not to wake me. I heard soft thuds and scuffles as he got dressed, then the whispery sound of the broom as he swept the floors. I lay still, trying not to move. I could tell the dishrag was soaked. I was scared, and I was embarrassed about the blood. I didn't want him to see it. When it was time for him to leave for school, he came in our room. He cleared his throat. "It's almost eight o'clock."

"I'll get up in a little while." My voice was low and strangled.

"Are you all right?" he asked.

"I'm feeling a little puny," I said, making a great effort to sound normal. "I think I need to rest today."

He asked if he could bring me anything, and I said no. He left the trailer and I heard the sound of his car's motor, the crunch of gravel as he drove away. I felt abandoned, and I wished that I had told him.

The pain continued. I was afraid the baby was hurting. I got up and found a fresh rag to put in my underwear. The blood was bright and full of thick clots; I had to do something. I washed my face and got dressed. I picked up my purse and walked slowly over the hill to Aunt Dayna's.

She was outside sitting on her porch swing. "You're late," she called out as I came into the yard. She stood and continued chattering. I don't know what she was saying. She suddenly

245

stopped when she saw how slowly I was moving. "Why do you have your pocketbook with you?" she asked.

I made it up to the porch and stood there, holding my stomach. "May I use your phone?" I asked.

It sat on a table in the hallway. I dialed slowly, watching the wheel turn around the numbers. I was afraid I might be calling too early, but Lorraine answered right away. She wasn't in a good mood; I could hear that in her voice.

"I need to go to the doctor," I said. "Can you come get me?"

Much later, I think about Lorraine alone in the house after I marry Joseph. Both of us are thrust into a new kind of solitude, though in her case nobody comes home in the evenings to break it. When I move out, she thinks it will be like starting over, a fresh party. She imagines that she and Jo Penny will go out more often, that she will call old friends and entertain. But when she calls, people aren't available. Jo Penny is always busy, either going to one of Marlene's recitals or going out with her new man, a guy she had met at her store. Denis is preoccupied and surly, and he's drinking too much. She doesn't want to be around him now.

She has a new neediness with customers. She asks them about their health, their relations, she plies them with Cokes and cookies and insists they sit down to eat them. In the early mornings and evenings, she takes on ambitious cleaning projects. She turns the volume on the TV loud while she scrubs floors and attacks the mildew in the bathrooms. The house seems to pulse around her, a live thing breathing. She lies awake in her bed, in the room where her parents once slept, and she thinks about them more than she has in years. She dreams about her father. They are in New York sitting in

246

a restaurant with white tablecloths and waiters wearing black suits. They are presented with foods of all kinds, huge, bright platters, and the table is so long she can't see the end. Her father has his arm around her, but then he's gone. She spends a long time looking for him, frantic then hopeless. She has no way home, so she has to walk.

One long evening, when she can't stand the silence anymore, she dials Information and gets Jack's telephone number. The operator gives her a new street name, not the one Lorraine last knew. So he's moved, she thinks. She tries to push the thought out of her mind. This is strictly business, she tells herself. He has a right to know about his daughter. It is just past nine o'clock, still a decent hour, early enough to call. Nine o'clock is fine. If his wife answers, she will simply ask for him. There is nothing wrong with a friendly call. Or maybe she will hang up. Years have passed since she last did that; they will never suspect her.

"Hello." His voice in her ear. Deep, intelligent, carrying a mix of his Kentucky childhood and all the countries he has visited since. Lorraine suddenly remembers that he knows how to speak Turkish.

"Jack? It's Lorraine." He won't guess she's been drinking. She makes sure she sounds clean, and she's only had two or maybe three. "Lorraine Stokes," she said.

There is only the shortest pause. "Well, hello," he says. "How are you?" The tone is one he might use with an old college buddy that he hadn't known very well. It is a tone used when a wife is in the room. Lorraine notices he doesn't say her name.

"I'm fine, doing really well. I won't keep you, but I just wanted to pass along some news." She is talking too fast, she can't stop. "Lily got married. She married a really nice boy. Joe Satterfield's son. Do you remember the minister?"

"No, I don't believe I do…"

"He's been at the Baptist church for years…but I guess you wouldn't know…Anyway, the Satterfields are lovely people."

"It's hard to believe she's out of school already," he says. "They grow up so fast. My boys are eleven and thirteen now."

He says it as if she knew about them, as if they had discussed them before. "Yes," she says, with an artificial laugh. "I still feel far too young to be a grandmother, but I suppose that's coming next." She laughs again, as if the possibility is still remote and absurd.

"Well, thanks for letting me know," he says. "Glad to hear you all are getting on well."

He is dismissing her. Lorraine feels a surge of rage. The blood rushes to her face. She grips the receiver tightly. "You have been glad to ignore her all these years." Her voice sounds ugly, but she won't be quiet, not anymore. "She needed you while you have gone on living your little Country Club life as if she didn't exist. She is so beautiful, Jack, and you have never seen her. You are a complete bastard." But by the time she says these last words, he has already hung up.

She picks up the base of the phone and rips it away from the wall. She hurls it with all her strength toward the dining room. It flies across a table that holds iced tea glasses and candle holders. It grazes those items, plus a tall pitcher, and lands with a crash against a mirror. An intricate web of cracks appears in the glass. The noise of crystal exploding is spectacular, like a million chimes. It seems to last for a long time. She has always wondered what it would sound like.

❧

Lorraine sped all the way to the doctor's office, but she drove slowly on the way back. It was dark, and drizzling a little; every now and then she turned on her windshield wipers. I sat in the passenger seat with my hands folded in my lap. It had hurt when they took the baby, it was still hurting. The doctor gave me a sample of pills. I took one pill from the bottle and swallowed it without water.

"How do you feel?" Lorraine asked.

"Fine." I didn't have words to tell her anything else, I never had.

"I called Joseph's aunt," she said. "She said she would let him know."

"Thanks," I said faintly.

"I'll come in with you," she said, but there was something tentative in her voice. "Maybe there's something I can do to help."

I couldn't imagine her in the trailer. "You don't have to do that," I said. "I'll be all right."

We rode in silence. I didn't know I was crying, but every now and then I had to swipe at my cheeks. I turned my head toward the window.

On Aunt Dayna's road, Lorraine drove slowly to avoid getting her car muddy. She pulled up in front of the trailer; I could see her trying not to look at it. "Maybe this is for the best, Lily," she said. "You and Joseph are young. Now you two can just have fun together."

Joseph had turned the armchair so it was facing the front door. He stood as soon as I came in, letting a book fall from his lap. I went straight to him, the way I might have gone to a father. He hugged me and held me close against him. "Are you okay?"

I swayed in his arms. The pain killer had begun to work. I felt groggy and bereft. I felt married.

"What happened?" he asked. "Do they know why?"

I shook my head. I thought about all I had ever lost, how I could trace my life from the beginning by following a trail of missing things: crayons, books, permission slips, hair clips, jackets. The fawn-colored coat bought especially for church. When that disappeared, it was the only time Lorraine switched me instead of Connie. I wished it had happened more. "I'm sorry," I whispered.

Joseph slowly let me go and leaned down to pick up the fallen book. "You should get in bed."

"Have you had supper?" I had an urge to begin making things up to him, to give him whatever small thing I could manage.

"I'm not hungry."

I didn't want to be away from him; I didn't want to be alone in our room. "Let's sit outside. The rain has stopped, I'm pretty sure it has."

He glanced at the window and frowned. "It's cold."

"Just for a minute. Please."

He put on his coat and carried out a towel to spread on the

top step. I sat down slowly. My thighs were sore from being pried apart so long at the hospital. The rain had stopped; a field of stars was out, bright and close.

"Have you told your folks yet?" I asked.

He nodded. "I called them from Aunt Dayna's."

"I bet they weren't sorry," I said in a low voice.

"Yes, they were," he said, sounding surprised. "We know it's God's will, it must be, but they were very sorry."

I wondered why they had never had us over to eat a meal with them, or even to drink lemonade or whatever normal church families did. "Do you think God wants babies to die?"

"I don't know," he said. "I just know He has a plan for all of us."

"So what's our plan now?" I whispered.

"What do you mean?"

"Do you want to stay married?"

He looked at me with a pained expression, almost angry. "I was so worried something would happen to you. I was worried about the baby...but mostly you."

Something lighter separated from the heaviness in my chest. He hadn't said he loved me, but he did. I leaned closer to him; our shoulders touched. I felt a flare of pure joy. "I didn't feel afraid for myself," I said. It was a truth that felt like a lie, because it made me sound brave. At some point I had known I would get through it and the baby wouldn't. Maybe everyone would have been better off if it had been the other way around. The baby would have had a crazy grandmother in Lorraine, and two more grandparents I didn't even know, but Joseph would have been a good father.

"You should go to college," I said. "You'll be a good preacher."

"It will take some time, but we can save some money. We

need to trust God, Honey."

I heard the "we." I heard God and Honey, too, but mostly we.

"You're so good," I said.

He shook his head a little, but I could see he was glad I said it, it was what he wanted. He took my hand and squeezed it. "You're shivering," he said. "We should go in."

When we said goodnight, we stood together, and he stroked my hair. He began to feel hard against my belly. I reached up to put my arms around him, but he stepped back. "I'd better do my homework. And you should get in bed. Do you need anything?"

"No, thanks."

He started to turn away, then stopped. He came back to me in two quick strides and gripped my shoulders. "I want to make love with you, Lily." His eyes were moist, and his cheeks had turned red. "It will be okay now."

"The doctor said to wait two weeks," I said softly.

He nodded, and let his hands slide from my shoulders down the length of my arms before letting go. I wanted to feel that touch everywhere. I lifted my face toward his, but he turned away. "Okay, then," he said. "Good night."

The next day I woke up at noon with only a hazy memory of saying goodbye to Joseph when he left for school. I had heard him tiptoeing around the trailer, and when it was time for him to go, he came in to say goodbye. He had given me a quick kiss on the mouth. I was pretty sure he had.

After that, I kept waking up and going back to sleep. Every time I woke, I felt the baby's absence in my body, the ache and the emptiness, before I remembered. I lay in bed and stared at our walls, which were made to look like old knotty pine, yellowish brown with dark blotches. The shapes they made looked like children's faces with no eyes. I wondered what I would have seen if they had showed me my baby, whether there would have been anything to recognize in the pulp they pulled out.

Sometime in the early afternoon, I got up and wandered in the kitchen and turned on the radio. I took a package of bologna from the refrigerator and listened to a news update on Patty's trial, which was winding down after five weeks. A reporter interviewed two people, a woman who thought the jury would find her innocent and a man who said they might not be able to reach a verdict. A crowd was hanging around the courthouse in San Francisco; I wondered if Connie was there. I turned off the radio and ate a piece of bologna.

As I stood in the kitchen and chewed, I heard strange noises outside. It sounded like someone imitating the creaks in a staircase. I went to the window. Aunt Dayna was striding toward the trailer with a knapsack on her back and a bundle under each arm. As she got closer, I saw she was carrying two of her chickens. They clucked and wriggled in her armpits.

I opened the door before she got to the porch. She was out of breath; sweat gleamed on her forehead and on her upper lip. She squatted down and opened her arms, and the chickens landed on the ground in a flurry of squawking and feathers.

"What are you doing?" I asked.

"Thought you could use some company, and some fresh eggs," she said, looking pleased with herself.

"Thanks," I said faintly. I eyed the chickens as they scratched around in the dirt outside. One was black and one was white. They had scrawny necks, beady eyes and feet shaped like stars. I was afraid of them. I suspected they would peck the stuffing

254

out of me if I tried to pick them up as Aunt Dayna had.

"It will do you good to have something to take care of," she said.

I held the door open, and she came in. In the narrow box of our living room, she suddenly looked big and even taller. She shrugged off her knapsack and set it down at her feet; it made a thumping sound on the floor.

"For pity's sake, it's dark in here," she said. "Let's get some light." She went around to all the windows and pulled up the shades.

"I've been sleeping," I said sheepishly.

"It's time to wake up. How do you feel?" She looked me up and down, then peered into my face.

"Okay." She kept looking at me. "Terrible," I added.

She nodded. "I lost two. Doctor said that was it, he didn't want me to try after that."

"I'm so sorry," I whispered.

"I'd be lying if I said it didn't matter. But you know what? There ain't much that matters forever. What do you have to eat?"

"Um, bologna. And crackers and pimento cheese, I think."

"Good, I brought everything else." She took her knapsack to the kitchen and began pulling things out. First she held up a bag of grain. "This is for the chickens," she said, putting it aside. Then she pulled out a bag of chocolate bars, a deck of playing cards, and a gleaming bottle of sherry. She held up the bottle and admired it. "You got any ice made? I like it cold."

"I'll just have a Coke," I said. "I'm training to be a preacher's wife."

She gave a brief snort, but didn't argue with me. She poured her own drink in a plastic cup, and we sat down at the kitchen table with the cards. "Want me to teach you how to play gin rummy?" she offered.

I picked up the cards and shuffled them several times, ending by making them fly back and forth between my hands like an accordion before I slapped them together and set them down in front of her for a final cut. "Do you want me to teach you how to play seven-card stud?"

"You're on, girl. What can we use for chips?" She jumped up and started searching the kitchen drawers.

I thought about Joseph walking in and finding us playing poker. "I was just kidding," I said. "Let's play gin."

As a gin player, she reminded me of Connie. She was strategic and ruthless, and she wasn't above cheating. More than once she claimed a spread when she had two kings and a jack.

"I'm surprised at you," I said. "I thought you were an honest woman." Even though she was the one drinking sherry, I felt giddy.

"It's not me," she said. "They make these damned cards so they all look alike." She slapped down a spread and grinned. "Gin again."

After Aunt Dayna left, I pulled out a package of macaroni and cheese and put some water on to boil. While the noodles were cooking, I opened a can of green beans and heated them up, too. I found an old muffin tin, washed it, and decided to make cupcakes. We wouldn't have any icing, but we could put jam on them.

By 5:30, twilight started creeping in. I kept looking out the window, expecting to see Joseph's car. Pacing around the kitchen, I noticed Aunt Dayna's bottle of sherry, still three-quarters full. Shit, I thought. Joseph can't see that. I hid it away in a cabinet behind a bottle of corn oil.

Six o'clock came, then quarter 'til seven. He had never been this late. I was just putting on my coat, preparing to walk over to Aunt Dayna's to see if she knew anything, when Joseph's car pulled up.

I started toward the door, then sat down at the kitchen table; I didn't want to be hovering. It seemed to take a long time, but finally the door opened. I heard him hang his keys on a nail, then he came into the kitchen. "Why are chickens in the yard?"

I searched his face, and he looked away from me. "Aunt Dayna brought them over this afternoon," I said.

"What for?"

"I don't know, she wanted us to have them. Honey, I've been waiting. You're really late."

"I'm sorry." He turned away as he said it, made himself busy taking off his jacket and hanging it up.

"What happened?" I asked. "You haven't been working outside in the dark, have you?"

"No, no. My father came by this afternoon when I was out in the field. He said he needed help over at their house, they're remodeling the basement. So I went over there, and I ended up staying for dinner. I didn't think it would take this long."

"Oh." Why didn't you come get me? I wanted to ask. They could have easily stopped at the trailer on their way out. "I guess you're not hungry now." I pointed toward the stove. "I made some macaroni. And cupcakes."

He shook his head. "My mom had roast beef."

"Roast beef?"

He gave me an apologetic look. "I could probably eat a little something. I'll sit down with you."

I took two plates from the cabinet and spooned out some food. I knew neither of us would eat much.

He sat down at the table, waiting for me. I settled myself in my seat and picked up my fork. As I lifted the first bite to my mouth, I saw his face darken. "Lily," he spoke quietly, too quietly. "Aren't you going to say grace?"

Joseph wasn't happy about the chickens. He said they were dirty and noisy. He said any eggs we might get wouldn't be worth eating. I told him it was good for me to have something to do when I was at home alone.

"When you get your license, you can get a job," he said.

"That's what I've been thinking." I didn't mean to lie; I just didn't know how to tell him I would never drive. There had been a baby and now there wasn't. I was even more certain the world was a dangerous place.

"I'll be late again this evening," he said, looking away from me.

For several nights I had barely seen him because he was still helping his parents with the basement. In the mornings, he discouraged me from getting out of bed before he left for school. I wanted to get up and have breakfast with him, but he kept saying I needed to rest. I wondered if I should give the chickens back to Aunt Dayna, but I couldn't bring myself to do it. I liked sitting out on our front stoop and watching them walk around with their bright little eyes and jerky movements. I named them Sylvia and June, after twins at school who didn't look alike except they both had big chests. Sylvia was the better behaved of the two. When I went out to scatter feed, she stood back politely, while June would make a run for me; I was still a little afraid of her. Aunt Dayna told me I had to show her who was boss. I flapped my hands around and scolded. In return, she cackled back at me and seemed to enjoy the attention. While they ate and scratched, I sat in the sun and watched them for long stretches of time. I felt tired, but the soreness in my stomach and thighs was gone. The lack of pain felt like something lost; more and more, it was like the baby had never been there.

I thought about Joseph, replaying in my mind the things he said the night I came home from the hospital. I worried that he had changed his mind, but I remembered Lorraine had always told me how hard it is for boys not to have sex. She would say, and maybe she would be right, that he was staying away from me to avoid the torment of blue balls. Our two weeks were almost up; I was sure he had been counting the days, too. I tried not to daydream too much about what it would be like to be close to him again, but it crossed my mind a lot.

When the weekend came, I got out of bed while Joseph was still asleep on the floor, and I found just enough bread and eggs in the refrigerator to make breakfast. I heard Joseph stirring around. When I called him to the table, he came to the edge of the room and looked at the dishes I had laid out. His hair was wet, and he was wearing jeans and a faded flannel shirt that had been neatly pressed. His shoulders filled the doorway. "Thanks for cooking," he said, but he didn't look pleased. We sat down, and after he said the blessing, we ate in silence until I put my fork down and sat staring down at my plate.

He finally looked up. "Aren't you hungry?"

I shook my head.

He tore off a piece of his toast, and in the silence between us, his chewing sounded too loud. He swallowed and cleared his throat. "When do you think you'll start working at Aunt Dayna's again?"

"She told me to take my time. I'll be ready to go back

Monday, I think."

He nodded. "What are you going to do today?"

I heard the "you," but ignored it. "I thought maybe we could have a picnic. I could fix a basket…"

"I'm sorry." I winced, because he wasn't calling me anything anymore: not Honey, not my name. "I promised Dad I would help out with the basement again. We think we can finish up today."

He shifted in his chair and looked down at his plate. He did look sorry, or maybe sorry for me. I felt like an ugly girl who had asked him to dance. "Can I go with you? Maybe I can help."

"I don't think so," he said, still not looking at me. "But thanks."

I pushed my chair back and got up; I couldn't stop myself. I went over and put my hands on his shoulders, breathing in his smell of soap and shaving cream. "Look at me," I said. I meant to plead with him to say what was wrong, but when he tilted his chin up and his dark eyes were so close, I didn't have any words. I leaned down and kissed him. For a second he didn't kiss back, it was only me, but then he pulled me onto his lap. He cupped my head in his hands and pressed his mouth hard against mine. As soon as his tongue slipped between my lips, he drew back. He took hold of my elbows and gently lifted me off his lap. It was all right, because I could feel it wasn't what he wanted.

"I don't like being away from you so much," he said.

I pulled my chair closer to his and sat down. "It seems like you don't want to be around me when you're here."

He looked away and sighed. "There's a lot on my mind, like how we're going to pay for things. I want to give you something better than this trailer."

"This might seem crazy to you," I said. "But I never want to leave this place. I love it here." My face felt warm; it was probably the truest thing I had ever told him.

He laughed softly. "After living in that big house all your life…You don't have to say that, Lily."

"I mean it."

"Well, this isn't a suitable place for a preacher."

"Suitable" wasn't a word I had heard him use; I knew it came from his mother or father. He reached across the table and took my hand. It didn't feel as if he took it to touch me, but to stop me from touching him. "I think we need to pray," he said. "Will you do that with me?"

I nodded. His palm felt warm and damp; my fingers twitched, then his did. I closed my eyes and waited for him to speak. Outside a blue jay screeched, stopped, then screeched again. When a long minute passed and he had said nothing, I looked at him. His eyes were closed, his face was clenched. Then I understood this was *his* prayer, silent and separate. I shut my eyes again and tried to think of something to say to God, anything.

Joseph whispered "Amen." When he opened his eyes he leaned over and kissed me on top of my head, and he squeezed my hand before he let go. "I'd better finish getting ready," he said.

He came back home late that afternoon with a fresh haircut, this one even closer than the one before. I watched him from the window as he got out of his car. He walked slowly toward the trailer, his head bowed, his feet scuffing the ground.

Something inside my chest tightened at the sight of the dark stub on his head. He looked like an exhausted soldier, like someone I had never known who was returning from a place far away. I moved away from the window. When he came in, I was sweeping around the armchair.

"Oh, hi," I said.

"Hello." He glanced my way without looking at me directly. I wanted him to see that I had taken time to primp. My hair was freshly washed and brushed, and I had put on clean jeans and a tight sweater. He picked up the day's mail and began sifting through it. "What did you do today?"

"Just worked around the house." I had done a few essential chores, but I had spent most of the day outside playing with the chickens and sketching them. I liked their shapes. The lines of their bodies seemed simple, but they were tricky to draw. I didn't want to waste too much of Joseph's notebook paper, so I made them tiny, drawing them over and over in different poses, trying to show how I saw them. If nothing else, I was becoming good at watching chickens. "Did you finish the basement?" I asked.

"No. Almost." He opened the electricity bill and frowned at it.

"But you stopped to get a haircut?" I meant to sound teasing, but it came out like a complaint.

"When do I have any time during the week?" He stuffed the bill back in the envelope and tossed it on a chair.

It was as if the morning had never happened. I kept sweeping the floor, which was always clean since he swept it every day.

"What do we have for supper?" he asked.

The broom stirred a tiny speck of lint, but I didn't have the dustpan. I swept it under the chair. "We need to go to the store," I said. "We're out of everything."

He sighed. "We should take your car. It's good to run the engine every now and then."

I went and got my pocketbook, even though I didn't have any money, and I brushed my hair. While I was in the bathroom, I heard him leave through the front door. He was sitting in my car when I went outside.

My car balked the first time, but then he tried again, and it sounded all right. He gunned the engine a couple of times, then pulled out to the dirt road, faster than he usually drove. I could see he just wanted to get the trip over with. The road was full of deep ruts, and it was muddy from recent rain. The car pitched up and down like a boat on rough water. I held on to the edge of my seat until we got to the main highway. "Do you mind if I turn on the news?"

"I heard it just a little while ago," he said. "The Patricia Hearst case is finally over, thank goodness. I'm tired of hearing about it."

I had been reaching for the radio dial, but I let my arm fall in my lap. "Did they let her go?"

"Of course not," he said. "She's guilty. They're sending her to jail."

I was stunned and wounded, as if he had said something ugly about me. "I don't believe it."

He glanced over with a surprised look. "Well, for gosh sakes, she did rob a bank."

"She was stuffed in a closet for fifty days, too."

He didn't answer, which made me furious. "I don't think it's surprising she did what they wanted," I said loudly.

He turned onto the main highway. "They told her she was free to go. She had a choice."

"Maybe it wasn't that simple," I shot back.

"What is this...Is something bothering you?"

I gave a bitter laugh. "You're asking what's bothering *me?*"

His mouth got a set look, which I took to mean he was determined not to speak. I prepared myself for silence during the rest of the drive. Then he suddenly turned on his signal, slowed down the car and pulled into the dirt parking lot of an abandoned country store. He parked on the near side of a rusty gas pump. Two dark birds were huddled on the ground near the road. When we stopped, they suddenly rose like large black kites and flew away, their wings alarmingly wide.

"What are we doing?" I asked. Joseph turned off the engine and pulled out the key, then put it back in. His hands were shaking, and he saw me looking at them. He clenched them in his lap.

Until then, I had been hoping he would tell me everything was okay, even if it really wasn't. Now I wanted his silence back.

"My folks are giving me a hard time," he said.

I looked out my window at the store. It was an old wooden building with a slanted tin roof. A battered rocking chair sat on the front porch, tipping a little in the wind. I knew what he was going to say; I had known for a long time without telling myself. "They don't want you to be married to me, do they? But they don't even know me."

He bowed his head and let out a breath. "They think they do because they know your mother."

I shook my head, not understanding. My mother knew his parents by name only. "They've never…"

"They've heard things about her."

"Oh."

He leaned back against the seat and shifted his hips, avoiding my eyes. My car was smaller than his, and the seat was still adjusted for me. The lower part of my steering wheel pressed into the top of his thighs, and the short bristles of his hair nearly brushed the stained ceiling above. He looked cramped and miserable.

"My mother had some hard times way back," I said. "She lost her father when she was young. There was a time when she…didn't always do right. But she's worked hard all these years…she goes to PTA meetings, she gives money to the United Way…"

"She doesn't go to church," he said.

"She prays, though." When I said it, I thought it was probably true; Lorraine was one to cover her bets. "If your folks met her, I think they'd see she's okay, she's really not a bad person. Do you think…maybe we could get them together sometime?"

He shifted in his seat, and I saw on his face it would never happen. His hands were a tight knot in his lap. "There's something else…"

I could see he didn't want to say whatever was coming, that it was something terrible. It wasn't possible, but I wondered if his parents somehow had found out about Denis and me.

"It's about your sister," he said.

Everything stopped. She's dead, I thought. He's going to say she's dead. One of the black birds swooped down in front of the car, returning to something in the dirt. I tasted vomit in my throat.

"I'm sorry to have to tell you this, Lily. She's in trouble…"

"Just tell me."

He took a breath. "She's living with Earl."

It took a moment for the simple meaning of the sentence to sink in, and then I knew there had been a mistake. "Connie's not here. She's not in Carlington."

"My parents told me," he said. "They're upset… Your sister moved into Earl's house, and she's working at the restaurant again."

No." I hit the dashboard with my palm and twisted in my seat to face him. "She was in Reedsboro, but she left back in December…"

"I haven't heard it just from my parents." He hesitated.

"Everyone at school has been talking about her."

I wanted to shake him until he said something that made sense. "Why do they care what she's doing?"

He reached for the steering wheel, gripped it, then let his hands drop. He spoke without looking at me. "Lily, Earl is a queer. I don't know how else to put it. She and Connie are queers."

I sat back in my seat. There was a part of me that wanted to argue, but I knew it was true, I knew it as soon as he said it. I tried to remember where Earl lived, and the street came to mind, the hippy neighborhood where people hung long metal chimes on their porches, where they had rain barrels and odd-looking lawn ornaments. The place wasn't more than five miles from Lorraine's house. "How long has she been there?"

"I'm not sure. At least a month or two."

"Why does anyone think..."

He sighed. "They're together all the time. People have seen them holding hands around the restaurant. It looks like they don't even mind if people know."

I leaned my head against the window. I didn't care whether Connie was a queer. It would have been okay if she had told me; even now, six months apart, it hurt not to be the one who knew, to be the only one who *didn't* know. She hadn't held my hand since I was six years old. Queer faggot lesbian bitch.

"Take me there," I said.

"To Earl's?"

"Yes."

"Lily, I don't think you want..."

"Take me now," I said in a voice he had never heard before, a tone I had never used with anyone.

"I don't know exactly where it is," he said, starting the car.

"I can get close enough. We'll find it."

We headed into town, and I told him where to make turns. "I don't know what you have in mind," he said, "but I don't think you should spend any time with your sister. Not until she changes."

I didn't say anything, because I didn't know what I had in mind, either. "Slow down," I said when we turned on Earl's street, which was longer than I remembered and lined with houses on both sides. A guy with a long ponytail was trundling a wheelbarrow down the sidewalk; we pulled over and I rolled down my window and asked him if he knew where a girl named Earl lived. He smiled at the mention of her name and told us it was on the next block, second house on the left. "It's painted blue," he said. "You can't miss it."

He was right; we had no trouble spotting it. The instant I saw the house, a modest-sized bungalow painted pale turquoise, I detested it for looking like a place where Connie would want to live. The front porch had a wide swing on one end, and there were two large windows on either side of the door covered with pale yellow shades. The yard was well taken care of, with bushy green shrubs in front of the porch, a dogwood tree on one side, and several rows of dirt furrows near the front where it looked like something had recently been planted. The front walk was lined with pretty white rocks of various sizes and shapes. I didn't see Connie's VW; there wasn't a driveway, and no cars were parked in the front. "Pull over," I said.

I got out of the car, and Joseph started to get out, too, but I shook my head and told him he didn't need to come. I stood in front of the house and stared, not caring whether anybody was inside or not. When I still lived at home, at Lorraine's, I easily could have ridden my bike here; it was that close. I felt like I might throw up, and I wondered what else Connie hadn't told me through all our years. She had always sheltered a secret place, I knew that, but I thought I was the only one who had been there with her.

I took a few steps down the front walk and set off a barrage of familiar barking from somewhere in the back yard. This is bad, I thought. If that dog and I meet now, one of us is going to die. I bent down and picked up a rock from among the decorative whites that marked the walkway. It was a good size, just right to hurt a big dog.

The dog kept barking, but she didn't appear, and I realized she must have a pen in the back. That's when I should have dropped the rock, but I liked the way it felt in my hands, cool and heavy. Carrying it in both hands like an offering, I walked closer to the house until I was within spitting distance of the front steps. The damned dog wouldn't shut up. I looked around, wondering if a neighbor might be watching; there was no one in sight except Joseph in the car. I took the rock in my right hand and swung my arm over my head and then forward as hard as I could, hurling the rock at the house. I was aiming at the house in general, it didn't occur to me to try for a particular spot, but I, who had hardly even thrown a softball at school, hit the perfect center of a windowpane. The glass exploded and tinkled, and then there was the satisfying thud of the rock hitting the floor inside.

I turned and went back to the car. Joseph started up the engine and drove away as soon as I closed my door. We didn't say anything until we got to the A&P. He stopped the car and sat back without looking at me. "I can't believe you did that," he said. I couldn't tell whether he was disapproving or admiring.

"Those girls are evil," I said. "I was called. God wanted me to do that, Joseph." As I said it, it sounded like the truth. I gave him an earnest look that I didn't need to fake. We were on the side of right, he and I were. He would preach the difference between right and wrong, and I would be there beside him no matter what happened. I would be baptized; I would change my ways and learn about God, and everything I had ever done wrong would be erased, just like that. I had never felt so grateful to Joseph, never loved him so much.

He shifted in his seat. "Lily, the police could come after us."

"No one saw except God," I said. "Everything is going to be fine." I put my hand over his; it felt both cold and sweaty. I felt as if I could tell him anything. "I love you," I said. At that moment, it didn't matter to me whether he said it back or not, but he did. His eyes went soft, almost wet, and he spoke in a soft, choked voice. "I've loved you ever since I can remember."

We sat there a while, holding hands and looking at each other, and then looking away when we couldn't stand it anymore. Finally I picked up my pocketbook from the floorboard. "I'll run in. What do you want for supper?"

"Whatever you want is fine." He reached in his wallet and gave me fifteen dollars.

Walking into the store, I wasn't sure what we would eat, but after all that had happened, I had a wicked craving to buy cigarettes. Just one more, that's all I wanted. One, and then I could throw them away for good.

Connie slips into Earl's life easily. She picks up her job at the restaurant and, even though she doesn't discuss her plans, not at first, they both know her plans have changed. When they talk, they speak tentatively and then in halting bursts, because neither of them has ever relied too much on words. When they don't talk, it's okay, and the differences between them are okay, too. For one thing, Earl is a non-smoker and near-vegetarian while Connie likes to top off a juicy steak with three or four Tareytons. So they compromise. When Earl cooks, Connie willingly eats eggplant and beans and rice. When it's Connie's turn, Earl tolerates the smell of hamburger, and Connie also makes plain spaghetti and cheese toast. After their meals, they go outside together to the back stoop so Connie can smoke. They sit hip-to-hip on the top step, and Earl throws a stick for Lola, who dashes to pick it up before trotting back to Earl and dropping it at her feet. Lola never gets tired of fetching, and Connie never gets tired of watching the two of them. She loves Earl's strength, the way she seems to accept the world without bending to it. She loves Earl's hands, which are large and graceful, with long slender fingers. She loves the way Earl doesn't take any of her shit. Once, without thinking, Connie tosses her finished cigarette. Earl gives her the same look she usually reserves for waitresses who bungle an order. "You just threw trash in the yard," she says.

Connie smiles and waggles her eyebrows. "What else would I do with a cigarette butt—save it for posterity?"

"There's this cool gadget nowadays called an 'ashtray.'" Earl picks up a container that sits next to the back door. It is an old coffee can painted in swirls of psychedelic colors. Connie takes it and sees there are several mashed butts in the can already.

"Whose are these?"

"You're not my only friend who smokes," Earl says.

Connie gives her a challenging look. "So we're just friends?"

Earl puts an arm around Connie and gives her a long, deep kiss. "We're very good friends," she says.

The biggest difference between them is the other people in Earl's life, people who seem threatening to Connie long before she meets them. To her, it seems like Earl knows everyone, or at least everyone outside the mainstream of Carlington life. Earl's friends are both women and men, ranging from late teens to some in their early thirties. A few rent houses in town, but most live out in the country in group arrangements that stop just short of being real communes. They have sporadic day jobs doing office work or construction, but their real lives are spent in their old farmhouses, listening to music, smoking dope, trying to raise soy beans or bees for honey. Earl has been a frequent visitor in these houses. She has helped her friends move in and paint them, she goes to their parties and just hangs out with them when she's not working.

After Connie comes, these visits stop. Earl knows instinctively that Connie isn't ready to meet her friends; she knows it will take time. For a while her telephone stops ringing as her friends absorb the new fact of Connie. Earl is the first lesbian any of them have known, and they spend long, pot-fueled nights discussing it among themselves. Some of the men say two girls together is okay, but two guys is weird. Most of them finally agree it isn't their bag but they can dig it. Anything that upsets everybody else in Carlington is probably cool.

While Connie and Earl are the subject of debate in their neighborhood and all around Carlington, they are in their own quiet world. It's as if everyone else chatters frantically on dry land while the two of them swim far below the surface of their own pool, where sounds are muted, colors are more intense, ordinary events seem novel and dreamlike. They love each other, that much they know. Otherwise, nothing is certain, they have no pattern to follow. They are both deeply private, and they share an unspoken contempt for the flimsiness of words. Instead, they float and dip around each other, circling and coming together in physical acts, not all of them sexual. They take care of each other in big and small ways. Connie repairs a broken rocking chair and paints it, she cuts Earl's hair, she figures out why the stove doesn't always light. Earl monitors Connie's wound from the accident and buys her a new pair of jeans and warmer shirts; she has come with so little. They touch each other constantly.

All of this is pure joy for Connie when they are together. But when Earl is away, working or even at the grocery store, Connie feels uncertain and sometimes panicky. She worries that Earl won't come back, or that things will be different when she does. She suddenly remembers some small thing Earl has said that strikes her wrong, and it nags at her. She begins to think about California again. By the time Earl returns, she has worked herself into a knot of irritation and suspicion. Earl notices, but Connie can't explain it, and Earl doesn't press. She waits until Connie lets her near again; it doesn't take long.

One night Connie is working at the restaurant until closing. Earl is there for a while, but everything seems under control, so she tells Connie she is heading home. They kiss quickly, ignoring the stares around them.

Connie feels happy. As she finishes her shift with her usual

273

competence, she thinks about Earl and the evening ahead. She will be home by midnight, which, for them, is still early for a Saturday. Maybe they will go outside and look at the night sky. Earl has a telescope, they haven't had a chance to use it yet, and tonight the sky is clear. On the way home, she stops and buys some cigarettes and a candy bar to share.

When she gets to the house, she notices more cars than usual parked on the street. She thinks nothing of it, since theirs is the kind of neighborhood where someone is always having a party. But as she walks toward the front door, the door she thinks of as "our" front door, she hears music inside and the sound of voices. She stops and listens for several minutes, her heart beating hard, and she's pissed. Why didn't Earl tell her?

She steps in the house and looks around. Loud, unfamiliar music is blaring, and the smell of marijuana is strong. A guy and a girl sit on the floor in the living room looking at cards that are decorated with Zodiac signs. Another couple—it's hard to tell whether it's two guys, two girls or one of each— is doing a slow dance near the stereo. Connie goes down the hallway without being noticed. She looks in Earl's painting room. Earl is there, standing in front of a canvas and talking to a girl; a woman, really. The woman is a bit older, probably in her late twenties, and she has long, wavy hair down to her waist.

Earl looks over the woman's shoulder and sees Connie. She smiles. "Looks like we're having a party," she calls.

Connie turns and flees to their bedroom. She closes the door behind her and sits on the bed, trembling. From the other side of the house, a new song starts on the stereo, louder than the one before. Earl strictly forbids smoking in the bedroom, but Connie shakes a cigarette out of her pack and lights it. She's puffing furiously when the door opens with a swell of sound. Earl comes in and closes the door behind her. "Hey,

274

what are you doing?"

Connie picks up a glass and jabs her cigarette out.

Earl wrinkles her nose and waves a hand against the smoke. "Great. We'll be sleeping under all this tonight."

Connie tries to keep any expression out of her face. "I didn't think a bit more smoke would matter."

"Leo started a joint in the living room before I made him go outside." Earl is studying her. "Hey, I'm sorry to surprise you. This wasn't planned. After I got home, Leo and his girlfriend dropped by and…it turned into this."

Connie shrugs.

"Come out and meet everybody," Earl says.

"I don't feel like it. I'm tired."

"Do you want me to ask them to leave?"

"No, you don't have to do that."

But Earl disappears, and within a few minutes Connie can hear the sounds of things winding down. The music becomes lower, then it's off. The front door opens and shuts several times, and she hears voices in the front yard and then the quick, chopped sounds of car doors shutting.

When Earl goes back to their room, Connie is in bed under the covers, her face toward the wall. Earl changes into her night T-shirt, gets in bed and cuts off the light. They lie in the darkness listening to each other breathe.

"Talk to me," Earl says.

Connie rolls over on her back. "It's time for me to get to California. I've put it off long enough."

The clock on their night table ticks loudly. Earl says, "I can't stop you if that's what you want."

"What I want…" Connie begins, then she pauses. "I wanted to come home and be with you."

"I was here. I'm still here."

275

"I'm not saying I make any sense," Connie says.

"I'm not going to hide from the world, Con."

"Who's hiding?"

There's a long silence before Earl speaks. "I think it would do you good to see Lily."

Connie pulls the covers closer to her chin. "I doubt if she would see me. Now that she's married to Mr. Holy."

"That's bullshit. I bet she would see you any time."

"Then why didn't she leave with me? She's such a coward. I feel sick every time I think about her and Denis. That boy would die if he really knew anything about her."

"She would be okay now if she had stuck with you," Earl says.

"That's right."

"None of this stuff with Denis and Joseph would have happened, maybe, if you hadn't left, or if you had gone back to get her."

Connie pushes the covers back and sits up. "Are you blaming me?"

"I'm not blaming anyone," Earl says. "I just see that you're quick to run away."

Connie sits up. "So you're saying *I'm* the coward."

Earl smoothes back Connie's hair. "We're all scared of something."

"Except you," Connie says bitterly.

Earl says nothing.

"What?" Connie asks.

"I'm scared you'll run away from me."

Connie wants to speak, but no answer comes. She's never been one to make promises, not since she and I were little girls. If Earl had pushed her then, it would have been over between them. Even if Connie ended up staying for weeks or even months afterwards, that moment would have marked the true end. But Earl lets her confession and implied question hang. The two of them talk a bit more, carefully and neutrally, and Earl rolls over to go to sleep. Connie slides toward Earl's back and tucks her knees into the crook of Earl's knees, shaking her head against the pillow.

26

I pushed a cart around the A&P, wandering from one aisle to another, putting things in the cart and then returning them to the nearest shelf when I saw something better. I felt grimly extravagant, ready to lunge at any small treat. All this time I had deprived myself for Connie. I hadn't even known it; I hadn't known anything. I picked up a bottle of ginger ale and a block of Swiss cheese. I wondered what I would have done if Connie had been there. I snatched up a package of roast beef and imagined knocking on the door and slapping Connie or Earl, whoever answered. Standing in line at the cash register felt odd when there didn't seem to be any ground beneath my feet.

Joseph jumped out of the car to meet me as soon as I walked out of the store. He took the bag and leaned down to kiss me on the side of my mouth. I saw that his love was back. I couldn't have named it then, but he had that feeling of closeness that comes when you finally say something true to someone. A rush of desire flowed through my hips and legs, an ache that almost hurt.

"What did you get?" He was looking at me, and I could see he didn't care, that he hardly knew what he had asked.

"Lots of good things." I didn't mention that I had no change from the money he had given me, that a man behind me in line had handed me a quarter when I was short. I could have put the cigarettes back, but I needed one, just one, as soon as possible; the pack of Tareytons was tucked away in my purse.

We drove home in a silence that seemed more shy than tense; there was too much between us to speak. We went to the kitchen together to unload the groceries. Joseph frowned a little when he pulled the ginger ale from the bag, we usually drank water, but he seemed pleased about the roast. "This looks like a good piece," he said. "It will take a long time to cook."

"I'll put it in right away," I said.

"You don't have to be in a hurry."

Something in his voice stopped me, and I looked up at him. He pulled me close, and we kissed until both of us were shaky. We stopped to breathe. "Would it be okay..." He cleared his throat. "Can I sleep in your bed tonight?"

I tightened my arms around him. "It's *our* bed. It's where you belong."

He stroked the back of my head. "I know," he said hoarsely.

So this is my consolation, I thought. Being really married to Joseph now. There was a lot about me he would never know. While Connie had become visible in the world, I was going underground. I smiled up at him. It was possible to imagine that I would be happy with him when I could be happy again.

He asked if I needed any help in the kitchen, and I said no. "I'll do my Bible reading and take a shower," he said. "Then I had better work on a history paper. It's due on Monday."

When he went back to our room, I felt too alone, I wanted to call him back, but I wouldn't have known what to say. I picked up the roast and examined it. I had never cooked one before. I turned on the oven and unwrapped the meat from its package. It was a cold and bloody lump. I tried to remember what Denis did with this kind of thing. I rinsed it and patted it dry with some toilet paper so I wouldn't dirty our one kitchen cloth. I stabbed it with a fork and poured some ketchup over it, making criss-cross lines like I had seen on meatloaf. Then I set it on an old cookie sheet and slid it in the oven.

From the back room, I could hear the shower running. I got my cigarettes and quietly slipped out the back door.

The back yard was a fairly large clearing, mostly dirt with a smattering of grass. Two dogwood trees stood in the exact center; someone must have planted them years before. Beyond the edge of the yard, there was a field with remnants of corn stalks, tattered things like broken skeletons. When I came out, the chickens sang out in a flurry of clucking, hoping for some attention, but after a moment they settled down. I pulled out a cigarette and lit it.

This will be my last one, I thought. There would be certain things I would have to give up, and a lot to learn about being a preacher's wife. There would be things I could never tell him. But I wouldn't lie anymore. He was the only person I could trust now; the least I could do was give that back to him. I took three long drags, then took the butt and the rest of the cigarettes to the woods and threw them in the brush.

The smell of the roast filled the trailer. Joseph was hunched over his desk with a book open next to him, working on his paper. "Supper will be ready soon," I said.

He looked up and smiled. "Good. I'm starving."

This is our honeymoon night, I thought. I took an extra bed sheet and folded it to cover our small, scarred table. I found a tall candle in a kitchen drawer. There was no candle holder anywhere; I would have to ask Lorraine to bring some from the shop. After some botched efforts, I made a make-shift holder out of aluminum foil and set the candle in it. I peeked at the roast. It still looked too red, so I turned up the oven.

I went into our room and rummaged through my clothes. Since our wedding, I had worn nothing except jeans and oversized shirts and sweaters. I wouldn't hide from Joseph anymore. I found a sheer cotton dress with a halter top, one that Lorraine had bought for me the previous summer. It was far too skimpy for the evening, which was turning cold. I put it on along with my one pair of high heels, and I looked in the mirror. The dress was short and tight. I felt like I was in a costume, like someone on TV. I smiled at myself. Connie had never liked playing dress-up when we were kids, but I had secretly loved it.

I combed my hair and put on a little lipstick. I looked at myself again, this time with Lorraine's eyes. "You need some jewelry"—that's what she would say. I only had one piece, a silver chain necklace. I tried to put it on, but I couldn't get the clasp to work.

I slipped out of the room holding the necklace. Joseph had his back to me and was still engrossed in his work. I stood there, watching him. One of his hands was splayed against the open pages of a thick book; with the other hand he was writing at a steady pace, pausing every now and then to refer to the text. I cleared my throat.

He glanced back at me, "The roast smells good..." He stopped and twisted around to face me. The book he had been holding open flapped shut.

His face flooded with color, and his expression seemed to shift between lust and mild alarm. I held up the necklace. "Would you help me put this on?"

He stood. "I would be happy to help you with that, Mrs. Satterfield."

He took the necklace and examined it. "The catch is bent," he said. He pulled his pocketknife out, found the blade he wanted, and gave a small twist to some part of the necklace. "Let's try this."

Just then there was a sound from outside, the noise of a motor. Joseph put down the knife and necklace and went to the window. He lifted the shade, then let it drop. "Shit," he said. He looked at me. "I'm sorry."

I thought he was sorry for saying "shit;" I was pleased. Now it wouldn't be so bad when I slipped. "Who is it?"

"My parents."

I went to the window and looked. A car had pulled in the yard and parked behind mine. The lights blinked off, and I saw it was his father's Cadillac. "Did you know they were coming?"

"They said…" he stopped. "No."

There was a loud knock at the door. I felt the same kind of panic I had felt when Denis came; it seemed important not to let them in. "Let's keep still," I whispered. "We can say we weren't at home."

For a second Joseph seemed to consider it, but then he shook his head. From outside, his father called his name and knocked harder.

"I have to let them in," Joseph said. He opened the door and stood back.

His father entered the trailer slowly, as if he expected an ambush. He was tall, taller than Joseph, and he had a long, thin face. He looked like a gray-haired Abraham Lincoln. Joseph's mother trailed behind him. She was plump, with dark hair and pretty skin. The hem of a pink dress hung beneath her coat, and she wore pink shoes. She slipped in the house quietly and stood with her purse in her hand. She gave me a quick, frightened smile.

Reverend Satterfield looked me up and down, taking in my halter-top dress. Joseph stood stiffly with his hands stuffed in his pockets. "Mom and Dad, this is Lily," he said.

I extended my hand to Mrs. Satterfield, as Lorraine had

taught me. She gave me a limp, fleeting shake. When I turned to Reverend Satterfield, he put his hands behind his back and looked around, surveying the trailer. He sniffed. "It smells in here. Has she been smoking marijuana?"

"No, Dad."

I realized the roast was burning, but I couldn't move.

"Why did you come here?" Joseph asked.

His father went and put his arm around Joseph. "Pack your things, son. You need to come back home."

Joseph's face darkened, and he pulled away. "You promised you wouldn't do this."

"Joseph, I have prayed over this night and day. I have never prayed so hard in my life."

"Dad, you need to give Lily a chance."

His father's neck jerked forward and his eyes widened. "Don't tell me what I need, boy. Only God tells me what I need." He whirled around to point at me. "Look at her, Joseph. Look at her. This girl is an abomination."

Joseph closed his eyes and shook his head. "No, Dad, you're wrong…"

"Do not contradict me," the Reverend thundered.

His mother sidled over to me, her purse held tightly in both hands. "Do you have a sweater to put on?" she whispered.

I saw that she meant to be kind, but I also saw it was a literal question: She wasn't sure I had a sweater. She wasn't sure I didn't walk around half naked all the time. "Excuse me," I said, backing away. I ran to the kitchen.

When I opened the oven, thick gray smoke poured out. I grabbed some towels and pulled out the meat. It looked like the black remains of a campfire. I laid the pan on top of the stove and fanned the air with a towel. Joseph came in and paced around the kitchen table. The candle I had lit was still burning. He leaned over and blew it out.

"What are they doing?" I whispered.

He stopped pacing and looked at me and the smoking meat. "You ruined our dinner."

I stared at him. "I'm not very hungry now. How about you?"

He sat down at the table and put his head in his hands. From the other room, we could hear his father giving instructions. "This is his, Denise. Don't forget this."

I sat down beside Joseph. "What are we going to do?" I whispered.

"Good grief, where is all this smoke coming from?" his father asked. He strode into the kitchen and went to the stove. "What was that?"

I stared at him without answering; Joseph didn't move. His father picked up a fork next to the stove and prodded the charred mass. "You wasted a lot of good meat," he said, looking at me.

I sat up as straight as I could. "This is our home. Joseph is staying here."

"I'll ask you not to speak." He said it almost politely, as if he were talking to a difficult parishioner. His eyes moved from my face down to my chest. Joseph still had his head down, he didn't see.

"Please go," I said. "My husband and I want you to leave."

"He's not your husband," he said. "Not in the eyes of God."

Joseph's shoulders were heaving, but he still didn't look up.

"If you love my son, you will let him go," the Reverend said. "He has a future. I will not allow you to ruin it."

"I haven't done anything…"

"You are just like your mother and your perverted sister. Do you think any church will take Joseph as long as he's married to you?"

285

"You don't know my mother or my sister."

"And it will stay that way," he said. "Denise," he bellowed. "Do you have all his things?"

Joseph got up and pushed his chair back from the table. He looked battered. I thought of a fight I had seen once, two boys who had rolled on the hard dirt ground behind the school, punching and kicking until a teacher pulled them apart. Joseph's face reminded me of the bloody one who had gotten up last.

His mother appeared in the doorway holding a paper bag. "I think this is all," she said cheerfully, as if she had been packing for a family vacation. "The rest is in the car." She took Joseph's arm. "Let's go, son."

Joseph pulled her hand away, and I felt a small flare of hope. He was breathing hard; his shoulders rose up and down. "Go on to the car," he said to them.

"Not without you," his father said.

"I'm coming," Joseph said. "I'll be there in a minute."

His father hesitated. "Do you swear to our Lord?"

"Yes," Joseph said. "Please go."

We watched them leave. The preacher let the screen door bang behind him.

Joseph turned to me. "We're young…"

"Don't," I said. "I don't want to hear it. Why don't you just go on?"

"I need to say this, Lily. Maybe I'll have my own church, maybe I'll end up in the next war, only God knows. But I'll never do anything harder than this."

"You're free to do what you want. You have a choice."

"God has called me to be a minister."

"Don't blame this on God. Do what you have to do, but know it's you leaving here, not God."

286

He stood there looking down. "Call me. We'll talk…"

"Do you think your parents will let you take a call from me?"

He kept on as if I hadn't spoken. "You can't drive, you'll be stuck here…We can take you home. At least let us do that."

"I never felt stuck here."

"Lily…"

"Who are you?" I took a step toward him and looked in his eyes. In the brief second before he looked away, I saw him, the man who had been coming to life, but then he was gone. If he had been strong enough to hold my gaze, I would have kissed him. Instead I said, "Go, they're waiting."

He turned to go, and I followed him. I stood at the top of our stoop, shivering in the cold but not feeling it. Later I would think of all the things I should have done, what I might have said. But at that moment I couldn't think; I could only be a witness to an ending I didn't want. In the short time of our marriage (a marriage that, within a month, Reverend Satterfield's lawyer would annul), I had grown older and stronger than Joseph, but I didn't know it then. I still didn't know there are worse things than being left.

Joseph's father had pulled the car closer, and the motor was idling. Joseph opened the door and got in the back seat. I watched the car drive away until the tail lights were just two small fireflies in the distance, flitting above the ruts in the road. If Joseph looked back, I didn't see it.

27

I sat huddled in the armchair listening to the trailer tick and breathe around me. When I couldn't stand it anymore, the near-silence that would go on and on, I got up and went to our room. The floor was bare where Joseph's blankets had been; he had brought those from home. My clothes, the ones I had been trying on before dinner, were no longer piled in a heap, but folded loosely on the bed. Joseph's mother had gone through them, looking for anything that belonged to him. It must have killed her to touch my things.

When I went to the bathroom, there was nothing of Joseph there, not even the faded blue towels we both had used. It was like I had dreamed living with him. Connie had taken so little when she left; it had been easy to believe she was coming back.

The smell of the burned roast had grown stronger. As I scraped it into the garbage, I nearly retched. I drank a glass of water and thought of Aunt Dayna's sherry, still hidden in the cabinet. I pulled it out.

It tasted sharp and sweet. I took small sips and thought of the word "chase." Lorraine and Jo Penny had sometimes chased one drink with another. I wished I had something else, like bourbon or Scotch. I lifted the bottle and looked: Aunt Dayna hadn't taken much, the bottle was nearly full. I was cold, I would put on a sweatshirt and drink a little more, just enough to warm up and get sleepy. Or maybe I would take the bottle over to Aunt Dayna's, and we could share the rest. But then I couldn't imagine seeing her, or anybody. She wouldn't say it, but she would be thinking what everyone would think:

Joseph had never really loved me.

My sweatshirt hung on a nail by the kitchen door. I slipped it on over my dress, turned on the radio, and took another swig of the sherry. It was tasting better; I tipped it up for a long swallow. I began to feel warm and calm, or at least a faint echo of those things. I drank more, and was definitely feeling better until the first slow chords of "Wild Horses" came on. A million years ago Connie and I had sung that song together in the car, and it was more than I could bear now. I turned the tuner until I found something fast and unfamiliar. Lifting the bottle to my lips became part of the rhythm, a sort of downbeat. The songs got better. I had stumbled into a long Saturday-night set, Robert and Rod and Elton and Bruce. I got up and swayed. Joseph had never seen me dance; no one had except Connie. I took off my sweatshirt and swung it over my head. The song ended and a commercial came on and then another song. I spun around; I did the pony and the jerk until the front of my dress was damp with sweat. Then the slow chords of "Color My World" came on. "God, no," I groaned, snapping off the radio. I collapsed in the chair, feeling light-headed and suddenly hungry. There was nothing but the roast. I pulled it out of the trash and tore off a piece. It tasted like wet ashes. I swallowed and ate another bite.

Without the radio, the silence in the trailer felt new again, louder and more permanent. I paced around the trailer, wanting a cigarette. No one was coming back, it was only me here forever, and my fucking cigarettes were somewhere in the woods. I stumbled out the back door, missed a step and nearly fell down. It was dark and noisy outside with crickets and strange birds. The sky looked smoky with clouds, and the wind had picked up. The ground was wet on my bare feet. There had been a soaking rain the day before, more was coming, I could smell it. I stepped on something sharp but

290

kept going, scanning the thick border of trees at the edge of the clearing. Where had I thrown them? I went to the spot that seemed right and fell to my knees. I groped around, stabbing my hands on sticks and rocks. Nothing. I crawled in every direction, sweeping the damp ground with my hands. My hair fell in my eyes and mouth, and I brushed it back, smearing mud on my face. The cigarettes were out here, they had to be. Maybe I had come too far. I wiped my face with the hem of my dress and went back toward the yard. A gleam of white paper caught my eye; I pounced on it. The package was sticking out of a shallow puddle. I fished it out carefully, treating it like the finest crystal. Hallelujah, I thought. Halle-fucking-lujah.

I carried the package back to the trailer, the place where nobody lived anymore. Now I can fill it up with smoke, I thought. I took the cigarettes to the kitchen table and inspected them. The package felt soggy, some of them would be ruined, but surely one or two would be all right. They were too damp to shake out, so I found a pair of scissors and cut the package down the middle. Carefully I took out each sodden stick one by one. I picked the one that looked the driest and tried to light it. The match flared against it, but nothing burned. I put the other end in my mouth and sucked hard. Nothing. I threw it down and tried another. The match went out as soon as it touched the tip. I crumpled up the package and threw it on top of the roast.

The sherry was nearly gone, only a small finger left. I tilted the bottle over my face and drained it. A draft of cold air blew against my legs: I had left the back door open. When I went to close it, I saw dirt on the floor and spots of blood. Then I felt the pain in my foot. I grabbed the back of the chair and lifted my heel; there was a bloody gash. Joseph's first-aid kit with the bandages would be gone. I limped to the bathroom and dampened a wad of toilet paper. It hurt when I pressed the cold water against it, but in a distant sort of way. I had liked seeing my blood on the floor. It looked good there.

Sherry. I moved to get it, then remembered it was gone. Nothing to drink, nothing to smoke. I picked up the bottle and threw it against the refrigerator. It shattered in a spectacular, satisfying way. I wished for a phone to call Joseph. He would find a way to talk to me, I thought, but then I knew he wouldn't. I wanted to call him so I could call him a goddam bastard. I wanted to see Connie. I wanted to call her a goddam bastard too.

The broken glass lay on the floor in shards and tiny pieces. The light caught them so they looked beautiful, like jewels. I lifted my good heel over a small shard and stepped on it. Nothing happened. I pressed down harder and watched the blood ooze. Whenever we had broken something at home, it had been an Event, whether we had done it or, in rare cases, when Lorraine herself had been dusting or rearranging things too furiously and some piece of crystal or glass got knocked over. To Lorraine, anything broken was an emergency, and often the cause for angry weeping. "Don't walk there, get away, go get the broom," she would yell frantically. I stepped on another piece with the ball of my foot. It didn't even hurt, not much. I wiped my foot against the floor, making a bright red smear. Not everything needs to be cleaned up. Some things are just a mess.

I wanted more sherry. I wanted a cigarette. Everything was gone and out of reach.

❦

I woke up in my car. I don't know how long I had been there. It was raining lightly but steadily outside. My feet throbbed, my head throbbed, my body felt damp and stiff. I shifted and heard the sound of metal. I looked down. The car keys sat in the lap of my dirt-smeared dress along with a crumpled dollar bill. Then I remembered: I had decided I would drive to town to buy cigarettes.

I looked over my shoulder at the trailer and saw that all the lights were blazing. I didn't want to go back there. I picked up the keys but I couldn't remember what to do. I sat staring, maybe even falling asleep again before I roused myself and put the key in the ignition. My hands were shaking. The motor coughed and sputtered then cut off. I tried again, and it started. I closed my eyes and listened to the motor idle. Closing my eyes was not a good idea; my head seemed to be spinning. I opened them again and grasped the gear stick and pulled it over to drive. The car gave a little jump forward. I grabbed the steering wheel and peered through the windshield, straining to see, but I didn't turn on the lights. When I pressed on the gas pedal, pain shot through my foot, but I kept it there and pushed harder. Slowly and then faster, I rolled out of the yard and was moving down the dirt road.

The speed scared me, even though I wasn't going fast. I let up on the gas pedal and slowed to a crawl, then gradually pushed harder until the speedometer moved up to twenty-five then thirty. The car vibrated beneath me, feeling like my own power. I marveled at how it obeyed my aching foot, but the road was tricky with all its bumps and ruts. Information seemed to come when I needed it: push harder, let up, turn a little to the right. I drove past the entrance to Aunt Dayna's long driveway. She might hear the motor, but her house was hidden by a grove of trees; she wouldn't see me. I didn't feel like myself and I didn't feel drunk; I felt like somebody I hadn't met.

The wheels hit a long muddy patch, like plowing through ooze. I remembered what Denis had told me about ice: Don't slow down, that's the worst thing you can do. I sped up and maneuvered around the worst banks of mud. Connie wouldn't have done it any better than I had. I thought of all the times I had ridden with her, long before she was sixteen, and for the first time I really knew how she felt. When you take a steering wheel in your own hands, the world is suddenly more possible to navigate. She wouldn't be driving me again, no one would. Up ahead I saw the road that turned off toward the lake. *That's where I'm going.* I made the turn as if I had been doing it all of my life, moving forward until the car and I were perched at the top of the hill, the same place Joseph had shown me on the night of the ice. My foot pushed on the brake until the car stopped.

The hill was steeper than I remembered. Down below, maybe a quarter of a mile, the lake lay like a dark plate of glass streaked with light from the moon. I wanted to fly down, to burrow in the water; it would be quick and quiet. My head was pounding, my feet were killing me, I wanted everything to stop hurting. I gripped the wheel with both hands and pressed on the gas pedal. The ground beneath the tires felt slippery. I pressed harder, going faster to avoid getting stuck. The car sped up to thirty, then forty. I was getting through the pain in my foot, making myself push harder, when something flashed at the edge of my vision. A deer sprang from the darkness and ran across my path.

I slammed on the brakes. The tires seemed to do a strange sort of slide and sink, as if the car had turned into a boat. The deer made its crossing a few yards ahead, then disappeared into the woods. I tried to move forward. The tires spun and mud flew up and sprayed my window. The motor roared, but the car didn't move.

Finally I cut off the motor, imagining what other people would do. Denis would swear and laugh and round up a gang of farmers to help push him out. Lorraine would sit in the car and smoke, waiting for Denis to fix it. Joseph *would* fix it. He would have all the right tools in his trunk, or he would figure out how to use sticks or logs to pry himself out. Connie never would have gotten stuck in the first place. Even if she had hit the deer, she would have done what she set out to do.

It felt all right to be there, just sitting. It seemed fine. I felt no need to do anything; it was enough to look out at the lake and the sky. Above the treetops, there were more stars than I had ever seen in one place. It was prettier, in a way, than the icy evening when Joseph had brought me here. I heard the distant sound of cars passing on the highway. Before the night was over, I would need to walk back to the trailer. There were blankets there, aspirin, something to put on my feet. It would hurt to walk back, it would hurt like hell. That's just the way it was.

In the daytime, my car looked out of place perched on the hill, nose pointed toward the lake. There was the sheet of shining water, the scrubby grass, the tall pines, and my purple machine mired in the mud as if it had been dropped from the sky. I circled the car, assessing its stuckness. The front tires remained partially buried, but the ground looked dry.

Nearly five days had passed since I had left it there. During that time I had slept a lot, day and night. When I was awake, I sat outside and watched the chickens. I spent a morning hunting for pretty stones in the woods; I planned to make a rock garden behind the trailer, a small memorial to the baby. My feet were healing. Aunt Dayna and I had gone to the grocery store together, and I had bought a box of heavy-duty bandages. She showed me how to wrap them, so now I could walk without much trouble.

I started the engine, put the car in reverse and tried to back up. It rolled a little, then stalled. I tried again, giving it more gas. There was a trembling hesitation, but the car heaved itself out of the mud. I backed up until I was pointing the right way, then drove up the hill. It was different, driving sober in daylight. The dirt road was dry and solid beneath the tires. I thought about heading to the open road, but decided against it. I wasn't ready for that yet.

As I pulled into the yard, I saw Lorraine's Thunderbird parked in front of the trailer, gleaming in the sun. She rose from my front stoop and shaded her eyes to watch me come in. I drove to my usual space and brought my car to a neat stop.

When I got out, she was standing with her hands on her hips and her mouth open. She was wearing bright yellow pants with a paisley top.

"Will wonders never cease," she said. "When did you get your license?"

"I haven't yet. Need to do it soon."

She was made up, but in the sun her face seemed pale and creased. She folded her arms against her stomach and looked worried. "Jo Penny called. I'm so sorry, Honey."

Everyone knows, I thought. Geese flew above, honking as they passed.

"It's all for the best," Lorraine said, "don't you think? Lots of people get divorces nowadays. It's not like it used to be."

"I think Joseph plans to get it annulled," I said. "Like it never happened."

"That's even better," Lorraine said, touching my shoulder. "A fresh start for everyone."

I stepped away, wishing she hadn't come. "Carlington hasn't had this much to talk about since you were a teenager," I said. Her face darkened, but I went on. "Between Lily the Loser and Connie the Queer, they can't get enough of us Stokes."

She looked hurt, then tired. She reached for her pocketbook and fumbled inside for her cigarettes. "Have you seen your sister?"

"No. Have you?"

She lit her cigarette and shook her head, appalled. "I can't appear to be condoning her behavior."

"Lorraine, no one will ever think you prefer women."

She laughed a little, but then quickly looked away. A hesitant expression crossed her face. "Come over here and sit down with me for a minute."

I followed her to the front stoop, and we sat. Her cigarette

298

burned quickly in the breeze. She took another drag before crushing it out against the concrete. "There's something I need to tell you. The timing is a bit awkward, but I didn't want you to hear from someone else." She held up her left hand. There was a band on her third finger. She gave it a twist, revealing a diamond. It caught the sun and flashed. "It's about time, don't you think?"

I felt a quick stab of jealousy, but also relief. Denis had always been hers; that had been the point of my revenge and his fantasies. I thought of the last time I had seen him, his nearly deranged performance at the trailer door. I had hated seeing him that way. He wouldn't change, of course, neither of them would, but Lorraine would get through her disappointment, and Denis would find ways to cope, and maybe they would stick it out.

"Congratulations." I managed to smile.

She looked relieved. "We've set a date," she said. "There's so much to do, so much to think about, but we're having it in June."

"Great." Already I could see it. Lorraine would get the fancy wedding she had always wanted. The ceremony would be a private affair in the house, though someone would play the bridal march as she floated down the staircase. Afterwards, the party would be out in the yard, where there would be an enormous yellow tent sheltering long tables, covered in white cloths and filled with flowers and food. Denis would insist on a live band; he had always said there would be music if he ever had a wedding. It was all so easy to see: The band would play music from the '50s. Denis would drink too much and flirt with the singer, a blonde in a tight dress. Nearly *everyone* would drink too much and it would be declared Carlington's best party in years.

"Presents are already coming in," Lorraine was saying, covering my silence. "I know it's silly, but I picked out new china. I can't wait for you to see it. Some people might say it's a waste, but I'm tired of using Mother's. I want something more contemporary. Don't you think?"

"You should get what you want," I said.

She looked down and smoothed a wrinkle out of her pants; I could see there was something more. "Lily, I don't know what your plans are now…things are going to be crazy at the house, getting ready for the wedding and all. I was talking to Jo Penny, and she said she and Marlene would love to have you stay with them as long as you want…You would be back in town, and we would see you all the time…"

I was already shaking my head. "I'm staying here."

"Here?" She looked at the trailer as if I had lost my mind. "You can't be serious."

"Not forever, but for now while I finish my senior year."

"Will the Satterfields allow you…?"

"It's not up to them. Joseph's aunt owns the place, and I've already talked to her. She wants me here, and she'll pay me to help her with things. I can get by."

We sat side by side, both of us looking in the distance. I thought about the dough that was rising inside my kitchen; it was probably time to punch it down. Aunt Dayna had showed me a simple way to make pizza crust. I was doubtful that the blob of sticky flour could turn into a crust, but she swore it would work.

"Oh," Lorraine said, brightening. "I have something for you." She went to her car and came back with a brown paper bag. "It's asparagus," she said. "One of my customers grew it herself. We have more than we can use." She thrust the bag toward me.

I held my hands in my lap. "Mother, I've never liked asparagus."

"Oh, I…" She stopped and bit her lip, looking bewildered and defeated. In that moment, I could see her as an old woman, someone who would drive too slowly on highways, gripping the wheel with both hands, someone who would need pills and ointments, someone whose bones would ache every time it rained. I thought about when she had seemed so strong, all those times she had stood at the back door and called Connie and me to come in, and how we had crouched behind the trees, silent and hidden, even when she got hoarse from shouting our names. We had all needed more than we had gotten.

"Are you sure…?" she was saying. "These are really fresh."

I stood and put my arms around her. I smelled her familiar scent, a mixture of perfume and dust, and my eyes began to burn. "Thanks," I said, hugging her tighter than I ever had. "I don't need them, but it's okay."

That early morning in June, the birds were already chattering loudly when I went outside, even though it was still dark. I had been lying in bed all night, wide awake. Finally it had made sense just to get up and get dressed. On my way out, I picked up my billfold, which contained a few dollars and my newly issued driver's license.

I got in my car and started it. By the time I reached the end of the dirt road, the first traces of pink and purple streaked the sky. I turned right; it was almost a straight shot to Carlington.

The bypass took me by the house. Lorraine had left a light burning on the front porch, or, more likely, Denis had, since Lorraine was fanatical about the electricity bill. Denis's car, with a smashed taillight, I noticed, was parked in the driveway by the oak tree. I smiled. Now that it was so close to the wedding, Lorraine wasn't making him keep it out of sight. I tooted the horn as I passed, even though I knew they wouldn't hear.

My plan was to drive directly into town, but I found myself veering off at a fork in the road and going a roundabout way. During all the hours of lying awake in the dark, I had never considered riding past Joseph's house, but now I turned onto the street where his parents had lived as long as I could remember. It was a tidy neighborhood of small, nicely painted houses with spacious yards. The Satterfields' parsonage sat across the street from their church. As I got near, I saw the white steeple looming above the trees. Everything was quiet in the dim morning light; no one stirred except a boy on a bike delivering newspapers. I slowed down, nearly stopping, in front of the brick ranch with a wooden cross hanging on the front door. The Satterfields had no garage, but the paved driveway formed a T-shape, with a wider part at the end. Three cars were parked there side by side: Reverend Satterfield's Cadillac on the right, under a basketball goal, and Mrs. Satterfield's Falcon on the left, near the house. Joseph's car was wedged in the middle so tightly I wondered how he would manage to open the door. Until then, I had felt sheepish about coming and nervous about being spotted. Looking at his car, I no longer cared if anyone happened to look out and see me. I stepped on the gas pedal and drove away noisily.

I had no trouble finding my way back to Earl's street, but I took my time and looked around on the way. It was an old neighborhood with small, tidy houses set close together, their yards decorated with abandoned toys and weedy beds of bright flowers. As I got closer, my heart beat fast. I spotted Earl's blue house and pulled over to park, but I didn't slow down enough. The right front tire banged against the curb and rolled up on the sidewalk before I stopped. When I put the car in park, my hands left damp spots on the steering wheel.

I sat for a moment in my lopsided position, catching my breath and staring at the house. The grass in Earl's yard looked recently trimmed; a pair of gardening gloves lay on the front steps. A birdbath stood in the center of the yard, a finely curved sculpture painted the same shade of purple as my car. One of the front windows of the house was cracked open, but the curtains were drawn, and there was no sign of movement anywhere. I reached across the seat of my car and rolled down the window on the passenger side. I looked up and down the street. All was quiet, even the birds. I laid my palm against the horn on the steering wheel and pressed it.

The horn blared. I made myself keep my hand down. The noise was loud and long, cutting through the silence of the neighborhood. A shade flipped up in the window of the house next door, and a lady's glaring face appeared. I kept pressing. The front door to Earl's house opened, and two figures stood behind the screen door. I released the horn as Connie came out.

She was not as tall or as thin as I remembered. She was wearing different glasses, rectangles enclosed by wire rims. Her face looked soft with sleep, and she looked annoyed. She strode down the sidewalk toward the car, and about halfway down she saw me. She stopped. Her arms jerked up, as if to block something, but then she let them fall. I could see her chest move up and down as she breathed.

"Come here," I called.

She walked slowly up to the open window and peered inside. I looked at her and she looked at me. "We have a doorbell," she said.

"It was hard enough to get here," I said. "I'm staying put. Get in."

She hesitated, and turned around. Earl was standing at the door. "Tell her we'll be right back," I said.

Connie turned toward Earl and some silent communication passed between them. Earl nodded and went back inside.

Connie got in beside me and looked around her hips and over her shoulders. "There's no seat belts. Will you get me back in one piece?"

"No guarantees, but that's the plan." I put the car in reverse and eased off the curb. The car came down with a bump. I pressed on the gas, and gave another honk as we pulled away.

ACKNOWLEDGMENTS

Thanks to Kristen Morris of Tigress Publishing for believing in the book and being a total pro, and to Carole Glickfeld for superb editing.

For comments or encouragement at just the right time, I am grateful to Walter Bennett, Celia Bland, Marie Bogan, Mia Bray, Joel Byrd, Ken Calhoun, Alex Charns, Lucy Daniels, Sherrie Dillard, Ann Eller, Phil and Martha Fonville, Stephanie Ford, Steven and Stephanie Gage, Melanie Iversen, Alice Kaplan, Lori Kikuchi, Genie Nable, Deborah Norton, Kathleen O'Keeffe, Alice Osborn, Peggy Payne, Martha Pentecost, Susie Powell, Jonathan Sledge, Lee Smith, and Elaine Souda. David Moon of Moon Productions provided a valuable jump-start on my website.

My siblings, John and Carolyn Moore, are my best friends and continuing inspirations. As the family's angel and professional editor, Carolyn offered perceptive suggestions early on. Linda Hanley Finigan, my other Massachusetts sister, was extremely generous with her support and thoughtful advice. Nancy Card has been a tireless reader, amazing friend and detail-person extraordinaire.

I'm blessed to have the best husband and son on the planet, and I'm especially lucky they don't think it's odd for a grown person to put made-up stories ahead of laundry and other practicalities.

Finally, the guidance, insights and friendship of Laurel Goldman have been pure grace, and I thank her for helping me see more again and again.

Mary Lambeth Moore has been a versatile, persistent and mostly anonymous writer for more than 20 years. Her paying and non-paying jobs have included government bureaucrat, freelance writer, corporate consultant, fiction editor, property caretaker, and, currently, fair lending advocate for low- and middle-income communities.

Through all of these jobs, Mary has written. She has been a ghost-writer for CEOs, national policy leaders and community advocates. She has published numerous articles under others' names as well as her own short fiction, most notably in the nationally-distributed magazine, *First for Women*. For three years she served as the fiction editor of Carolina Wren Press in Durham, North Carolina, where she edited the short story collection *In the Arms of Our Elders* by William Henry Lewis.

Mary graduated from the University of North Carolina at Chapel Hill and also the Harvard Kennedy School. She grew up in Reidsville, North Carolina and now lives in Raleigh with her husband and 13-year-old son. *Sleeping with Patty Hearst* is her first novel.